A Seeking Heart

While running from the past, Samantha O'Brien discovered a way of life she hadn't known existed...

A Seeking Heart

While running from the past, Samantha O'Brien discovered a way of life she hadn't known existed...

KIM VOGEL SAWYER

ACW Press

Phoenix, Arizona 85013

A Seeking Heart
Copyright ©2002 Kim Vogel Sawyer
All rights reserved

Cover Design by Alpha Advertising
Interior design by Pine Hill Graphics

Packaged by ACW Press
5501 N. 7th Ave., #502
Phoenix, Arizona 85013
www.acwpress.com
The views expressed or implied in this work do not necessarily reflect those of ACW Press. Ultimate design, content, and editorial accuracy of this work is the responsibility of the author(s).

Publisher's Cataloging-in-Publication
(Provided by Quality Books, Inc.)

Sawyer, Kim.
    A seeking heart / by Kim Sawyer. -- 1st ed.
    p. cm. -- (Mountain Lake series ; Bk. 1)
    ISBN 1-892525-86-0

    1. Abused women--Fiction. 2. Life change events--Fiction. 3. Christian life--Fiction. 4. Mountain Lake (Minn.)--Fiction. I. Title

PS3619.A884S44 2002   813'.6
                      QBI33-560

Printed in the United States of America.

Dedicated lovingly to Mom and Daddy.
Thank you for making sure my heart
never felt the need to go seeking
for love and acceptance.

Klaassen Family Tree

Simon Klaassen (1873) m. Laura Doerksen (1877), 1893
    Daniel Simon (1894) m. Rose Willems (1892), 1913
        Christina Rose (1915)
        Katrina Marie (1916)
    Hannah Joy (1895-1895)
    Franklin Thomas (1896) m. Anna Harms (1900), 1918
    Elizabeth Laurene (1898) m. Jacob Aaron Stoesz (1897), 1915
    Adam James (1899)
    Josephine Ellen (1901)
    Arnold Hiram (1903)
    Rebecca Arlene (1906)
    Theodore Henry (1908)
    Sarah Louise (1910)

Hiram Klaassen (1872) m. Hulda Schmidt (1872), 1898

O'Brien Family Tree

Burton O'Brien (1870) m. Olivia Ruth Stanton (1873-1901), 1891
    David Burton (1894)
    Samantha Olivia (1901)

*"...great is His love toward us,
and the faithfulness of the Lord endures forever."*

Psalm 117:2 (NIV)

Chapter One

August, 1917

On the outskirts of Mountain Lake, Minnesota, a young girl rested. Her back was settled comfortably against the gnarled bark of a century-old cottonwood, one of the few trees left standing when the farmers cleared the land to plant their Turkey Red wheat some seventy-five years ago. The shade offered a welcome respite from the stifling August heat, and the gentle whisper of the wind through the leaves was as pleasing as a lullaby to the tired girl.

She *was* tired: bone-tired, her father would say. She had come a long distance, sometimes hitching rides—in the backs of rattling wagons and once in the leather seat of a Model T—but mostly walking. Her feet wore blisters that told of the miles covered, and now she pushed them into the soft soil beneath the tree to cool them. Her inner thighs were chafed from being rubbed by the four-sizes-too-large overalls she had donned for her journey, and her wrists were grubby and dirt-streaked from constantly pushing up the sleeves of the loose flannel shirt that was so inappropriate for the heat of the summer. Yet she had dressed carefully before setting out, taking care to assume the appearance of a young farm boy rather than the almost seventeen-year-old young lady she was. She had her reasons.

What bothered her most was the abominable itching on her head. She had tucked her nearly waist-length hair up into a disreputable-looking brown suede hat that had been discarded by her father years ago. She longed to pull off the hat, shake her hair out and scratch her skull until it tingled, but she didn't dare. She might not be able to put it all back. So she satisfied herself by shifting the hat around on her head. It offered some relief.

Now she leaned back with a sigh, closing her eyes. A rumble in her belly caused her to grimace. She patted her empty stomach consolingly and spoke to herself, "I know, I know. I can tell you need nourishment." She scowled and popped her eyes open as the rumbling deepened and her stomach cramped painfully.

It had been noon yesterday when she had eaten last, and then only a handful of soda crackers and a wormy apple she'd snitched from an apple barrel in the Blue Earth mercantile when no one was looking. The problem was her cash supply was fearfully low, while her hunger immeasurably high. She rubbed her belly thoughtfully, pondering her alternatives.

Truth of the matter was she'd been formulating a plan under her battered suede hat ever since she'd passed the neat farm house about a mile and a half back. The whitewashed two-story with its big wrap-around porch and bright marigolds lining the pathways from the house to the dirt road bespoke of no little wealth. And judging from the number of dungarees, work shirts, and stockings hanging on lines strung between the barn and outhouse, it also bespoke of a whole passel of youngsters—too many for one small-town shopkeeper to keep track of, the girl reasoned.

Luckily for her, the owner had proudly painted his name, in neat block letters for all to see, on the roadside of the barn: KLAASSEN FARM. It was as if he was unwittingly asking to be her benefactor. Still, she stayed seated, pushing the plan back and forth in her mind. Hungry as she was, the thought of stealing wasn't an easy one. Oh, she'd done her fair share of pilfering apples, and, if you came right down to it, she'd really stolen the clothes she was wearing from the trunk in the cellar. But thievery didn't set easily on her shoulders; it was a necessity rather than a choice.

Another rumbling, this time not from her stomach, brought her to attention. She straightened up tensely, prepared for flight if need be. From around the bend came a high-sided boxy wagon painted celery green, pulled by two largely-muscled horses well along in years. Atop the wagon seat, holding loosely onto the reins with elbows resting lazily on knees, sat a young man. He wore a gray plaid shirt with its sleeves rolled above the elbows, faded blue britches, and a relaxed smile below a straw hat.

He spotted the girl and nodded a greeting: "Howdy, son!" The girl gave a barely perceptible nod in return and watched warily as he clucked to the horses and continued on, disappearing over the gentle rise in the road.

Having been acknowledged as a boy gave her the boost in confidence she needed to go ahead and carry out her plan. She waited a few minutes to be certain the wagon and its driver were well ahead of her, then pushed to her feet. She reached for her boots, but couldn't bear the thought of confining her feet again. Instead, she tied the rawhide laces together and slung the boots over her shoulder. With a sigh—and another loud growl from her middle—she began following the wagon tracks toward town.

"Whoa, there, Bet, Tick," Adam Klaassen intoned as he pulled the team up in front of Tucker's Lumber & Hardware. With a fluid motion, he wrapped the reins around the brake and leaped off the wagon, landing with a soft *jump* in the dirt street. He yanked his straw hat from his head and banged it against his pant leg a time or two to chase the dust off, ran his fingers through his hair, leaving it standing in dusty sun-bleached ridges, then slapped the hat back on his head.

Three long strides and he was entering the dim interior of Nip Tucker's store. He stood in the doorway a few minutes, allowing his eyes to adjust from the bright sunshine to the dismal gloom of the store's interior. Although the building boasted two large windows, one on either side of the wooden entry door, Nip didn't deem it important to clean them with any regularity. As a result, the accumulated dust and grime from the wind adequately blocked the sun from entering the shop.

"Mr. Tucker?" Adam called, finally stepping a few feet into the building. He glanced around at the wild disarray that made up Nip's stock. Barrels of nails, makeshift shelves holding a variety of tools, and stacks of lumber in various lengths created a mind-boggling maze of disorganization. Adam moved closer to the tall, dusty counter at the rear of the store and called out the owner's name again.

Adam cocked an ear as he heard a rustling from behind the counter, followed by the squeak of tin upon tin, and finally a resounding burp. He smothered a grin as Nip Tucker's huge frame straightened from his hiding place. Nip slipped a slim tin canister into the hip pocket of his overalls before greeting Adam with a face-splitting smile, revealing a gap in front from one missing tooth.

No one knew Nip's real name, but everyone knew why he was called Nip: it was after his habit of partaking frequently of the tin canister he now concealed in his ample pocket. Despite Nip's obvious weakness for the "spirits," he was an honest businessman and well-liked in the community by townspeople and farmers alike.

"Well, howdy-do, Adam," Nip cheerfully bellowed, his face wreathed with a grin. He had more smile lines than anyone else Adam knew. His fuzzy white hair stood in tufts around his over-sized head, and with his round belly and red-veined nose he resembled a jolly, giant elf. Adam couldn't help but smile hugely in return.

"Howdy to you, Mr. Tucker," Adam returned, leaning one elbow negligently on the unkempt counter. "Pa sent me in for some two-penny nails and a leather piece, say—" he gestured—"so big."

"That I c'n do, I shorely c'n do it," Nip nodded, then stuck out his lower lip and scratched his raspy chin thoughtfully. "Let's see now…two-penny nails." He ambled around the counter and waddled between aisles of barrels, peeking into each speculatively.

Adam knew the minute Nip found what he was looking for by the happy hiccup he released. As Nip waddled back to the counter for a paper sack, Adam wondered at the seemingly miraculous ability of Nip's to find anything he wanted; Adam had never been able to spot any kind of organizational system at work in the cluttered shop. Yet, to his knowledge, Nip had never disappointed a customer.

Nip dropped two huge handfuls of nails in the sack then carefully weighed them, squinting at the rusty scale with great concentration. "Pound an' a quarter," he announced, peering at Adam over his shoulder. "That enough?"

"Oughtta be," Adam answered.

"An' a strip o' leather, so big?" Nip held out his beefy hands in query.

Adam nodded. "Yep. It's for a hinge on the chicken coop. Pa says the busy rooster just wore the other one out."

The men shared a snort of laughter as Nip located a pocketknife in the depths of his pocket and then used it to whack off a piece of leather about four inches long from a much longer strip. He dropped it in the sack with the nails.

"Can you add it to our tab?" Adam asked, taking the sack and rolling the top down. "Pa will be in at the end of the month to settle with you."

Nip waved a big paw in agreement. "No problem, Adam. Your pa's always as good as 'is word."

"Thanks a lot," Adam said, heading for the door with his purchase in his fist.

Before he had a chance to swing open the squeaky door, Nip was calling him back.

"Adam, would'ja mind playin' delivery boy for me?" he asked, huffing his way around the counter again. "I got a roll o' screen to replace that what's tore on the back door of your uncle's store. Could'ja run it over fer me?"

Adam watched the effort it took for Nip to pull his big frame around the confined spaces of the shop and readily agreed to deliver the screen.

"Thank ya much, boy," Nip bellowed good-naturedly, giving Adam's shoulder a friendly slap of thanks that nearly sent him through the door.

"Sure, no problem," Adam managed to reply through clenched teeth. When Nip turned his back, Adam rotated his shoulder gingerly and stepped out into the August brightness. He dropped his small sack over the edge of the wagon bed, tucked the roll of screen beneath his arm, and headed across the street toward the mercantile.

The girl stood at the south edge of Main Street beside a scrolled sign that stated "Mountain Lake—Est. 1849", surveying the area with practiced nonchalance. Her pa had been in the habit of calling her dimwitted, but she was as bright as a new penny, and her cornflower blue eyes missed very little. But, she acknowledged disdainfully, there wasn't much to see. Mountain Lake was hardly a town at all, compared to where she came from.

Meandering on bare feet past the livery barn where the pleasant ring of a hammer against anvil could be heard, she stepped from the dirt road onto a raised boardwalk that ran the length of the scanty business district. The first of the tall, false-fronted buildings was the Mountain Lake Bank and Trust with surprisingly ostentatious stained glass windows. Four limestone posts with iron rings imbedded in their tops were standing in a precise row at the edge of the walkway. One lazy horse with a fancy, two-seater buggy hitched to his hindside stood dozing in front of the second post, his tail swishing in slow motion.

A narrow alleyway separated the bank from two-storied Maudie's Cafe, the biggest building on that side of the street. The painted letters on the square plate glass window next to the door arched the message "Good Home Cooking"; the aromas that escaped as two older men opened the door and stepped out lent credence to the words. The smell of ham and fried potatoes sent the girl's stomach into spasms of hunger, and she side-stepped quickly past the men who were lingering in the walkway to chat.

She stifled a giggle as she paused in front of Emma's Millinery Shop which advertised "The Finest In Ladies Headwear" in a flowery script on a board above the door. The shop was tidy with its lapped siding and narrow windows with matching ruffled curtains, but it was barely a wart on the nose of a hippopotamus when compared to the towering Maudie's. It was so small, about all it seemed capable of housing was a dozen hats. She scratched the back of her left leg with her right big toe as her eyes took in the stores lined up along the opposite side of the street.

Koehn & Sons Milling, where there was a lot of activity, was directly across from the livery barn and had no planked walkway fronting it. Two plain, signless wood buildings crunched side by side next to Koehn & Sons Milling, separating it from a narrow, two-story brick building with a tell-tale doctor's shingle sticking out beside the solid wood door on ground level. A painted stairway on the far side led to a small landing above. The upper story appeared to wink proudly with twin windows—one of which had its shade pulled—bearing white painted shutters and empty flower boxes. Obviously, the doctor lived above his office.

Next to the doctor's stairway sat the Mountain Lake Post Office, a small, square, red brick building with a wide, wood-planked stoop and benches out front. Then came an empty lot sporting clumps of weeds and wildflowers. On the other side of the deserted lot was a large, once-gray building with "Tucker's Lumber & Hardware" painted on the side in child-ish letters. The green wagon she'd seen on the road earlier was hitched to the crude wooden rail in front of the store.

She swiveled her gaze back to the west side of the street, noticing with no small amount of relief that next to Emma's was the mercantile of Mountain Lake. This was the business she was most interested in.

Like the bank and Maudie's, the mercantile was a two-story wooden structure with a square, false front. Also like the bank and Maudie's, it was painted neatly with a white background and dark green window trim, but it possessed the only porch along the length of the boardwalk. Spooled posts decorated with bands of green and yellow held up each corner of the porch roof, giving the mercantile a pleasant, homey appearance.

South of the mercantile was a wide street that ran east and west, dividing the town into two neat halves. Railroad tracks lined the south edge of that street, with the freshly painted brown and gold train station standing sentinel at the southeast corner of the town's center. Its spanking new appearance made the girl wonder if railroad service had only recently arrived in Mountain Lake.

Further down, on the west side of Main Street, sat what the girl immediately recognized as a church with a tall, white bell tower and doors at each corner on the front. Further yet, on the east, was another familiar building—a schoolhouse with a much shorter white bell tower of its own. Two small, shirtless, barefooted boys in striped overalls were bouncing each other wildly on a plank teeter-totter in the schoolyard while a little girl in a ruffled dress and bright hairbows stood nearby, swinging her arms and seemingly cheering them on.

Behind and beyond the business district, on either side of the street, extended what the girl took to be mainly residential houses. While there wasn't a great deal here, she had to admit that every business—with the exception, perhaps, of the lumber and hardware store—and all of the houses she could see were well-kept with neat yards and recent paint jobs. Mountain Lake was small, but the people here apparently took pride in their town. For some reason she couldn't understand, it rankled her a bit.

Turning to wrap an arm around the nearest post in front of the mercantile, she spent a few more minutes planning her best course of departure. *West along the railroad tracks then around the bend and through backyards until I hit the edge of town is the quickest and safest escape route*, she thought. The decision made, she sucked in a big breath of fortification and began moving purposefully toward the screened door of the mercantile of Mountain Lake.

Chapter Two

The girl paused briefly outside the screen door of the mercantile to dampen the dirty palms of her hands with her tongue and swipe them roughly against the seat of her equally filthy overalls. She peered at her hands in vexation, puckering up her face with a scowl. Still dirty! *Well, they'll have to do,* she decided.

One last tug on her hat brim brought it comfortingly low around her ears. Ready now, she assumed a casual pose by hooking her thumbs in the rear pockets of her britches. The shoes still swung over one shoulder, thumping her chest and back rhythmically. With the shoeless shoulder she bumped the door open. A cowbell that hung above the screen door clanged a noisy greeting, startling her out of her nonchalance. She regained her posture quickly, though, as the shopkeeper lifted his bald head from measuring flour for a young woman with a shopping basket in her hand and a straw bonnet on her head. Looking at the neatly dressed woman, the girl at once felt dowdy and unkempt, and she was hit with the desire to turn tail and run.

"Be with you in a minute, son," the shopkeeper called out in a surprisingly deep voice for someone who was so small of stature, and the girl felt his eyes measuring her as carefully as he measured his dry goods. Running would look plenty suspicious, she knew, so she nodded a silent reply and quickly turned her back on him.

The store was as tidy as Gran's pantry at home, the girl noted, and it smelled wonderful! Tangy pickles, malty yeast, and pungent apples combined to create a heady aroma that sent the girl's nostrils twitching, her salivary glands spurting, and her stomach into spasms of desire. She turned a slow circle, examining, sniffing, enjoying. Everything was neatly categorized and displayed attractively: can goods lined up with military precision on homemade pine shelves, household items arranged for easy contemplation. The store epitomized order and cleanliness, as well as a real pride of ownership. For a moment, the girl felt a pang of guilt for what she had to do. But another sharp pain of emptiness shot through her belly and overrode any feelings of guilt.

The store contained everything from household supplies to clothing to toys. A wondrous selection of fabrics and sewing notions beckoned from the northeast corner of the store, stirring a very feminine rush of pleasure. But wouldn't she look silly examining them all decked out in her overalls and lumpy hat! Besides, she was *hungry*. She moved resolutely to the west side where the canned goods were stored on plank shelving.

The cowbell clanged, announcing the exit of the woman customer, and the shopkeeper began dusting small bottles of medicinal cures lined neatly along a narrow shelf behind the counter. The girl could feel his watchful eyes following her.

The girl tried to appear as if she was checking off a mental list as she made her selections: a large tin of Edgemont crackers, two cans of spiced peaches (even though she wasn't sure she'd be able to pry them open), several cans of Van Camp's beans, and, with a burst of extravagance, an egg-shaped tin of ham. While she shopped, she went over the simple plan. The mercantile owner would keep an account book for customers to charge their purchases, with balances due at the end of the month. (It worked that way at home, but she and Pa were never allowed to charge since Pa couldn't be trusted to "pay up.") She'd just tell him to charge her selections to the Klaassen account, the owner would do it, the Klaassens would probably never even notice the small discrepancy on their account—from the looks of that fine farmhouse, they could sure afford it!—and she'd have food for a couple days until she hit the next town. It was a good plan, and no one would be hurt by it.

Balancing her load precariously, she leaned back and waddled awkwardly to the counter where she dropped it all with a series of resounding thuds. The shopkeeper placed his feather duster beneath the counter, smoothed a pink palm across his equally pink dome, and inquired, "Is that all?"

The girl paused as her eyes settled on the large glass jars displayed prominently on the countertop. Each wide-mouth jar contained a different goodie to satisfy the most discerning sweet tooth. From peppermint sticks to sour balls, to licorice whips, to brightly colored gumdrops and jelly beans her eyes roved, mouth watering.

The shopkeeper followed her gaze then smiled in understanding. He popped the cork on the jar closest to him and fished out a walnut-sized, sugar-coated red gumdrop. He extended it on his open palm almost beneath the girl's nose.

She looked up at him uncertainly, and he bobbed the candy invitingly and said, "Go ahead, on the house."

The girl licked her lips in anticipation and reached appreciatively for the proffered treat. Suddenly in her mind a voice snapped—*"Never take charity, girlie!"*—and her hand drew back as if slapped.

The shopkeeper thrust the candy forward and repeated, "Go ahead."

She reached again, apprehensively this time, peeking over her shoulder as if afraid someone might be watching. *Dummy,* she told herself, *Pa's not here!* She snatched the candy from the man's hand before she could change her mind again. It was settled in a bulky wad in her jaw before she remembered her manners and said belatedly, around the candy, "Fank 'oo."

The shopkeeper's eyebrows rose, but he simply swished his palms together to dispel the leftover sugar and said, "Yes, well, let's tally this up, shall we?"

He produced the stub of a pencil from behind his ear, licked the point once, and began figuring on a pad of paper near a large tin box which the girl presumed held his cash supply. After scratching out several numbers, he announced the total and inquired, "Will that be cash or charge?"

The girl had chewed down the gumdrop considerably and now swallowed with a visible bob of her Adam's apple before answering confidently, "Charge, please."

The shopkeeper reached below the counter again to bring up a leather bound book which he plopped on the countertop with a slap and then opened to the first page. He looked at her expectantly.

She gazed at the book, hands resting on the wooden counter, elbows splayed outward. When he made no move to record her purchase, she glanced up to find him staring at her strangely. Her heart began to pound. But he just cocked his head and asked, "Account name?"

"Oh," she breathed with relief, mentally kicking herself for being so dense. She drew herself up and announced, "Klaassen."

Her gaze dropped back to the leather bound book. When his hand still didn't move, she looked up again. This time the man's stare was accompanied by a scowl that brought his bushy eyebrows downward and created a series of deep furrows across his pink forehead. The girl gulped, her bravado fading fast.

"Klaassen, did you say?" the shopkeeper queried, his voice low and steely.

She nodded weakly, bringing her hands down to her sides. It hurt to breathe. She choked out nervously, "Y-yessir."

"*Simon* Klaassen?" he pressed, his voice a little louder.

She couldn't be sure that it was Simon Klaassen's house she'd seen, but she felt agreeing was the safest bet. So she nodded with her heart pounding in her throat.

The man shut the book with a bang, and for a moment the girl wondered if Mr. Klaassen hadn't paid his account regularly. His eyes pinned her in place as effectively as a nail holds a shingle. He asked, "And just *which* of the Klaassen boys are *you?*"

She felt like she had a hairball stuck in her gullet, but she somehow managed to answer, "Uh… S-Sam."

The man nodded. He lowered his head and glowered at her through the curly hairs of his eyebrows as he slowly rounded the counter. The girl backed up a step as he neared. Her muscles were tense and she was poised to run.

"Sam," he repeated, his arms crossed and forehead so furrowed it looked painful. His eyes were like granite. "Funny. My brother Simon has five sons, but I don't recollect a one of them's named Sam."

The terror that had been climbing now rose to a crescendo peak. *His brother!* The shopkeeper was *kin* to those Klaassens!

The girl's middle jumped, and as the man reached for her, she reacted instinctively. She kicked him as hard as she could in the shin—which no doubt hurt her bare toes as much as it did his leg—grabbed up the tin of crackers, and careened out the screen door, sending the cowbell clanging angrily behind her. Risking a glance back over her shoulder at the furious shopkeeper, she missed seeing the tall, straw hat-topped young man stepping up on the planked walkway. She ran full-tilt into his solid chest. He lost a roll of screen he was carrying, and her tin of crackers fell to the boardwalk with a tinny clunk.

The man caught her by the shoulders to steady them both, laughing an amused warning. "Whoa there! What's your hurry?"

She gave him a wild-eyed look and pushed on his chest with both hands. The shove off-balanced him, dislodged his hat, and nearly threw him on his backside. His hands flew from her shoulders, and she leaped from the boardwalk, running a zigzagged pattern down the dusty street.

Adam shook his head indulgently, watching her go, and leaned down to scoop up his hat and the roll of screen that had rolled against the side of the building when it fell. The cowbell above his uncle's shop door clanged, and Adam looked up to see his uncle in the doorway, shaking and pointing after the fleeing youth.

"Uncle Hiram, what—" Adam started, but was cut off by his uncle's excited shout: "Get'im! Catch'im! He's a thief!"

Without a second thought Adam thrust the roll of screen into his uncle's middle and took off after the girl. She'd gotten a good head start, but Adam's stride was twice the length of hers, and his feet were protected by sturdy work boots. It wasn't hard to overcome her. He reached out a long arm and caught her by an overall strap, swinging her around.

"Hold still!" he barked as the girl spun in circles, trying to free herself. Suddenly she swung her boots by the laces, the heels smacking him hard on the shoulder and bouncing off the side of his head. It hurt, and he released his hold, stumbling sideways a few steps. She took advantage of his over-balance and charged furiously, barreling headlong into his belly. Even as her head connected with his hard stomach, she realized it was a foolish, angry move, but there was no reversing it.

The impetus carried them both backwards several feet before he fell, catching one of her overall straps as he went and pulling her with him. He landed flat on his back with her sprawled across his chest. Now instinct kicked in, and with a simple maneuver Adam rolled over, pinning her neatly beneath him. He was panting with exertion from the brief chase and subsequent scuffle, but he managed to hold her down by the shoulders as she bucked and bellowed.

"Git offa me, you durn honyocker!" she squawked, kicking wildly.

"Not 'til you promise to behave yourself," Adam retorted in a stern voice, stung a bit by the rude term she'd called him. He sat on her stomach a little harder to subdue her as he continued, "Now if you'll be still, I'll—" But he stopped in astonishment as the battered hat flipped back, revealing a mane of tangled auburn curls. The girl realized that the hat was slipping, and her arms scrambled to retrieve it, but Adam had her pinned. She couldn't reach it.

"Why, he's a *girl!*" came a startled voice from behind Adam's shoulder, and Adam looked up into the surprised face of his uncle Hiram. Beyond Hiram's shoulder, lining the boardwalk, Adam now noticed several spectators—overall clad men, women in go-to-town dresses and bonnets, and a cluster of snickering youngsters who apparently were heading out on a fishing venture as cane poles were propped on their shoulders and they cheerfully swung syrup buckets filled with worms. Even the banker had left his desk and stood in his doorway, watching with an amused look on his mustached face.

Adam leaped up as if hornet-bit, never in his life having been as embarrassed as he was at that moment. Why, he'd never tackled a girl before! Not even his *sisters*! And to do so in the middle of Main Street with half the town watching yet! He blushed from neck to hairline.

The girl was pushing herself to her feet, and Hiram reached out to assist her, hauling her up by the straps of her overalls. She tried once to pull away, but he gave her a firm shake, commanding, "You're coming with me, missy!" and began herding her back toward his store. Shame-faced and still somewhat in shock, Adam grabbed up her ugly brown hat and followed.

Hiram's feet pounded the dirt street, sending up angry puffs of dust with each step. The girl walked stiffly with her chin held at a defiant angle, but she seemed to have lost her fire. Back in the store, Hiram gave her a push towards the apple barrel and demanded, "You sit right there, young lady!" She did so without a fuss. She held her knees together with her palms pressed between them, her back ramrod straight and her head tipped down. When Adam held her hat out to her, she didn't even glance up, just reached out a dirty hand to grab it and throw it to the floor by her feet, then resume her stiff pose. Hiram was in a state of agitation. Adam had never seen him so upset—even his nearly bald head was glowing red from compressed fury.

"Uncle Hiram, what's she done?" Adam asked in an intentionally calming voice.

Hiram wasn't calmed. He spun towards Adam, his arm outflung as he gestured towards the girl and exclaimed, "Done? What's she *done?!* Why, she tried to make out with half the store, and put it on your father's account, no less! Stood right there at my counter and claimed to be Sam Klaassen! *That's* what she's *done!*"

Adam's right eyebrow shot up and he peered at the girl curiously. She reacted not a whit to his uncle's accusation, just sat there stiff as a board and as poker-faced as a judge. If she was scared or nervous, she was certainly good at hiding it.

"I'm going for Sheriff Barnes," Hiram announced, and Adam turned his attention back to his uncle. "Adam, you stay here and see that she stays put." Then to the girl he added in a stern voice, wagging a finger almost under her nose, "You stay put, hear?!"

If the girl heard, she gave no indication of it. She didn't even blink. Hiram snorted and shoved his way out the door, sending the cowbell into clamor again. Adam reached up and caught it, stilling the sound. He stayed by the doorway, his arms crossed over his chest and watched the girl as Hiram's stomping steps faded away. Adam speculated that his uncle really didn't want to file formal charges but wanted to put the fear of God into the young thief—wanted her to sweat a little bit. The girl sat still, staring at her hands in her lap, a sullen expression on her face. If Adam hadn't known better, he might have thought she was carved of stone. He'd never seen anyone who could sit without even a muscle twitching.

It didn't take long for the silence to grate on Adam's nerves. He broke it by clearing his throat. The sudden sound caused the girl's jaw to tighten, but she didn't look up. Adam dropped his arms and moved toward her casually, seating himself on a keg close to her right leg. She shifted slightly to lengthen the gap between them. Adam had to grin at her belligerence. She sure was a funny little thing.

"What's your name?" he asked in a friendly tone. No response. "Who are your folks?" he tried. The girl lifted her head and shook back her hair, still refusing to meet his gaze or answer him. Adam tried another tack: "You do realize stealing is a crime, don't you?"

This time the girl turned her face to him and gave him a look that said very clearly, *Leave me alone.* Their eyes

29

locked—Adam's amused, hers stony—and both were stubborn enough to hold that gaze for an eternity.

Hiram burst back into the store, and Adam turned away from the girl to meet his uncle halfway across the floor. The girl retreated back into her sullen pose.

"What'd the sheriff say?" Adam asked.

Hiram paced in agitation. "Oh, he wasn't even there! Old Hilarius Schwartz's cow wandered away again, and he was out helping hunt. Honestly, if Hilarius would put a bell on that animal it would certainly make for a lot less fuss and bother!"

Adam hid his smile. Uncle Hiram had to be mighty upset to complain about Mr. Schwartz. Everyone knew Adeline the cow was 90-year-old Hilarius's best friend, and Hiram himself had helped seek her out in the past. Hilarius believed a cowbell would just make Adeline nervous, so he refused to hang one around her neck. Whenever the cow took a mind to wander, finding her was a challenge without the tell-tale clang of a bell to guide the seekers. Any other day, Hiram would have laughed about the sheriff being called out on a cow hunt in the heat of the afternoon. But not today.

Adam leaned against the counter, watching his uncle pace. He ventured to inquire, "So what are you going to do with her?"

Hiram stopped pacing to angle an angry glare at the still-silent girl. "Do? Well, I guess just send her home." He marched across the room to stand in front of the girl, hands on bony hips. "Okay, young lady, what's your name?" he fired.

The girl didn't give him any more attention than she had paid Adam.

"You've got a name besides *Sam Klaassen*," Hiram spat, "so what is it?"

When the girl did not so much as move a muscle, Hiram threw up his hands in exasperation. To Adam, Hiram said, "I guess I'll just have to keep her here 'til Hank comes back, then hand her over to him. Maybe a night in the hoosegow will loosen her tongue."

"Jail?" Adam asked in surprise. "Do you really think that's necessary?"

"The last I knew, stealing was still a crime," Hiram countered evenly. "Besides, there's also the matter of assault and—"

"*Assault?*" Adam interrupted, his voice rising.

Hiram glared at him. "Yes, assault!" he snapped, daring Adam to argue. "She kicked me hard enough in the shin to raise a welt, not to mention how she barreled into you!"

"Well, I'd as soon forget—" Adam started, turning red again.

"Besides," Hiram continued, "you know as well as I do there'd be nobody at the jail except old Fitz sleeping off his weekday drunk. She'd just be out of harm's way until her family could come and get her. Assuming, of course"—and he shot the girl a meaningful look—"we figure out who she is."

Adam leaned in close to his uncle and spoke softly, but loud enough for the girl to hear if she wanted to. "Uncle Hiram, I'm not sure jail is the answer here."

"What then?" Hiram queried, lowering his voice to match that of his nephew.

"Look at her, Uncle." Adam waited until Hiram's gaze was pinned on the scrawny child so bent on ignoring them. "She's just a kid, probably no older than Arn," Adam said, refering to his fourteen-year-old brother who was rather a pet to Hiram. "And look how thin she is. Stealing isn't right, but doesn't she look hungry? Seems to me what she needs is a bath, a good meal, and a warm bed, in that order."

Hiram was mellowing. Adam could see the lines around his eyes softening. He plunged on. "Now, since she tried to charge the food on Pa's tab, maybe I ought to go ahead and take responsibility for her. I'll take her home, let Mother see to her needs, and you can get hold of Sheriff Barnes and see that he gets word to her family. I reckon her own pa will have a dose of medicine waiting for her when he hears of her mischief, so let's let him handle it."

The men, engrossed in their conversation, didn't notice the girl's reaction to Adam's last words. Fear flashed in her eyes, and her fists clenched convulsively. Her thoughts raced, *Can't let 'em tell Pa where I am! I gotta get away!*

Hiram shook his head in defeat. "Okay, Adam, you win," he conceded. "You take her home. I'll walk over to the post office and leave a message for the sheriff that we've got a runaway on our hands. I imagine he'll come out and get her name out of her."

But he shook a finger at his nephew. "But you watch her! Don't let her rob you blind!"

Mockingly Adam crossed his finger across his chest, tongue in cheek. Hiram snorted. "You and your strays," he said fondly, shaking his head. "Never could stand to let so much as an abandoned kitten starve in an alleyway, could you?"

Adam just grinned. "'Whatsoever you do for the least of these...'" he quoted, letting his words drift away. Hiram just shook his head again and gestured toward the girl.

"Take her home with you," he said, and headed behind the counter to gather up the things the girl had dropped earlier and return them to their places on the shelves.

"Ain't going."

The low voice from the thus silent girl startled both men into staring at her.

She lifted her head and fixed Adam with a steely glare. "Ain't going," she repeated, adding icily, "an' you can't make me. I'm no *stray*."

So she had been listening! Adam thought, *Cocky little thing. Sits there so tough, but with all that hair falling around her face, she just looks ridiculous.*

32

"Well, now," Hiram drawled, his hands going back to his hips in a stubborn stance, "I don't recall you being given any choice in the matter."

"Ain't going," the girl returned, her jaw set at a determined angle, arms crossed.

Hiram's jaw thrust forward in aggravation, and he opened his mouth to scold, but Adam held up a hand to silence his uncle and offered an ultimatum: "You can come home with me to a good meal and a warm bed…" he paused for effect, "or you can spend the night in the city jail. Actually, it's just the cellar under the post office, so it's not so bad except for the mice and spiders. And Fitz is harmless."

The girl winced at the mention of spiders, but quickly regained her composure. "I don't cotton to charity," she said, her chin thrust out sullenly.

Spunky! Adam thought.

Sassy! Hiram thought, and hollered, "You'll steal, but you won't take what's offered? Why, I ought to—"

Adam put a quieting hand on his uncle's arm. "My home, or the jail. It's your choice. What'll it be?"

Her chin quivered in anger, and for a moment Adam thought she might cry, but pride kept the tears at bay. She was silent several long seconds in thought before conceding, "I reckon I'll come with you." *It'll be easier to sneak away from a bunch o' honyockers than a lawman.* "But I'm leaving at first light. And all I want is the meal and bed—no bath."

Chapter Three

Once home, Adam handed a stiff, sullen girl to his mother's capable hands. He noticed the way Laura's eyes softened with maternal caring as she looked at the skinny, filthy waif before her. Adam felt the familiar swell of pride in his mother's innate compassion for the underdog.

"I still don't know her name," he admitted. The girl hadn't uttered a word on the bumpy ride home.

"That's all right," Laura said reassuringly, placing a soothing hand on the girl's flannel-covered arm. The girl jerked away as if struck. Laura's brows came together momentarily in concern, then smoothed out as she added gently, "We can get acquainted when you're cleaned up. Come with me and we'll get a bath drawn for you right away." And she placed an arm around the girl's stiff shoulders to gently guide her.

Adam watched the pair enter the house, one smiling and one scowling in what was already a familiar look of defiance. Turning away with a shake of his head, he sought his father. He found him in the tool shack where he was braiding several thin strands of leather together to repair a broken harness.

"Pa," Adam drawled in greeting as he leaned lazily against the door frame.

Simon Klaassen looked up and shot his son a lop-sided grin. "Hey, son, I thought maybe you decided to spend the night with Nip," he chided gently, as close as he would come to scolding Adam for his late arrival.

"No, no," Adam countered, "not this time. But I did bring someone home to spend the night here."

Simon asked cheekily, "Nip?"

Adam gave an amused snort. "No, not Nip." Briefly he explained his encounter with the young lady he'd left at the house, being careful to leave out the part about tackling her in the street. Just thinking of it made the blood rush to his face—the fewer who knew, the better!

"You did the right thing, son," Simon assured him at the end of his monologue. He let escape a throaty chuckle. "I sure would've liked to have seen Hiram's face when he realized the thief was a girl."

Adam chuckled, too, in spite of his own embarrassment at the revelation. "I left her at the house with Mother. She had sworn off a bath, but knowing Ma I expect she'll be convinced of the benefits one way or another."

"Reckon so," Si agreed. "Now, about the chicken coop…"

"First thing in the morning, sir," Adam promised as he headed back to the wagon to unhitch the horses and give them their supper and a good brushing. As he loosened the horses from their riggings, he saw Teddy and Becky filling buckets at the iron pump while little Sarah waited by the back door, ready to open it for their entrance. He grinned to himself as he led the horses to the barn. It looked as if there'd be a clean young lady at the supper table after all.

Adam came in from putting up the horses and crossed straight to the wash basin tucked below the stairs, next to the pantry. He dropped his suspenders from his shoulders and let them dangle at his knees. After pushing his shirt sleeves well above his elbows, he leaned over the basin to splash water on his face once, then again. He lathered his hands with his mother's homemade lye soap, scrubbed his face, washed clear to his forearms, then rinsed. Only when he had dried himself with the rough towel hanging conveniently on a nail hammered into the pantry door-jamb did he realize he was being watched. As he pulled his suspenders back in place, he looked over his shoulder to find himself under the careful scrutinization of a young girl.

She sat on a chair in the corner of the kitchen. A light spattering of freckles danced across her cheeks and the bridge of her nose. Her hair was clean and hung in damp curls well below her shoulders; in the yellow lamplight of the kitchen it had a reddish cast. Had it not been for the unwavering stare from her unusual eyes of cornflower blue, he might not have realized it was the same girl he'd tussled with in the street only a short hour or so ago.

He was amazed by the transformation. Gone were the grimy overalls and man's hat. In their place she wore a light-weight calico dress that Adam recognized as having belonged to his sister Liz. She looked small and vulnerable… and painfully young. Adam felt a swell of sympathy. He sent her a smiling nod, but her only response was to turn her head toward the commotion in the kitchen. And there was quite a commotion.

At mealtime, the children "melted out of the wallpaper," as Laura Klaassen was fond of saying. It must have appeared that way to the Klaassen's dinner guest. The girl's bare feet were tucked under the straight-backed chair on which she perched, left foot over right. Occasionally she rubbed her left foot up and down the top of her right one in apparent nervousness. The only other movement she made was the widening of her eyes as the number of people in the kitchen multiplied with the slam of the back door or a clatter of feet on the stairs. It was obvious the girl didn't come from a large family.

And as for the Klaassen children, they eyed their guest with friendly interest, some smiling and others speaking a polite "hello." The girl responded to each overture in exactly the same way: blankly. She simply remained still and silent on the chair, watching with wariness the bustle of activity. Each Klaassen had a job to do, and these were accomplished amongst teasing comments and much laughter. They never would have guessed that behind the closed expression on the freshly-scrubbed face of the young girl there lurked a wild jealousy for the enjoyment they took in one another.

When Simon Klaassen entered the house, the children all greeted him noisily, the smallest girl running to him to be swung up in his arms. She rode his hip as he crossed the floor to deliver a chaste kiss on his wife's upturned cheek. The girl noticed his gaze traveling in her direction so she turned her head sharply away. She watched out of the corner of her eye as he lowered the little girl to the floor and whispered something in her ear. The child scampered off happily, and the girl focused on a small tear in the wallpaper near her elbow as she fought the building of a strange pressure in her chest.

While Si took his turn at the wash basin, Adam crossed the kitchen to lift the lid of a heavy black skillet resting on the stove.

"Here, now, no sampling!" his mother teased, taking the wooden spoon he'd picked up for that purpose and replacing the lid on the pot. When he made as if to reach around her, she slapped at him playfully. "You can wait a few more minutes."

"Yes, ma'am," Adam grinned, planting a kiss on his mother's cheek. It never ceased to amaze him that his tiny mother had brought ten children into the world and still had the energy to keep up with all of them. He respected his father, he loved his sisters and brothers, but he adored his mother. It was on her lap that he'd snuggled to hear his first Bible story, and it was beside her he'd knelt in the chicken coop (of all places!) when he was only five years old to ask Jesus into his heart. Yes, his mother was special.

Si joined the pair at the stove, and reached past Laura to sneak one of the pickled eggs that she had arranged on an oval platter. Adam noticed Ma didn't slap Pa's hands.

"So what's the story on our little beggar?" Si asked quietly behind Laura's ear.

Laura shot the girl a quick look, then told her husband and Adam what little she'd managed to pry out of the child. "She says her name is Frances Welch," she said, "and that she's traveling. Says she's nineteen years old"—Si's eyebrows raised to his hairline and his wife nodded in understanding—"and on her own."

Adam then repeated what he had shared with his father earlier about the attempted grocery theft, and Laura shook her head sadly. "Poor thing. She must have been awfully hungry to try something like that."

They both looked over to observe the girl. Little Sarah was animatedly entertaining her with a picture book. Frances Welch, as they knew her, was wearing the closest thing to a smile as one can get without actually smiling.

Si exchanged a look of indulgence with his wife, then clapped his hands together briskly twice, announcing, "Come, family. Let's eat!"

With much foot stomping and careful shoves, the family members slid into place on long benches which lined both sides of the plank table that took up much of the center of the kitchen. Laura, the platter of pickled eggs in her hands, stood at one end of the table, and Si moved to the opposite end. Laura set the platter down and held out a hand to the girl who still sat in the corner.

"Children," Laura introduced when the girl came to stand self-consciously beside her, "this is Frances Welch. She is going to be staying with us for a few days."

The girl shot her a startled look, but said nothing.

"Frances," Laura continued, eyeing her warmly, "you won't be able to remember all these names right at first, but..." She started with the small child who'd been talking with her and introduced each member of the family in turn. "This is our youngest, Sarah." Sarah beamed a bright toothless smile. "Then there's Teddy, Becky, and Arn." Teddy, nine years old and scared of girls, ducked his head and blushed when his name was mentioned. Becky, eleven years old and fearless, nudged him and snickered. Arn's freckles seemed to glow like copper pennies in his friendly face.

"On the end is Mr. Klaassen," Laura continued. "You met Adam in town"—Adam waved a hand in casual response—"then there's Frank and Josie." Frank was just a slightly older, slightly huskier version of Adam, and Josie seemed friendly enough with her soft brown eyes and upturned lips.

Laura finished the introductions by saying, "We have two more children, Liz and Daniel, but they're married and living on their own now. You might meet them later." The girl looked doubtful, but Laura just gestured to the spot on the bench next to Josie and said, "You slide in here next to Josie now."

Josie smiled and patted the seat next to her invitingly. After a moment of hesitation, the girl sat down.

Simon clasped his hands in front of him, and, as if on cue, everyone around the table followed suit. Then all heads bowed in unison. That is, all heads but the clean shiny head of one Miss Samantha O'Brien, alias Frances Welch. While the Klaassen family listened to the head of the household deliver thanks for the evening meal, Samantha O'Brien silently filled her pockets with two pickled eggs, a funny little double-decker roll, and a chunky piece of sausage, all the while watching carefully the bowed heads to be sure she wasn't caught.

At the other end of the table, Si concluded his prayer with a reverent "Amen," that was echoed by all family members, large and small, in various vocal tones and volumes. Then the bowls and platters of food were sent around the table, with healthy servings spooned up to fill the well-used Blue Willow plates.

Samantha could hardly keep from licking her lips in anticipation as she helped herself to crisply fried potatoes, garden fresh tomatoes and green beans, puffy browned rolls—funny-looking buns with a top that was smaller than the bottom—sausage links, and a host of relishes. She slathered the buns liberally with butter that had been churned only that morning and Laura's own mulberry preserves. It took a great deal of self-control to avoid sneaking bites between passing bowls.

At last each plate held all it could hold, and the eating commenced. Samantha ate with the single-minded purpose of filling herself to the limit. Her nose hovered a mere four inches above her plate, the fork moving steadily between plate and mouth. The conversation that buzzed around her, as well as the clinks of silver utensils against china plates, was lost on her as she was totally absorbed in the meal. Her eyes didn't leave her plate until every bite was gone, and even the remnants of grease from the sausage and potatoes was sopped up with one last two-level roll.

The speed with which Samantha's food was being consumed had not been lost on the Klaassens. At one point or another, everyone from Frank on down to Sarah had stared in disbelief at Samantha's obvious hunger. The frowning shake of their father's head had stilled their tongues and turned their attention back to their own plates.

When she was finished, Samantha sat up and wiped her mouth with the cloth napkin resting beside her plate. She suffered a moment of embarrassment when she realized no one else was even close to finishing, but when they didn't seem to take notice, she relaxed.

Laura turned her gently lined faced to Samantha and asked, "Frances, would you care for anything else?"

Samantha offered a barely discernible shake of her head, and when Laura asked if she'd like to be excused, she stood wordlessly and stepped out the back door.

Adam helped clear the supper table when everyone was finished. That wasn't normally one of his chores, but since he had spent an extra amount of time in town that day, his sister Josie had thrown hay to the cows for him. He felt an obligation to help her out a little in return. However, he felt no such compunction when it came time to wash the dishes. Instead, he stated his intention to locate Frances and be sure she hadn't run off into the night. His mother answered dryly that she was certain the young lady wouldn't run far barefooted, but felt it was a good idea to offer her a bed, so Adam was sent out with her blessing.

Dusk had settled during the supper hour, and Adam stood still for a few minutes, enjoying the sounds of evening on a farm: gently lowing cows, the scratching of the chickens as they settled down in the coop, frogs calling to one another.

Adam loved the farm; he couldn't imagine ever leaving it. His brother Daniel had gone off to college to be a lawyer, and while Adam was proud of him, he didn't envy his city life one bit. The country—and the wheat—was his choice.

Taking a deep drag of the cooling air, Adam twisted his head this way and that, trying to spot their young visitor. For a moment he wondered if she had taken off, shoes or no shoes, when he didn't locate her anywhere in the yard. Then a thought: *Maybe she's ridden off.* He crossed quickly to the barn. Nope, all of the horses were standing contentedly in their stalls, and he called a "good night" when the yearling Pepper raised his head and snorted a greeting. He closed the barn door again and stood, hands on hips, deciding where to check next.

His feet carried him softly across the grassy yard to the front of the house where the scent of marigolds hung heavy in the humid air. Inhaling, he decided the German name of *schtinknelke* sure fit—they were rather stinky flowers. He started around the corner, then froze when he heard the murmur of voices. He cocked an ear, listening. What if she had a friend—a partner in crime, so to speak? He strained, then catching the words, his shoulders slumped in relief. It was only one voice, he was certain. He could see her now, seated in the shaded corner of the porch where Mother's lilacs partially shielded her from view. She was talking to herself, completely unaware of her audience. He wouldn't embarrass her by catching her at it. He turned to sneak away, but his foot came down on a twig and the snap rang out in the stillness of the evening.

"Who's there?" he heard her call out, and he sighed. *Might as well face the music*, he decided, and clumped up on the porch.

Chapter Four

amantha had located the porch swing by accident, but once she was settled in the shadowy
corner, surrounded by lilac bushes, she felt
more secure than she had for quite a while. She needed a
quiet spot to think—not only about her plans to move on,
but also about that funny feeling in her stomach. Her brow
furrowed in puzzlement. Such a strange feeling it was, not
the fearful churning her father's drunken rages had produced, and not a hungry emptiness. Indeed, she was more
than full! She'd not only eaten the plateful of food in the
house, she had eaten everything she'd stashed in her pocket,
too.

Maybe she was just feeling sick from eating too much,
she pondered. But no, it wasn't a sick feeling, either. It was

more of a hollowness—an emptiness that food wouldn't fill. And she didn't like it.

If she were to be honest with herself, she'd recognize the feeling for what it was: jealousy. She'd sat and watched the family inside the house preparing for their supper, working side by side with smiles and laughter. She'd seen their genuine enjoyment from just being together, and it had touched something in her. When she'd watched the father swing his little girl high in his arms for a hug, she had wondered for just a fleeting moment what it felt like to be lifted high in a father's strong, capable arms and held there. Even the praying part had stirred a reaction. All those heads bowed together, sharing something that they all believed and respected.... She started the swing in motion, suddenly restless, wanting to escape—but how could she escape these feelings?

Coming home next to Adam in the wagon, she had determined that they wouldn't outsmart Samantha O'Brien! She'd concocted the name Frances Welch, reasoning that if they didn't know her name, they couldn't send her home. That mother—Laura, her name was—had accepted her words as fact without a question. It should have pleased her, knowing that she'd fooled them. But instead it left her with vague feelings of remorse. They were obviously good people, and they deserved better than a lying thief in their midst. *And that's what I am,* Samantha told herself fiercely, *nothing but a sneaky little liar and a thief!* Those feelings made her angry with herself. *A bunch of farmers shouldn't be making me feel this way!* she scolded herself. *Don't think about it.*

But her thoughts pressed onward in spite of herself....

Samantha remembered a time when she'd been loved, when she'd been taught to kneel beside her bed and recite her "God blesses" at the close of a day. There was a time when grace had been spoken before meals, too, but it was a long time ago. When Gran was alive. Even now, after more than ten years, the lonely ache of missing her was still there. Samantha wrapped her arms tightly across her tummy and spoke softly to the slight breeze that whispered through the lilacs.

"Oh, Gran, I miss you so much. Why'd you have to go? Why'd you have to leave me? And David... Gone, too. Everybody I loved, gone. Why? Why..."

No answer came. Not that she expected one. She'd asked the questions before. Her father had caught her talking to the wind one day and had called her foolish. "Real smart," he had sneered disparagingly, "yappin' at the breeze. All it does is grab your words and carry 'em away." And he had made her come in the house.

She still did it, though—talked to the wind. It was comforting somehow, talking to something more powerful than she was. She was just careful about staying far away from her father when she did it.

"It's not foolish, Gran," she said now, lifting her head proudly. "'Cause maybe, just maybe, someday those words will be swept up to heaven and you'll hear me. And you'll send me somebody who will listen when I talk, like you used to, and maybe even care about what I say. And then I'll feel good again. Can you do that, Gran?"

She paused, face turned to capture the faint breeze, breathing in the sweet scent of lilacs and the aromas from supper. Her eyes were lifted heavenward, and she held her breath as her heart begged for a response. Then she heard a twig snap, and she went cold all over.

"Who's there?" she called out loudly, her hands clutching the swing seat, feet planted firmly, ready for flight.

"Just me," Adam said as he stepped up on the porch, stopping a few feet away from her to lean against the railing that separated the slender posts. He gave her a brief glance over his shoulder and commented, "Nice night, isn't it?"

She looked at him sideways, distrust written all over her face. "Yes," she finally acknowledged, "it is." Her voice was clipped and didn't invite further conversation.

He turned his face to the sky where the first stars were beginning to appear. "I thought maybe you had lit out, 'til I remembered we had your shoes. You couldn't go too far with bare feet."

"No." Gradually she relaxed back into the swing, allowing it to move slightly. Apparently he hadn't heard her babbling. *I'm gonna have to be careful 'til I can git outta here! Too many cotton-pickin' ears around this place!*

"Are you tired?" Adam inquired, still observing the stars. "Mother sent me out to find you and offer a bed."

Samantha shrugged. "I guess." Then, defensively, she added, "But just for one night. What she said at supper, about me being here a few days? That's not right. I'll be on my way tomorrow."

Adam shifted his weight on the railing and crossed his arms casually. He finally turned his head to look directly at her. "Well, I haven't got a problem with that, but I imagine the sheriff will want to talk to you first. I tell you what, come on in now and let Mother get you tucked in for the night, then we can worry about arranging your travel plans in the morning."

Indecision marred her face, which, Adam noted, was a rather pretty face, partially lit by the lamplight shining through the parlor window. Curling lashes threw a soft shadow on high cheekbones, and her blue eyes were almost luminous in the pale yellow light. Her full, bow-shaped lips were now set in a tense pout and Adam wondered what she would look like if she would just let down her guard once and smile.

Samantha stared outward, unaware of the scrutiny she was receiving. For several minutes she sat in silence, trying to decide how to respond to Adam's request. At last she sighed, and pushed to her feet. "All right. I'll talk to your sheriff. But after that, I'm leaving!" she finished adamantly, the stubborn thrust back in her jaw.

Adam raised his hands in defeat, and she marched past him and headed for the back door. Shaking his head in amused exasperation, Adam followed.

Sheriff Barnes turned up unexpectedly on the Klaassen doorstep later that evening, sent out by Hiram. The youngest Klaassen children were already settled in bed, with their guest tucked in next to Josie in her big feather bed. Laura came downstairs after calling her customary, "*Schlop Die gezunt*," to find the swarthy sheriff seated at the plank table with Si, enjoying a cup of strong, black coffee. Adam was leaning in the doorway, and he moved aside to let her pass. Si and Adam had already filled the sheriff in on what they knew about the girl. It hadn't taken long; they knew so little.

After offering a piece of rhubarb pie which the sheriff politely declined with a humorous pat on his extended belly, Laura poured herself a cup of coffee and seated herself across from the sheriff. Si shifted a bit closer to her and put a hand on her shoulder.

"Our young guest feels compelled to leave first thing in the morning," Laura informed the men, one hand curled around her coffee mug and the other reaching up to hold Si's hand. "Although I think she's very good at hiding her feelings, she still seems frightened of something." She turned her worried gaze to her husband. "Si, you don't think she's running from the law, do you?"

Si shook his head and rubbed Laura's shoulder consolingly. "Well, I realize she was trying to steal from Hiram, but she hardly seems old enough to have gotten into too much trouble yet."

Sheriff Barnes stroked his bushy mustache thoughtfully with a forefinger. "My guess is that she's a runaway and wants to be on her own. I suspect a mighty big hunger led her to attempt the food robbery. She didn't threaten Hiram in any way"—he chuckled—"although she did give him a pretty good bruise on the shin. She's probably got a very worried mama sitting at home, waiting for her return."

Laura and Si exchanged glances, and Adam shifted against the door frame. Si asked what they all were wondering: "So what do we do in the morning when she tries to leave?"

Sheriff Barnes sighed. "Whatever her reasons for being here, her family will have to be contacted. Despite her claims to the contrary, it's obvious that she isn't old enough to be on her own, and she'll have to be sent home. If we find she doesn't have a family…. Well, we'll just cross that bridge if we come to it. To keep her here, threaten her with criminal prosecution for attempted theft, if you have to. For good measure, throw in battery for that kick on the leg Hiram got. I'll do some checking—her family will have turned her in as a runaway, so someone will know something."

Si and Laura nodded in agreement, and the sheriff stood to leave. After thanking Laura for the coffee, he took a big breath that expanded his middle, then he rolled back on his heels—a sure sign that he had something important to say. Everyone waited attentively.

"Si, Laura, you're good people," he said at last in a deep, serious voice. "You mean well, and I know I'm leaving that girl in good hands. But I feel I should offer a word of warning. *Be careful.* No telling where she comes from or what she's learned. I'd hate to see you taken in by a little con artist."

"We'll be careful, Hank," Si promised, standing and reaching to shake the sheriff's hand. "Thanks for coming out."

"Just my job," Sheriff Barnes grinned, plopped his hat back on his head, and left.

Adam quickly sat down next to his mother, and, as his father turned back from closing the door behind the sheriff, he spoke earnestly. "Pa, I know what Frances did was wrong, but I really don't think she's bad."

Simon and Laura looked at their son expectantly. He felt the beginning of a blush staining his cheeks, but continued, "I think she's scared, and I think she was really hungry and desperate. I don't think stealing is something she does as a habit." He paused, suddenly feeling self-conscious about his intensity. Finally he asked, "Do you?"

Laura laid her hand on Adam's arm and smiled gently. "I think you're right, Adam. I think beneath that sullen exterior is a hurting little girl in need of a friend."

Adam nodded. He rose. "Well, I guess I'll turn in. I've got a chicken coop to work on tomorrow in addition to my other chores. 'Night, Mother, Pa." He gave his mother a kiss on the cheek and squeezed his father's shoulder as he headed for the stairs.

Safely behind the closed door of his bedroom, Adam let his head drop into his hands. He could hear a sad little voice echo, "Maybe my words will be swept up to heaven…and you'll send me someone to listen when I talk…" Then came his mother's words: "A hurting little girl in need of a friend." Adam lifted his head, his mouth set with determination. Well, for whatever time Miss Frances Welch was with them, he'd be her friend, her listener. And maybe, with someone around who cared, they'd all see a change for the better in that lonely young woman's life.

Chapter Five

*S*amantha drifted slowly awake as the soft patter of raindrops against cedar shingles cut through her dreams. She stretched lazily beneath the patchwork quilt covering her, eyes still closed, savoring the comfortable feather bed and sweet smelling sheets. She brought her fists up and rubbed her eyes, yawning widely as she did so, then opened her eyes slowly to squint into the dusky room.

She jerked upward and sat on her elbows, disoriented. *Where am I?* Then, remembering, she fell back on the thick pillows and sighed. *Oh, yeah…*

She threw back the quilt and padded on bare feet to the window where she drew the curtains aside and peered out at the late-summer rain. She groaned.

"Oh! You're up!" came a voice behind her, and she spun around, surprised.

"I'm thorry," said the littlest Klaassen contritely, peering up at Samantha with large blue eyes. "I didn't mean to thcare you."

"You didn't," Samantha lied, entranced by the child's china doll features and endearing lisp. "I just didn't hear you come in, that's all."

Sarah laughed, a tinkling laugh that reminded Samantha of sleigh bells. "Frank thayth I can be ath quiet ath a cat when I want to be. He thinkth I try to be thneaky, but I really don't. I'm jutht not big enough to make a lot of noithe yet."

It was difficult for Samantha to stifle the chuckle rising in her throat. The child was animated and lively—and completely irresistible.

"Sarah Louise," came Laura's stern voice from the doorway, "did you wake up Frances?"

Sarah twirled and rushed to her mother, wrapping her arms around Laura's waist and turning an innocent face upward. "Oh, no, Mama, Frantheth wath awake already. I jutht came in to talk to her."

Laura's eyes crinkled. "I'm not surprised, little chatterbox. Why don't you go downstairs and tell Josie that Frances is awake and needing some breakfast, hm?"

"Okay," Sarah returned cheerfully. She waved to Samantha, calling, "Thee you later, Frantheth!" as she skipped out the door.

Samantha took a step forward, a frown on her face. "Thanks for the bed an' all, Mrs. Klaassen, but I don't have time for any breakfast. I really need to get my hands on my own set of clothes, and then I'll be on my way."

"On your way?" Laura asked in surprise. "But, my dear, it's raining! You surely don't expect us to allow you to run off in the rain? No, you'll stay until the weather clears. Why, you'd catch your death out there!"

Samantha stared in disbelief as Laura moved into the room, scooping up the dress Samantha had been given after her bath the evening before and handing it to her. "I doubt this got soiled at supper last night, so just slip it back on after you clean up. Your clothes are in need of washing, and wash won't be done 'til Friday. Surely by then, the rain will have let up, and you'll be able to be on your way."

Laura paused by the door, gesturing to the washstand with its full bowl of water. "Just wash the sleep from your eyes, dress, and come down. One egg or two?"

Samantha's mouth dropped open. *How do I get out of this?* she wondered frantically. Laura waited expectantly. "Uh, one'll be fine, thank you," she answered.

"Very well," Laura smiled. "Now don't dally! The water's still warm." And she left, closing the door firmly behind her.

Well! Samantha thought, hands on hips, glaring at the door. *She sure takes a lot for granted!* But after a moment's worth of stewing, she sighed and moved to the washstand.

Samantha's breakfast was eaten—two eggs after all, along with three more of the rolls she'd enjoyed at supper the night before (Becky called them *zwiebach*), coffee, and a glass of milk—and her dishes washed within the thirty minutes after rising. The day stretched ahead endlessly, and Samantha was on tenterhooks, wondering how to fill it.

Sarah and Becky seemed determined to entertain, and "Frances" seemed determined to be aloof. It made for a rather dreary undertaking on the parts of the two younger girls, and they soon tired of being ignored and moved up to the attic to play with their rag dolls. Samantha sighed with relief at their departure. She had no desire whatsoever to form any sort of attachments here.

The men, from Si on down to Teddy, were outside some-where, Samantha assumed. There wasn't a male in the house, and that suited her fine. Samantha wasn't much on the com-pany of men. In her experience, men were demanding and temperamental—not the type of company one sought out for any length of time. Of course, Samantha's experience with females wasn't a whole lot better. Where she came from, the girls were catty and condescending, seeming to take great pleasure in making one feel foolish and gauche. Trust in humankind had definitely not been developed in Samantha. She had been a loner since she was six years old, and she did-n't see that changing in the near future.

Now she wandered hesitantly into the parlor. She looked around with interest. Although the house wasn't fancy—the wallcoverings were plain and the furnishings were simple—it seemed opulent when compared to Samantha's three-room cracker box of a house. The Klaassens didn't own many extras, but what they had was cared for with pride; all was as clean as rain-washed flowers. It smelled good, too, Samantha noted, wondering where the pleasant herbal scent came from. Had she gathered up her courage to ask, she would have learned that Josie enjoyed mixing herbs and dried flow-ers into potpourri which was tied into cheesecloth and hid-den in discreet corners. When combined with the typical Minnesota humidity, it made for a nose-pleasing back-ground aroma.

Samantha seated herself stiffly on the edge of the camel-back sofa, taking care not to touch the highly polished wood-trimmed armrests. She was nervous of smudging anything. She stared out the window, watching the rain continue to fall, and her thoughts ran faster than the raindrops racing down the long, narrow windows.

Despite her misgivings of last night, she felt pretty smart now, having come up with a false identity. If she was stuck here, being only known as Frances Welch would make it nigh on impossible for them to trace her back to Pa. A small-town sheriff wouldn't be terribly bright, she was sure, so no doubt he'd only look into the name she'd given, not her description.

She gave an audible sniff at that thought. She could imagine how Pa would have described her when alerting the authorities that she'd run off again. "Jest a sawed-off runt, spindly, with a long ol' rat's nest o' hair on 'er head... an' dumber'n a rock, that'd be my girl," she'd heard Pa say about her to one of his cronies. At the time she'd trembled with rage and had wished him dead for the hundredth time.

Well, she decided with no small amount of smugness, *Pa's right about one thing—I'm not so awful big. But I'm not so dumb. I managed to get away and he hasn't managed to find me this time. And I plan to keep it that way!*

If only the rain would stop and she could get moving! The longer she stayed in one spot, the more likely it was that somehow, some way, Pa would catch up to her. He seemed to possess some sort of sixth sense peculiar to drinking men— he always found her. And she was determined to escape the prison that had been home, just as Davey had escaped.

As always, thoughts of her brother brought a lump to her throat. She swallowed hard, trying to force it down. That lump of longing brought the desire to cry, and Samantha didn't cry—not anymore. Tears were for weaklings, and Samantha was no weakling! She'd been able to keep the tears at bay since she was six years old, and she wasn't about to change that now. She was going to prove to Pa and to anyone else who cared to look on that she was strong enough to stand on her own, just like Davey was. Davey had proved it when he'd run off almost seven years ago. He'd promised to come back for her, but she figured once he'd gotten settled, he'd decided it was easier not to have to worry about a kid sister. She had waited, but he hadn't come back. And after all this time, Samantha was tired of waiting. She couldn't depend on Davey—she'd have to depend on herself.

From the kitchen came the murmur of voices. Josie and her mother must have finished their upstairs chores, for they'd come down the stairs, laughing at something together. Samantha could tell from the tones of their voices and the occasional burst of laughter that the conversation was a lighthearted one. She felt a pang of desire to join them, to feel just once what it was like to be part of a family such as this one. But Samantha was well-schooled in putting a stop to such yearnings. Instead of joining in, she interrupted the conversation to ask, "Would it be okay if I went out and sat on the porch swing?" If she was outside, she wouldn't be tempted to pretend she belonged.

"Certainly, Frances," Laura nodded. "I enjoy that swing, too. Perhaps I'll join you when Josie and I have finished mixing the bread dough."

Samantha shrugged noncommittally and slipped out through the parlor door which led directly to the swing area of the large, covered porch. She sat down in the direct center of the swing, kicking her feet against the wooden porch floor to set it in motion, drinking in the scent of rain and lilacs.

Suddenly, unbidden, a memory surfaced, aided by the quiet patter of rain and the fresh smell. She was a little girl again, standing in the rain at a gravesite, holding a large cluster of wildflowers beneath her chin, listening to the droning voice of a minister give his final farewells. Samantha squeezed her eyes tight, trying to shut down the replay in her mind, but behind her closed lids she could see clearly the plain pine box which held the dear body of her Gran. She could see her pa, too, standing sullenly beside her, chin thrust out, hands behind his back, his hat firmly on his head to shield himself from the falling rain. And Davey was there, hat in hands, his tears mixing with the raindrops that ran in rivulets down his thin cheeks.

She stood abruptly and moved to the porch railing, digging her fingers into the hard painted wood. Had Pa been sad that day? Had he cried on the inside only, as she had, afraid that if the tears began they would never end? Gran was his grandmother. Did he miss her at all? Somehow, Samantha doubted it. Someone as self-centered as Burt O'Brien had thoughts for no one but himself.

Pa was probably just wondering who was gonna do the cooking an' cleaning, with Gran gone, Samantha thought resentfully, remembering how he had ranted that night, complaining about the scanty meal six-year-old Samantha had put together for them. David had eaten silently, uncomplainingly, but Pa.... But then, Pa always complained about everything. Gran was the only reason she and Davey had stayed.

Samantha scowled, despair filling her once more as she remembered helping Davey pack, whispering in the dark so Pa wouldn't hear. "Soon as I'm settled, Sammy, I'll send for ya. Just wait for me, okay, Sammy?" And Samantha, trusting, had waited. Waited seven long years, years of Pa's drunken rages, years of lying awake in the dark, thinking, *This is the night Davey'll be comin'.* Well, she wasn't waiting anymore. From now on, Samantha O'Brien was responsible for Samantha O'Brien, and the fewer people she trusted, the better.

Across the wide yard, she saw young Teddy splashing through a mud puddle, a huge grin splitting his face. The boy was soaked and muddy to the knees. Samantha cringed, imagining the trouble he'd be in when his pa caught him fooling around so. She saw Si appear in the doorway of the barn, and she held her breath in sympathetic apprehension. But then she took a good look at Si, and the breath she held was released in a rush of relief.

Although Samantha couldn't make out Si's face from this distance—he stood in full shadow in the barn doorway—she could tell that his stance was relaxed, not angry: feet planted wide, torso leaning back, hands resting loosely in his overall pockets. Then, much to her surprise, he bent down and yanked off his own boots and thick socks. With a gallop he crossed the ground to join his son! She could hear the man and boy hoot with laughter, and something thick and stifling rose within her. She turned away only to catch Laura's laughing face in the parlor window, watching their antics with obvious pleasure.

As a child, if Samantha had come home dirty, she got a good licking for soiling her clothes. She had learned early to sidestep mud puddles and hold her skirt high to avoid being splashed by others sloshing through them. But here was a grown man, playing like a child, and his wife was laughing about it! Samantha looked from Si to Teddy to Laura, then back again. It was puzzling, the way these people acted. They were making her very uncomfortable.

She turned her face to the rain and sent a silent wish for sunshine so she could be on her way before this family and their cheerful manner of living created a desire to stay.

Chapter Six

The rain lasted three days—three of the longest days of Samantha's not-so-long life. During those days she spent a lot of time looking and listening and spent a great deal of energy trying to look as if she *wasn't* looking and listening. By the end of the third day in the Klaassen household, Samantha was convinced there was something seriously wrong with the whole family.

For one thing, Si didn't go into town with the men, and certainly didn't seem to require any whiskey to keep him happy. Samantha couldn't get over how hard he worked, and how hard the boys worked, trying to keep up with him. She'd never seen such an industrious man in her life. What was he trying to prove, anyway? Yet as hardworking as he was, he was lighthearted, too—she'd seen that the day he'd pranced in the rain with Teddy. The children all minded him, but Samantha never once heard him raise his voice, and certainly never saw him raise his hand to any of them. Samantha couldn't figure out for the life of her how he managed to keep everybody doing what they were supposed to be doing.

And Laura was a puzzle, too. She had permanent lines around her eyes from smiling. Her face was always carrying a hint of a smile that was more in her eyes than on her lips. Most people who grinned all the time got on Samantha's nerves because it made them look rather feeble-minded, but Laura was far from that! She had tons of work to do, too— chickens to look after, wash for a family of nine as well as meals three times a day and all the baking that went with it, a garden to care for, a house to keep clean…. It all seemed overwhelming to Samantha, who was accustomed to a very small home and very few people around to look after. Yet Laura never complained about the heavy work load. She smiled and teased her way through the days, completing her tasks in a cheerful manner.

Samantha had always been a hard worker—more by necessity than design—but she couldn't claim to be overly cheerful about it. It had always aggravated her that she'd no more than get things straightened around when Pa, alone or with some of his buddies, would come through with dirty feet and lips full of snuff and muck things up. Samantha didn't understand Laura's lighthearted attitude toward work, either.

Then there were the Klaassen children! Here was Frank, nearly as big as a barn himself, still living at home and minding his Pa. Samantha figured once kids grew to be big enough to take care of themselves, out they'd go. But Frank, and Adam, too, were more men than boys, still following their father's lead and seeming to not mind it a bit. Josie and Becky had lots of jobs to do, helping their mother keep things in order. Arn was always out with the men—every time

Samantha looked at him he'd go red in the face which made his freckles glow—and didn't seem to mind the work, either. Teddy and Sarah weren't as tasked as the others, being the youngest, but they had their responsibilities. Only once had Samantha seen any of them shirk their duties, and that was Sarah, who Samantha had decided was just a wee bit spoiled. Scuffles between siblings were few and far between, too. Seemed to Samantha that with this many people in one house, they'd be feuding all the time, but they all got along.

Yep, something was definitely not right here.

But if this was "not right," Samantha had to acknowledge, it wasn't exactly wrong, either. It sure wasn't normal—not from her standpoint—but it was rather nice. It was peaceful, a feeling Samantha hadn't known heretofore. And she wondered if, when she left, she'd be able to find it somewhere else on her own.

Adam had been spending some time in deep thought as well during the rainy days that kept him and the other men holed up in the barn doing busy work to fill their days while wishing they could be in the fields. The promise he had made to himself to be a friend to Frances Welch turned out to be a pie crust promise—easier made than kept. The girl eluded him at every turn! Any attempt at conversation was met with an even stare that seemed to look past a person, and if any answer came at all, it was monosyllabic at best.

Adam scrubbed at the old paint on the hay wagon, thinking of the way Frances's big pale blue eyes watched all of them. Usually you could look into a person's eyes and tell what he was thinking, but not this Frances. She could hold a blank face better than anyone he'd ever met. Often he'd watch her watch them and wish he knew what she was thinking. It was obvious she was uncomfortable—she was restless, almost like a caged animal, pacing from place to place in the house and avoiding all of them whenever possible. He had to wonder if she'd been mistreated at some point in her life, she was so distrustful of everyone, particularly the older male family members. He'd also noticed that whenever his mother tried to touch her—Laura was a very demonstrative person, and touching came naturally to her—she would pull away as if the touch hurt.

His hands stilled momentarily as he tried to pinpoint what it was that made her so different. After a moment, it came to him: she seemed emotionless. She didn't smile, didn't laugh, didn't cry…. Her face wore a mask of indifference to everyone and everything around her. What kind of life had she led that would bring about such a closed, empty shell of a person? What a barrier she had built around herself! But why? He was certain by now that, whatever the answer was, he wouldn't hear it from Frances's lips.

He set to work again as his thoughts tumbled onward. He hadn't known such close-mouthed females existed! Had the situation been less serious, he might've had some fun with that little idiosyncrasy of hers. The one person he'd seen her relax a bit around was the youngest family member, Sarah. With her bright smile and endless chatter, Sarah seemed to win Frances over from sheer innocence.

There had to be some way to gain Frances's trust and let her know that someone cared about her. Adam wasn't thinking so much of himself at that point, but of the One Adam had come to know personally as a very small boy in the chicken coop. If only he could let Frances know of the loving God Adam and his family were so secure in, she would have a permanent friend—a listener, as she had put it that night he'd heard her on the swing—to be with her no matter where she ended up.

Adam ceased his rubbing and paused to look out the open barn door. He could see Becky and Josie busy at the washtubs, scrubbing what looked like bed sheets. He sighed.

With everyone busy at chores, there wasn't much time to talk to Frances about God's unwavering love for her.

But, he conceded to himself, *even if we can't let her know with so many words, we can certainly show her with our actions, even when we're working.* Everyone down to Sarah could help in that regard.

Adam got back to his job, determined once again to somehow break through the barrier his family's houseguest had built around herself. He decided to talk it over with his pa as soon as he could find him.

Just then Arn burst through into the barn, hollering, "Hey, Adam! Pa says come quick and help! Hilarius's Adeline is loose again!"

Adam dropped his scrub brush over the edge of the wagon and answered, "I'm a-comin', Arn." His talk with Si would have to wait.

"Frantheth, gueth what?" Sarah stopped right under Samantha's elbow as she stood in front of the parlor window, staring silently outward. Samantha had been inwardly rejoicing that the rain had stopped, so freedom was near! Now she turned her gaze to Sarah, who peeked up at her with those blue, blue eyes that always caught Samantha off guard with their depth.

Once she'd captured Samantha's attention, Sarah gushed, "Thinthe tomorrow is Thunday, Lith and her huthband Jake are going to come here for dinner! Mama'th gonna make a thcripture cake, too! Won't that be nithe?"

Samantha nodded dumbly, wondering what in the world a "thcripture cake" was. By now she knew what scriptures were, that's for sure. After three days of being stuck in this house with Laura, she'd been introduced to a fair amount of it. Laura had a verse for every occasion, and her children were often seen winking at one another when she got to quoting. Plus the day got started with everyone sitting around the table, holding hands and listening to Si read a few passages from the Bible, then praying. As a guest, Samantha had been invited to join them, but she'd felt foolish sitting there holding hands with Laura and Josie, so after the first time, she'd stayed out of the kitchen 'til all that stuff was done.

"Lith ith going to have a baby, too," Sarah continued as she nearly danced through the parlor, tugging at Samantha's arm, giving her no choice but to skip along beside her to the kitchen. "It'll be jutht a while now an' that baby will be here. That meanth I'm gonna be an aunt again!"

Samantha's eyes grew wide. "You're an—an *ahnt?*" she asked, pronouncing the word the same way Sarah had. "But you're just a little kid!"

Sarah laughed. "I'm little," she agreed, "but Lith ithn't. She'th real big—and real fat now!" Sarah more or less pushed Samantha onto the nearest kitchen bench, then straddled the wide plank seat and swung her feet as she continued, "After Lith hath her baby, there'll be three babieth in the family. My biggetht brother got married to Rothe, and they have two babieth already—two girlth. Their nameth are Chrithtina and Katrina an' they're real cute! Daniel and Rothe live way in Minneapolith tho we don't get to thee them much, but Lith and Jake jutht live on the other thide of Mountain Lake, tho we thee them a whole lot. I'll get to know thith baby a lot better than Chrithtina and Katrina, that'th for sure."

Sarah finally stopped talking long enough for Samantha to absorb it all. If Sarah was an aunt already, then Laura was actually a grandmother! Samantha swiveled her gaze to watch Laura at the dry sink, rolling out dough to cut noodles. Laura looked nothing like the grandmother Samantha remembered. Laura was tiny—eleven-year-old Becky was only an inch shorter than her mother—and her nut-brown hair was swept back in a tidy coil that sported less than a dozen white hairs. Her brown eyes sparkled with vitality, and she looked far too young to be a grandmother!

Now Laura looked up and pinned Sarah with her gaze. She allowed her eyebrows to pull down just a bit as she asked, "Sarah, aren't you supposed to be helping Josie and Becky with the wash? If everything is to be dry by evening, they'll need your help."

Sarah gave Laura her best pleading look. "Oh, Mama, I wanna thtay here and talk to Frantheth. It'th tho hot outthide! Why do *I* have to hang clotheth?"

"Because when everyone does his or her share, the work gets done much faster," Laura replied in a tone that brooked no nonsense. "Now scoot!"

Sarah seemed to consider another argument, but thought better of it. She sighed. "Yeth, Mama," she said in a resigned little voice, and swung her leg over the bench to leave. As she stood, she looked at Samantha and asked hopefully, "Want to come too, Frantheth?"

Samantha looked to Laura is if for approval, and Laura smiled. "Go ahead, dear. Just don't let Sarah try to talk you into doing her share of the hanging!"

"Come on!" Sarah demanded, capturing Samantha's hand and pulling her out the back door.

Samantha hop-skipped after Sarah, who refused to relinquish her hand until they had reached the other two girls who were wringing out the wet wash and hanging it over the lines to dry. Becky turned, spotted Sarah, and made a sour face.

"It's about time," she scolded. "We're practically done! You sure know when to show up!"

"Now, Becky," Josie put in, trying to restore harmony, "you weren't much better about your chores when you were

Sarah's age." Becky opened her mouth to protest, but Josie cut her off with a gentle suggestion, "Let's not spend time fussing or we'll be out here all afternoon."

Sarah stuck her tongue out quickly at Becky, smiled at Josie, and ran to the basket to wrestle out a towel and wring the excess water from it. Samantha noticed Sarah's ineptitude with the task and crossed to help her. As she hung the heavy towel on the line next to similar items, she noticed her own overalls and flannel shirt hanging amongst the men's things closer to the barn. Her heart did a happy flip-flop. With her clothes back, she could be on her way! Maybe even by this evening!

Josie started singing a nonsense song about little children eating oatmeal, and Becky joined in. Sarah lisped her way on the words she could remember, just singing "la, la, la" in place of the ones she couldn't. Samantha listened in while moving between the baskets of wet laundry and the clothes lines, her hands busy and her heart light.

Before they knew it, the baskets were empty and three long lines of wet clothing, sheets and towels flapped in the warm, end-of-summer breeze.

Becky stood back, hands on her hips, and surveyed the rows of clean items with satisfaction. "Sure feels good to have that done!" she announced to no one in particular.

"Sure does," Josie agreed, stacking the empty baskets and scooping them up. "It will feel nice tonight to sleep on those sun-dried sheets, too."

Sarah skipped along beside her older sister as the four girls headed back to the house. "I jutht love the thmell of fresh sheetth, don't you, Jothie?"

Josie reached out a hand to rustle Sarah's soft blonde curls. "That I do, *liebchen*," she said, using the endearment Samantha had heard Laura use when addressing the child.

As the girls reached the back door, they heard a shout. "Hey! Girls!"

All four twirled to see Arn coming from behind the barn at a trot. He came to a stop in front of them, panting from his run, his face beet red. "Hey," he repeated, "guess what we found?"

"Can't guess," Josie retorted, "just tell us."

"Mushrooms!" Arn replied, a huge grin splitting his freckled face. "Pa says if we get 'em picked now, Ma'll have time to fix 'em with our gravy. Want to help?"

The three Klaassen girls immediately gave an enthusiastic "Yes!" in reply. Samantha merely shrugged.

"Let me put these baskets on the back porch and check with Mother to make sure she's done with us for now," Josie said, being practical.

"Well, hurry up, grandma!" Arn encouraged in a teasing voice.

Josie made a face at him and slammed through the back door.

Becky pulled at Samantha's hand. "Have you ever hunted mushrooms, Frances?"

Samantha shook her head, gently freeing her hand from Becky's grasp. These were the touchiest people she'd ever met! "No," she said. "I never ate one, either."

Arn, Becky, and Sarah stared in amazement. "Never eaten a mushroom?!" Sarah exclaimed. "Din't they have 'em where you uthed to live?"

Samantha shrugged. "I don't know. I never asked."

Becky opened her mouth to ask something else, but just then Josie came back out. "We can go as long as we're back in time to remake the beds before supper. Come on!"

"Great!" Arn exclaimed, his voice cracking. He was at that awkward age between boyhood and manhood, and his voice tended to change, running the scales like an inept piano tuner. His sisters giggled and poked at him as they dashed off at a pace that wasn't sensible considering the August heat. It didn't occur to Samantha not to follow along. She was wondering what a mushroom looked like and why you put it in gravy. Between these mushrooms and the promised scripture cake, meals around here were getting to be quite an adventure!

Arn led the girls past the grazing area behind the barn clear to the stand of maple, apple, and mulberry trees that bordered the Klaassen property. The children called this part of their land "the woods," and all loved any time spent there. It was particularly nice on hot summer days, because the thick foliage cut back the sun's heat, and the breezes that moved the trees picked up the scents of ripened fruit, damp earth, and decaying leaves. It was colorful thanks to the wildflowers that grew in profusion. Samantha admired them all, from the delicate white angel's breath to the chubby lavender bluebells.

Fallen mulberries lay like a purple and magenta carpet, and Josie warned in a happy voice, "Watch where you step or Mother'll be scrubbing the hide off your feet tonight!"

Samantha knew what she meant—mulberries stained! She watched her step.

Finally Arn pointed and yelled, "There's the spot!" He dashed ahead to a row of spine-covered bushes, one of which wore a red bandanna tied to a spindly branch.

"Look out for prickles," Arn said, carefully pushing back the branches so the girls could pass. "The mushrooms are under the trees there."

As they came through the bushes, they saw Adam already hard at work on his knees, plucking mushrooms from the soft ground and dropping them into a burlap sack.

Samantha came up short. Sarah ran to him immediately, obviously delighted to find him here. "Adam!" she squealed. "How come you're not in the fieldth?"

"Because, *schnigglefritz*," Adam replied, poking a finger into her round middle, "the fieldth, as you say, are too wet to be worked. We'll get out there Monday if the sun holds through the weekend. But for today, I hunt mushrooms!"

Samantha was far from delighted to find Adam there. Being with the girls was one thing, but being close to Adam was another. Every time she ventured within his range, she immediately remembered the humiliation of being sat on in the middle of the street. Of course, he'd done nothing remotely close to that to her since; he'd been the perfect gentleman, kind and considerate. That only added to her shame, as she recalled calling him a "durn honyocker," a term she knew to be quite uncomplimentary. Adam hadn't deserved to be called that awful name, and she wished she had the nerve to apologize. But to apologize, she would have to engage him in conversation, and that was harder to do than bear her guilt. So she turned her flustered gaze away from him and became overly interested in a tear in the cuticle on her left thumb.

Now Adam grinned at his family and invited, "Pick away! That rain probably brought them out! There must be a hundred!"

Josie and Becky immediately knelt and began picking the smooth, brown-capped mushrooms. Sarah danced around excitedly, stubbing her toe at one point and howling in indignation. Adam spared a moment to give her a consoling hug, then went back to his collecting. Samantha, thinking the mushrooms looked like ugly toadstools, sat off to the side and watched. Arn squatted close to her. Apparently he felt his job had been to fetch more pickers, not pick the mushrooms himself.

"Ma will cook those in butter, then mix them in with some gravy to pour over potatoes or cornbread stuffing," Arn offered to Samantha. "They're really good."

Samantha sneaked a glance at him. She'd not spent time talking with Arn at all. He seemed gangly and awkward to her with his long limbs that hadn't yet filled out and his wide face full of freckles. If she was going to spend time in the company of any of the Klaassen males, she'd probably choose Teddy since he was small and unassuming and, if she had to, she could probably beat him up. But Arn was looking at her expectantly, as if a reply would be a gift. So she gathered her courage and ventured to ask, "Do you eat them a lot?"

Arn shook his head, making his cowlick bounce. "No, they're pretty hard to spot. We look at 'em as pretty much of a treat."

That explains the way they all came runnin', thought Samantha. "How'd you find them this time?" she asked.

Arn chuckled low in his throat. "I didn't really, it was Adeline."

Josie looked up from her task. "Adeline?"

"Yep! Hilarius's Adeline." To Samantha he explained, "Hilarius Schwartz is our nearest neighbor, and Adeline is his old milk cow." Then to all, "She wandered clear over here this morning, and Pa asked me to herd her back before Hilarius called out the sheriff. When I was taking her home, I spotted the mushrooms."

"Maybe we should take a few to Hilarius as a thank you," Becky suggested, wiping at a trail of sweat running from her temple.

Josie and Arn exchanged glances, then chorused, "Or maybe not."

Those mushrooms must be pretty special, Samantha thought, watching Adam carefully tie shut the burlap sack now full of the funny-looking plants. As she followed the others back to the farm, keeping well behind Adam, she decided maybe she'd stick around just one more night. She could start out fresh after a good night's rest. Besides, she had a sudden hankering to sample some of those mushrooms!

Chapter Seven

The mushrooms proved to be sumptuous fare indeed. Laura could sure put out a meal, Samantha decided, her belly full and aching. There'd been fried pork, stewed tomatoes, fresh ears of corn, and cornbread stuffing which they doused with brown mushroom gravy. What amazed Samantha the most was that every last bit of food on the table was provided by the Klaassens themselves! She had learned by now that they raised and butchered their own hogs and chickens, kept a massive garden and canned enough vegetables to last the winter, had their own wheat ground into flour, and cared for three milk cows which provided milk and butter for their own needs as well as for Simon's brother Hiram and his wife in town. All this, plus raising a money crop and keeping up with a house and horses besides! If she hadn't seen with her own eyes how much Si and Laura genuinely loved their children, she'd wonder if they'd had a big family just to have help in keeping the farm running smoothly.

After supper, Samantha automatically joined the female family members in clearing the dishes and preparing for the washing. The idea of accepting charity still stuck in her craw, so helping out with the chores off-set their providing her with meals, she figured. Besides, it helped pass the time.

Laura began pumping water to heat, and asked Josie, "Would you and Becky please get all the wash off the lines? Everything should be dry now, and you two can get the beds made while Frances, Sarah, and I do the dishes."

"Sure, Mother," Josie agreed quickly. "I'd rather make beds and fold laundry than wash dishes any day!"

Sarah looked hopeful. "Can I make beds, too, Mama?"

Laura's eyes crinkled. "Why, certainly," she agreed, reaching out to tap the end of Sarah's nose with a blunt finger, "you can make your own bed *after* the dishes are done."

Sarah stuck out her lip in a pout, but when no one paid any attention to her she bounced over to the dry sink and began stacking dirty plates together.

As Laura scraped bits of lye soap into the enamel wash pan, she casually asked Samantha, "What are your plans now, dear?"

Samantha blinked. "Well, ma'am," she answered, "I reckon since my clothes are clean again, I'll just be on my way. I reckon I've eaten up enough of your food by now."

Laura waved a hand at that. "Oh, that's not what I'm worried about. I'm thinking about you, dear, and how you'll manage. I'm assuming you don't have a definite destination in mind?"

Samantha looked at her blankly. Sometimes when Laura talked, she sounded like a fancy lady, and the words didn't match the picture of a farmer's wife.

Laura seemed to understand. "I meant, have you thought about where you'll settle?"

Samantha felt herself color, and stammered, "Well, no, ma'am, not exactly yet."

"Well," Laura said in a brisk tone, scrubbing vigorously at the gravy on the plate she held, "I've been thinking about that. You'll need money for the journey, and money to pay for lodging once you've decided where to stay. I can imagine you're a little low on cash, am I right?"

Laura looked sideways at Samantha. After a moment of hesitation, she gave a slight nod of agreement.

Laura went on. "It seems to me that before you leave, you need some money."

Samantha suddenly suspected where this might be heading, and blurted out firmly, "Now, ma'am, I know I've been eating an' sleeping here, but I won't take money from you, too! Don't ask me to do that, ma'am, because I won't!"

Laura's eyebrows shot up, and she quickly reached for a dishtowel to dry her hands. Once her hands were dry, she caught Samantha by the shoulders and looked her straight in the eyes.

"Frances, I wouldn't shame you by offering you money," Laura assured her, keeping a hold on Samantha's shoulders even though she felt the girl stiffen. "I was going to offer you a chance to *earn* some traveling money."

Samantha gulped. "Earn it?" she asked.

Laura turned back to the dishes. After instructing Sarah to be careful with the glasses, she continued, "Yes. You see, as Sarah told you, our daughter Liz is expecting her first child. Now, I would dearly love to go and spend a few days with her after the baby is born, helping out. But this is such a busy time of year, I really can't afford to be gone. Too many vegetables are awaiting canning; and school will be starting soon so I must be thinking of getting clothes ready for the

children. Then there's all the work that goes with harvest....
There are too many needs here to be met for me to be somewhere else."

Samantha began picking up the dishes that Sarah had dried and stacking them back in their places on the cupboard shelves. Laura followed her with her eyes, judging her reaction to her suggestion.

"Can't Josie help out?" Samantha wanted to know.

"She could, if she weren't going to be in school," Laura told her. "This will be Josie's last year of schooling, and then she'd like to test for a teaching certificate. It's important for her not to miss any of the school year if she plans to teach. Besides, I depend on Josie quite a bit for help with canning and sewing. I really can't spare her."

Samantha moved on about her task, thinking. She paused in front of the possum-belly cabinet that housed the larger bowls, chewing on the inside of her lip. It *would* be nice to have some traveling money, not to have to worry about where the meals were coming from. But by taking the job, she'd be stuck here in Mountain Lake for awhile longer—maybe a *long* while longer.

Samantha turned back to Laura. "I'd like to dwell on it some, if I could. Maybe meet Liz and see how we'd get on and such..."

Laura smiled, and reached out a hand to smooth Samantha's cheek. "I think that's sensible," she said. "You just sleep on it. Come along, Sarah, we'll make your bed."

Samantha watched the mother and daughter turn the corner of the stairs, hand in hand. She could still feel the whisper-touch of Laura's hand on her cheek. There hadn't been time to back up and avoid it, and now emotion was building in her chest at the longing that touch inspired. Quickly she put the last of the dishes in the cupboard and headed out to what was already her favorite spot—the porch swing behind the lilac bushes—to give this job idea some serious thought.

Sunday morning reminded Samantha of a whirlwind—everyone flew around in a near-frenzy, readying themselves for church. Laura had already had each of the children give their Sunday shoes a good going-over with a cold biscuit the night before so they'd be shiny for the service, but she had last minute pressing to do on Becky's church dress, and Sarah couldn't find her good hair ribbons, and Teddy pulled a button from his pants.... Samantha would have been yanking out her hair had she been in charge, but Laura just took it in stride.

"Josie, quickly grab a needle and thread and help Teddy with his button," Laura's mild but firm voice directed. "Becky, if you don't move back you'll be burned—that iron is hot! Sarah, stop sniffling and try looking under your bed. That's where we found your ribbons the last time. All right, Teddy, now no need to take your pants off, just hold still. Josie won't stick you."

Samantha had been given another of Liz's hand-me-downs and even a pair of black button-up shoes to wear over her borrowed stockings. Josie had offered to braid her hair for her, but instead Samantha had just brushed the top part of it back from her face and tied it with a ribbon loaned by Becky. She'd had a Saturday night bath just like everyone else, so her hair was clean and tumbly and she felt fresh to face the day. Of course, if she'd been offered a choice, she'd be wearing her own overalls and shirt and wouldn't be going to church at all, but everyone seemed to expect it of her, and she hated to cause a scene when there was already so much going on.

After a cold breakfast, everyone climbed into the back of the clean hay wagon and settled in amongst the pile of straw Adam had thrown in for the occasion. The Klaassens sang all the way to church, rivaling the goldfinches that called "perchickoree" as they rattled by. Everywhere Samantha looked, there were fields of golden wheat. The wind passed across the prickly tops of the shafts, creating a soothing waving motion that Samantha found pleasing.

Josie had told Samantha that harvest would begin soon, with all the men in the community pitching in to help in their neighbors' fields in return for help with their own harvests. According to Josie, harvest was an exciting time, and when it was complete there would be a big party at the schoolhouse to celebrate. Josie seemed to assume that Samantha would still be here by then, but Samantha wasn't so sure.

The church was a simple white clapboard building with doors at opposite sides of the front. She noticed that men and women separated as they walked toward the building, with the men entering from the door at the right, and the women entering on the left. She might have asked about that practice, but the bell in the belltower began ringing loudly and conversation wasn't possible.

As they pulled into the yard, she looked around with practiced disinterest at the number of buggies and wagons lining the dirt lot next to the church. It seemed as if the whole town turned out for services.

Samantha wasn't much of a churchgoer. As a small child she had gone with her Gran, but Pa hadn't shown any interest in taking her or David after Gran died, so Samantha had stayed home. She noticed how spit-shined everyone looked, and figured they were all turned out in their best clothes, just as the Klaassens were this morning. Ladies wore straw bonnets with little flowers instead of the everyday calico poke-bonnets, and most men had on black coats over their white shirts even though the late August heat was stifling.

Adam helped Sarah and Becky over the edge of the wagon and reached a hand to Samantha, but she braced herself on the edge and leapt out without his assistance. The memory of their Main Street tussle was strong in both of their minds, and neither had an easy time meeting the other's eyes. As they turned to go into the church, Adam was hoping fervently no one brought up the embarrassing wrestling match, and Samantha was pleading inwardly that no one realized she was the same girl who had been rolling in the dirt just a few days ago.

The Klaassen family took up quite a bit of space in the aisles, and Laura and Si ushered their offspring toward familiar benches. Samantha followed blindly, just wanting to find an inconspicuous spot to sit. Hovering between Josie and Becky, Samantha saw Laura move into the center aisle to greet a pretty young woman with a hug, and as they pulled apart, she realized the young woman had Laura's soft brown eyes and long, thin nose—plus a popping belly. She presumed this must be Liz, and the handsome tall man beside her must be her husband, Jake. They were a nice-looking couple, and they held hands even in the church. Samantha tried not to stare—public displays of affection were foreign to her.

When they were seated, Samantha found herself pressed between Sarah and Becky, with Laura, Josie, and Liz taking up the rest of the bench to Sarah's left. Samantha peeked back over her shoulder and realized with a start that the whole left section of the church was filled with ladies, and the right was all men. What an odd setup! But there wasn't time for further wondering; things were starting.

She did her best to pay attention, but Sarah and Becky kept leaning across her lap to whisper, and Laura would reach over and frown. The unpadded benches weren't terribly comfortable, and she was relieved that they at least stood up for hymn singing. Samantha wasn't familiar with the hymns, which were sung in some foreign language, so she stood silently, listening to the others. She could easily pick out Laura's sweet soprano, and, if she strained, Josie's pleasant alto. With Adam and Frank to her right across the aisle she got an earful of their resonant voices. It was obvious they all enjoyed singing, and even though there wasn't a hymnbook in sight not a one of them missed a note or a word. She guessed they were as familiar with church and its goings-on as they were with their own backyards. And she had to wonder if that was what made them so different from the families she knew back home who weren't churchgoers by any means.

Afterwards, no one seemed in too big of a rush to get home. They milled around outside, gathering in small groups to visit. Samantha found herself corralled with Josie and a small cluster of giggling girls who peeked over their shoulders at a larger group of young men in which Adam seemed to be the center of attention.

As Samantha watched, a husky youth with a shock of red hair poked Adam hard in the chest, said something behind his hand the girls couldn't hear, then threw back his head and laughed. The other boys joined in, and Adam shrugged, looking sheepishly downward at the toe of his boot which he pushed into the loose dirt.

Someone tapped Samantha on the shoulder, and she turned to come face to face with a petite young woman with sparkling, deep blue eyes, a tiny upturned nose, and full, rosy lips. Her face was framed by a wondrous mass of glossy black curls that contrasted shockingly with her bright eyes. She was by far the prettiest girl Samantha had ever seen, but the prettiness was spoiled by the haughty angle of her head, the superior glint in her eye, and the snooty twist to her lips. Samantha was immediately on guard.

"Aren't you the girl who tried to steal from the mercantile last week?" the wearer of the snide smile asked.

Samantha felt herself flush with sudden anger, but before she could answer Josie cut in, "Oh, Priscilla, leave her alone. This is Frances Welch, and she's staying with us."

Priscilla tossed back her curls with the flip of a slim wrist. "So nice to meet you, Frances," she said, holding her chin at a pert angle and fixing Samantha with narrowed eyes. "But you didn't answer me. Wasn't that you?"

Samantha tightened her fists and answered through clenched teeth, "Yes, it was me. But I don't see how it's any of your business."

Priscilla held up her hands in a mock show of apology. "Oh, dear, I didn't mean to offend you," she said, a sly little grin on her face. "I had heard that Adam carted home another stray—this time one that had been caught stealing. I just wondered if it might be you. I meant no harm."

Josie put a protective arm around Samantha's shoulders, but Samantha shrugged it off. She answered in a firm tone, her eyes never wavering from Priscilla's, "He didn't *cart* me home—he invited me. And I'm not a stray. And I'm smart enough to know you meant harm, all right. But you don't bother me any. I'm used to your ilk, and worse. So you can just keep your wonderings to yourself."

Priscilla gave a little giggle and turned to the other girls who had the good grace to at least look a bit uncomfortable, "I seem to have offended poor Frances here. Actually I envy her. Wouldn't I love to have a chance to be chased down the street by Adam Klaassen and then be taken home by him. Oh, my!" And she fanned herself with both hands, as if singed.

"Come on," Josie said at that, and steered Samantha toward their wagon. On the way, Josie said in a sympathetic voice, "Don't pay any attention to Priscilla Koehn. She's nothing but a troublemaker. She's had her eye on Adam since we were in pinafores, but if Adam ever so much as *looks* at Priscilla, I declare I'll never speak to him again!"

Becky had come up behind them and overheard her sister's last comment. She exclaimed, "Oh, Josie, give Adam *some* credit for sense! He knows Priscilla's nothing but a fickle flirt!"

Samantha just shrugged and said, "Makes me no nevermind either way. But *she* better stay outta my way!"

Samantha seethed all the way back to the farm, and it wasn't until after the dinner dishes were cleared and the scripture cake was served that she relaxed her tense jaw. By then her teeth were aching from being clenched, and she wished she'd never stepped foot in that church! She had come to one conclusion—her speculations that churchgoing was what made this family unique were completely off-base. That awful Priscilla attended church, but she sure didn't possess the sweet spirit that emanated from the Klaassens!

It had to be something else, but what?

The family retired to the parlor after dessert to relax and enjoy the one day of the week that wasn't filled with endless chores. Si and Laura sat together on the camelback sofa with Sarah snug between them, drowsing against her father's chest. Teddy and Arn sat on the floor near the bay window, each with a leaflet in hand, reading. Josie was running an embroidery needle through a piece of muslin in a wooden hoop, creating flowers, and Becky leaned over her shoulder, providing unwanted advice. Frank had disappeared upstairs to rest in his room, planning to use the buckboard later to visit his girlfriend, Anna Harms. Adam was perched on the window seat of the bay window, trying to read over Arn's shoulder. Jake and Liz shared the narrow courting bench that sat across from the sofa. With Liz's extra girth, it was a tight fit, but neither of them seemed to mind.

Samantha had gone upstairs immediately after kitchen clean up to change into her own set of clothes. She came back downstairs and peeked hesitantly through the parlor doorway, wondering whether or not she should intrude upon this family scene.

Laura spotted her and motioned for her to come in. She gently pushed Sarah onto Si's lap and scooched over to make room for Samantha. "Here, Frances, sit down," she invited. "Liz and I were just talking about you."

Samantha paused before sitting to ask suspiciously, "What about?" Did they know what Priscilla had said to her after church?

"We were wondering if you had decided to stay and work for Liz," Laura said.

"Oh," Samantha said with relief, and seated herself on the edge of the sofa.

Liz added, "I'd love it if you could, Frances. Even though the baby isn't here yet, I could use you now. I'm so big, it's hard just to pull myself around! Jake has had to take on many of my chores—"

"And he's not complaining," Jake interrupted, placing a loving kiss on his young wife's temple.

Liz smiled at him and patted his hand as she continued, "Which he's done cheerfully, but it makes for an awful lot of work for one person. He has his own work to do, and he really doesn't have the time to spare for mine."

Jake linked his strong fingers with Liz's and agreed, "She's right, Frances. I've kept up so far, but mostly because of the rain we've had. Now that things are drying out and we'll be starting harvest, Liz needs someone close at hand. We'd both appreciate it if you could see your way clear to helping us out."

Samantha hesitated, looking from Liz to Laura. As much as she needed the money, she was still afraid to stay in one spot for so long. She didn't know how to ask how long she'd be needed without explaining her reasons for wanting to be gone soon.

Jake apparently thought she was hesitating for another reason. "As for wages," he said, "I was thinking four dollars a week. We can raise that after the baby's born, as I'm sure your workload will increase then."

Samantha's mouth dropped open and her eyes popped. "Oh!" she exclaimed, "No! That's more'n enough. That's plenty, even *after* the baby's born. I just—well, I just don't know how long I can stay around here. How long do you reckon you'll need my help?"

Liz and Jake looked at each other. Liz shook her head and shrugged. "I'm really not sure, Frances. I've never had a baby before! Mother here was up and around in three weeks or so after her children were born. Could you stay that long?"

Three weeks! Pa could cover a lot of territory in three weeks—an' that baby's not even here yet, Samantha thought fearfully. Yet, if she had three weeks' worth of wages in her pocket, maybe she could buy a train ticket and get clear across country. Pa'd never find her then!

"Okay," Samantha agreed. "I'll hire on. I'll just head on with you folks when you go home tonight, and stay 'til the baby's born and Liz is back on her feet."

Liz broke into a relieved smile and leaned against Jake who squeezed her shoulders. Laura patted Samantha's knee and said, "Oh, Frances, thank you. You're an answer to prayer."

Adam looked up from his spot on the window seat to see Samantha blushing—from pleasure or discomfiture, he wasn't sure. But he had to admit, he was relieved, too. Not only that Liz would have the help she needed in the weeks ahead, but that they would all have a chance to give a soul-thirsty young lady what she needed as well.

Chapter Eight

Samantha settled in with Liz and Jake easily. Neither of them were much older than she was—Liz was only twenty, and Jake one year older than that—but they seemed eons older in experiences. They lived in a small, square house with only a kitchen, which also served as a sitting room, a bedroom, and a small pantry lean-to on the ground floor. A narrow stairway split the little house down the middle and led to two small rooms in the attic. Since the upstairs rooms were tucked in under the rafters, the ceiling slanted on either side of the door, ending with a four-feet high wall. Across from the door was one small four-pane window, the frame of which was painted white and covered with a bleached muslin curtain. The walls and ceiling had been plastered by Jake and his father, and the floors were wide pine planks over which Liz had thrown several small rag rugs for color and warmth. Next to the door in the room Samantha used was a narrow bachelor's chest, and pushed below the eaves was a white iron bed. Beside the bed sat a small washstand with a chipped china pitcher and bowl. It was unpretentious and had no unnecessary trappings of any kind. To Samantha, it was paradise.

Samantha's room was to the left of the stairs, and Liz had been fixing up the other one for the baby. But poor Liz was so heavy now, it was too hard for her to get up there, so it became Samantha's job to finish the curtain hanging and furniture placement. Liz had already painted the walls a pale yellow and Jake had moved a cradle, dresser, and oak rocker into the room. The day Samantha hung the curtains of goldenrod gingham and arranged the furniture was such fun! Liz was working on sheets and tiny gowns and flannel diapers. Samantha watched the pile of baby things grow beside Liz's feet as she sat in the kitchen rocker and worked, and in the evenings she would carry everything carefully upstairs and put it all away.

Samantha's days, though quite full, were very pleasant. The work was hard—she was responsible for all the house cleaning, the gardening chores, washing clothes, feeding the chickens, and milking the cow. Although Samantha was no stranger to work—she'd been largely responsible for her own house since she was quite young—she'd never realized how pleasant tasks could become when performed for people who appreciated your efforts and weren't adverse to saying so. At night she would fall into bed, blissfully exhausted, with words of thanks echoing in her ears. She'd never been happier.

"Frances," Liz said on the fourth morning of Samantha's employment, "I'm sure the strawberries are ripe and ready for canning. How would you like to make strawberry preserves today?"

Samantha hunched up one shoulder and admitted, "I never did that before. I don't reckon I could do it on my own. Might mix something up."

Liz heaved herself with difficulty from her rocker and crossed to Samantha, placing a hand on the younger girl's shoulder. "Now, I realize I've been more than just a wee bit lazy lately, but I would not expect you to do something as time-consuming as making strawberry preserves on your own!"

Samantha let the hint of a smile crease her face. "Well, if you're helping, I reckon I can do it. Should I pick the berries now?"

Liz nodded. "Yes. It's been wonderful to eat fresh berries this summer, but they won't keep through the winter unless they're made into preserves, so we better hop to it. I'd pick with you, but I just can't take the heat these days—makes me so dizzy!"

Samantha had never considered the miseries that went along with carrying a child. It made her wonder if it was all worth the trouble. She told Liz, "You just sit and stitch on some of your baby things. I'll fetch a basket from the cellar and get to pickin'. It won't be so bad in the morning—sun's not so high and hot yet."

The humidity was certainly high, though, Samantha realized, and by 9:00 she was wringing wet with sweat. Often she had to pause to swipe at her forehead to keep the salty sweat from stinging her eyes, and she pushed constantly at strands of hair that fell in her way. She'd filled one basket, and was well on her way to filling a second when a shadow crossed her path. She shielded her eyes with one hand and looked up, expecting to see Liz. Instead, it was Adam, wearing his familiar straw hat and easy grin.

"Well, you're certainly hard at it," was his greeting.

Samantha dropped her hand and pushed at her hair fussily. She must just look a sight, sitting here in her overalls, fingernails dark with earth and hair standing on end! But if Adam thought she looked a mess, he certainly didn't indicate it to her.

"Could you use a little help?" he asked, squatting down and picking up one large strawberry from the basket and bringing it to his lips. Samantha watched him bite down on the berry, saw a tiny spurt of juice hit the side of his mouth and run towards his chin. He brought the back of his hand across his face to catch it, grinning all the while.

Samantha smirked cheekily and surprised them both by asking, "With picking or eating?"

Adam's eyebrows raised to the skies, and, after a moment of shocked silence, he snatched the hat from his head, banged it against his knee twice, and let out a whoop that startled Samantha as much as her teasing had surprised him.

"Just maybe a little of both," he retorted, pleased more than he could understand with her small attempt at humor. He lifted out another strawberry, but this time offered it to Samantha.

She looked at the berry held with the tips of his blunt fingers, then up into his smiling face. His brown eyes sparkled at her in a friendly manner. Hesitantly she gave a quick flash of a smile in return, and took the strawberry and popped it into her mouth. The warm sweetness exploded against her tongue, and she closed her eyes while murmuring, "Mm."

When she opened her eyes again, Adam was still squatting beside her, his eyes glued to her face, his hat back on his head.

"So, Frances," he said, his eyes unwavering, "do you want my help or not?"

Without averting her gaze, she asked, "Are you sure you can spare the time?"

"Wouldn't be here if I couldn't," was his reply.

Samantha let her gaze sweep across the remainder of the large berry patch. "There is a heap of picking to be done," she acknowledged.

Adam took that as a yes. With a nod, he scooped up a basket and headed to the opposite side of the patch. Samantha watched him go, feeling a little flustered—yet pleased—to have him near. She gave herself a little shake. *Quit thinking that way about him!* she told herself firmly. *If he knew how your thoughts were flying, he'd turn tail and run! Now get to work!*

And, reluctantly, she obeyed that self-imposed demand.

Probably without even realizing it, Adam was sure, Samantha had been assuming some of the mannerisms of her hostess. Only thirteen months separated Liz and Adam in age, so he was closer to her than his other brothers and sisters—age-wise, and otherwise. Adam and Liz favored one another in looks, with their brown eyes and sandy hair that insisted on curling. They favored one another in temperament, too. Both were good-natured deep-thinkers, and sometimes found they knew what the other one was thinking without saying a word.

As Adam stood side-by-side with Samantha in the kitchen, washing the berries that she then cut into small pieces in readiness for boiling, he kept a close watch on her out of the corner of his eyes. Being with Liz had been good for the girl—she was relaxed, the deep furrow of distrust smoothed away from her brow. He caught her lips curled into the hint of a smile more than once as she and Liz exchanged idle chit-chat and Liz offered instructions on the task at hand. She had all but lost her sullen exterior, and while she wasn't quite cheerful, she was, at least, peaceful.

Adam made a mental note to give his sister a very long, very grateful hug for working this small miracle in her helper's attitude.

Liz, on the other hand, had been very aware of the way her young helper watched her every move, picking up not only on ways to handle the chores, but ways to handle situations. Liz had never been a person to let little things affect her, and her even nature seemed a direct contradiction to the girl's mercurial disposition. Realizing she was being used as a role model, Liz took extra care with her grooming and speech, her actions and reactions to what went on around her.

She noticed that Samantha, although still dressing in the men's shirt and overalls, was giving her clothes a good brushing before bed to freshen them a bit before wearing them again. She had requested the use of a brush which she used regularly on her long mass of wavy hair, even shyly asking for a piece of yarn to tie it back when the afternoon sun made it unbearable to have it on her neck. She had seen, too, how the girl seemed to absorb the conversations between Liz and Jake, and though neither had ever resorted to loud arguments, they became even more aware of tone of voice and choice of words when tired or upset. The girl seemed to need a great deal of gentling, as well as kindness, and Liz was giving her a healthy dose of both.

While Adam was appreciating the changes in the young lady by his side, Liz was wondering why Adam seemed so intent on the girl's appearance. Liz knew better than anyone how soft-hearted Adam was, and she wondered if Adam was feeling brotherly towards the girl, or if it was something entirely different. Adam, at nineteen years of age, had never had a steady girlfriend. Not that he wasn't interested—Liz had seen him indulge in his fair share of harmless flirtation, and many young girls responded eagerly. But he wasn't one to use people for his own pleasures, so she knew he held himself off until he was ready to give his whole self to one girl. In a burst of sisterly pride, Liz admitted to herself that Adam was one of those special men who were not only handsome on the outside, but beautiful on the inside, as well. When the right girl finally captured Adam's heart, Liz knew it would be a lifelong commitment, and the girl would never want for anything with Adam as her partner.

Her eyebrows came together sharply. Surely Adam wasn't looking at the girl in *that* way! Oh, she was sweet enough in her unassuming way, and she certainly was a good worker—Liz would give her that. But no one *knew* anything about her—she was such a secretive, private person. It was one thing to take her in, see to her needs, and be her adviser. However, Liz wasn't quite ready to throw her to Adam's head—*or* heart.

Samantha turned to Liz and said, "Okay, the strawberries are clean, the stems are gone, and I've got 'em cut in nice pieces. Do I cook 'em now?"

Liz nodded. "Yes, they'll need to boil with sugar until the sugar is dissolved and the juice looks clear and shiny. Adam," she motioned to the tiny lean-to off the kitchen, "my boiler pot is out there, would you get it, please? It'll probably need wiping out before we put the strawberries in. And, Frances, you know where the sugar is. You'll need one cup of sugar for every two cups of berries, so measure the berries first."

Adam and Samantha moved to obey, stepping around each other too carefully, Liz thought, as if they were afraid to touch. Liz felt that prickle of awareness again. *Adam, be careful,* she thought, *Don't let your sympathetic heart lead you down pathways you shouldn't be traveling.*

Samantha scooped the clean strawberries into the boiler cup by cup, counting to herself. Once the boiler was half-full of berries, she carefully counted out proper amounts of sugar, and then Adam lifted the pot onto Liz's wood-burning stove. The heat of the fire combined with the heat of the day made the room quite uncomfortable. Adam propped open the front door, the lean-to door and all the windows in the house, as well.

"I realize we need the breeze, dear brother," Liz scolded from her chair, her hands busily twisting a crochet needle through a snarl of yellow yarn, "but now the dust will come through here and ruin the cleaning job Frances completed yesterday afternoon!"

Adam reached for the window above the dry sink. "Oh! I'll shut us back up."

Samantha grabbed his sleeve, and when he looked at her, she pulled her hand back quickly. "No, leave it open," she begged, "the breeze feels good, an' I can always dust again. I'd rather be cool."

"Okay," Adam shrugged, and watched Samantha pull the collar of her flannel shirt away from her neck as she stirred the strawberries with a long-handled wooden spoon.

"I bet you're really warm in that get-up," he told her sympathetically. "Wouldn't you rather change into something else?"

"Don't *have* anything else. I'm okay."

Not willing to let it go at that, Adam asked Liz, "Don't you have a summer dress Frances could put on? She's cooking faster than the strawberries!"

Instead of answering, Liz drew in a breath and clutched at her distended belly with two hands, dropping the half-made baby afghan to the floor.

"Liz, what's wrong?" Adam asked in alarm, moving to kneel beside her chair and take her hand. He forgot all about locating summer clothes for Samantha.

It seemed a lifetime passed before Adam felt Liz relax. Little beads of sweat had popped out across her forehead. A weak smile creased her face.

"Oh, my," she sighed, "that one was a whopper."

"Whaddaya mean, *that* one?" Adam demanded, scowling fearfully. His eyes widened as realization dawned. "You mean, you've been having pains?" At Liz's nod, he asked sternly, "How long has this been going on, missy?"

"Awhile."

"Awhile? *Awhile?*" Adam exploded. Samantha quivered with shock. She had never heard Adam sound as angry as he did right now. "So why on earth have you been messing around in here, preserving strawberries, for Pete's sake? You should be in bed!"

"Adam," Liz said calmly, squeezing her brother's hand, "you sound like a mother hen. I hope you're ready to calm down now and quit your scolding, because you're about to become an uncle."

"You mean," Adam gulped, his eyes wide, his face going white beneath his summer tan, "it's *time*?"

She laughed at his stricken face. "Yes, it's time, and don't look like that, Adam. You didn't think I was going to carry this baby forever, did you?"

"Well…well," Adam sputtered, his anger completely dissolved. From the stove, a startled Samantha swung around, spoon in hand, flinging strawberry juice in an arc across the kitchen.

"Don't make a mess, Frances," Liz said. "Adam, help me into bed, then get Jake for me. I want him here. After that, run for Mother. I'm not having this baby without her!" When her brother remained on his knees in a shocked stupor, she slugged his shoulder and demanded, "Adam! Help me into bed now!"

Shaking from nervousness, Adam obeyed, lifting his sister as gently as if she was made of spun glass. With an arm across her back, he guided her to the bedroom, watched her sit on the edge of the bed, and lifted her feet for her as she leaned against the pillows.

"Now I'll get Jake," he promised, moving to the door. "And then I'll get Mother," he said, coming back to stand beside the bed. He didn't know what to do with his hands, and they flew around convulsively as if trying to shoo flies.

Liz shook her head. "Adam, Jake is in the east field, and Mother is probably at home in her kitchen. Do you think you can find them?"

Adam was at the door again. He said, "Yes, sure, I'll get them. I won't be long." Then he stomped back to give his sister a kiss on the forehead. "Take it easy, sis."

Liz touched his cheek, a smile on her pretty face. "*You* take it easy—I'm fine, really."

Adam dashed past Samantha, who stood hovering in Liz's bedroom doorway, the smell of scorched strawberries filling the air.

"What can I do for you?" Samantha asked Liz, wanting to help yet frightened that Liz might actually need something.

Liz just smiled and said, "Stir the strawberries, Frances. I can't abide burnt preserves!"

Chapter Nine

Of anyone had stopped to think about it, they might have found it amusing that the only calm person in the little house seemed to be Liz, who also happened to have the best reason for being alarmed. Samantha could tell by the low moans being issued from the bedroom that having a baby wasn't exactly fun, but so far Liz seemed to be taking the whole thing in stride. Between the pains, she managed to smile at her husband, squeezing his hand and assuring him that she was just fine. Whenever a pain hit, Jake would lean over his wife helplessly, his own face contorted, seemingly in pain himself.

When Adam had returned, he'd brought not only Laura, but had Si and Josie in tow as well. Adam had paused just long enough to peek in at Liz and assure himself that Jake was by her side, then he rushed off again to fetch Dr. Newton. Liz had told him to slow down or he'd give himself heat stroke, and she wanted the doctor focused on her, not her brother. Adam had grinned and replied, "You always *did* have to be the center of attention," and Liz had laughed a little bit at that.

Neither Si nor Laura were laughing, though. Samantha was relieved of her berry stirring by Josie, who said she absolutely *had* to have something to do, so Samantha had relinquished the job. Instead, she busied herself by hauling in water and bringing extra sheets down from the big *schrank* that sat on the small landing at the top of the stairs. Laura had indicated these items would be helpful, but no one else seemed to have the ability to go beyond planning to doing.

Josie stirred strawberries. Si paced back and forth, hands behind his back, his brow furrowed worriedly. Laura hovered beside Liz's bed, wiping her daughter's face with a cool cloth and murmuring to her in German words Liz seemed to understand. Jake kept a grip on his wife's hand and his face grew whiter with each pain, asking repeatedly, "When will Doc Newton get here?" No one answered him.

Samantha, her tasks completed, stood at the window and watched for Adam's wagon to return. When she finally spotted it, followed closely by the doctor's little black buggy, she turned around excitedly and exclaimed, "Adam's here! The doctor, too!"

Si gave a huge sigh of relief and went to the bedroom doorway to relay the news.

Although Adam pulled in first, the doctor beat him to the door. He was a small man with a narrow pencil line of a mustache, green eyes, and cropped hair that stuck up in the back. His suit was rumpled as if slept in, and his wire-rimmed glasses sat on the tip of his stub of a nose in a way that made him appear foolish. But he'd proven himself time and again to the people of the community, and everyone looked past his appearance to the ability he possessed.

He acknowledged the people waiting in the main room of the house with a nod but didn't slow down for pleasantries. Instead, he passed straight to the bedroom and ordered without preamble, "Jake, kiss your wife, then kindly leave. We'll all do better without you." As Jake rose to obey—albeit grudgingly—the doctor said, "Laura, please stay. I'm sure you'll be a comfort to Elizabeth here."

Jake paused in the doorway for one last look at his wife, and the doctor promptly shut the door in his face. The young husband backed away from the door, hands in his pockets, lines of worry creasing his handsome face.

Si put his arm around the younger man's shoulder and said soothingly, "Come sit down, son. Liz is in good hands, and fretting and stewing won't speed things up any."

Samantha hid a smile. Si was better at giving advice than he was at taking it—as soon as he got Jake settled at the table with a cup of cold buttermilk, he took up his pacing again.

Adam had taken the time to rub down his own team as well as the doctor's mare before coming back to the house. He was sweaty and breathless, and he cornered his father immediately with, "Is Liz okay?"

"Liz is fine," Si told him, not slowing down in his walk back and forth across the narrow floor. "The doc is in there...and your ma. Liz'll be fine." And Si paused to squeeze Jake's slumped shoulder on the way by.

Josie requested canning jars—the preserves were ready to be poured out. Adam crawled down into the under-the-kitchen cellar and brought up a wooden box full of canning jars. Samantha wiped them clean, then handed them to Josie who filled them by spooning out the bright red preserves. Adam sealed them tight, wiping the rims with a wet rag. No banter accompanied their task; all ears were cocked toward the bedroom door, listening for any sound that would give a clue as to what was taking place behind that closed door.

The jars of preserves marched across the wooden work table like so many jewels in a crown. Lunch time came and went without anyone even thinking about eating. The whole house seemed to be laying in wait.

By late afternoon, the men had headed out to take care of the milking and feeding the chickens and geese. Si had extracted a promise from Josie to fetch them immediately if anything happened. While they were gone, Josie and Samantha put together some ham sandwiches and cut up radishes and carrots to go along with them. The girls admitted they really weren't hungry, but it had been hours since break-fast and they all needed to put something in their stomachs.

The animals were cared for, and the sandwiches were gone (although they might as well have been eating sawdust for all the pleasure anyone took in the simple meal). Si leaned back in his chair to let Josie reach his empty plate. He sighed. "Well, I guess maybe I'll run home and check on the children, then—"

A sound cut through the quiet kitchen, silencing Si and turning everyone's attention to the closed bedroom door. Jake jumped up and placed both hands flat against the wooden door, his face nearly pressed against the painted wood. Adam half-stood, his hands pressing the table top tensely. Si covered his mouth with a shaky hand, and Josie reached blindly for Samantha who clutched at her thankfully.

Samantha had never heard a noise like that before. It had been low, guttural—a harsh, anguished sound that seemed to cut through the hearts of everyone in the room. Now they heard the doctor's voice, tense and authoritative, "Come on, Liz, bear down. Push, girl! I need your help!"

Jake leaned his forehead against the door, and his hands curled into tight fists which thumped at the door softly. Si rose and placed a hand on the younger man's taut back. Jake seemed unaware of Si's presence. Adam had crossed to stand between Josie and Samantha, and Josie turned into his chest, leaning against him. His arm curved around her protectively, and he reached for Samantha with his other arm. Samantha, so caught up in fear of what could be happening to Liz, unthinkingly moved into his embrace. They stood thus, silent and straining for any sound that could reassure them.

Then it came—a new sound, a soft, mewling sound that brought joyous smiles to the faces of the group in the kitchen. Josie hugged Adam, crying against his neck. Adam squeezed his sister, saying, "Here, now, it's all right now. No need to cry." But when Samantha looked up at him, she saw tears glinting in his eyes, too. She had a lump in her throat, and she swallowed hard, trying to dislodge it. She became suddenly aware of the weight of Adam's arm across her shoulders, and she stepped quickly away.

The bedroom door opened and Laura came out, moving directly into Si's arms. She smiled a weak but happy smile at Jake, saying, "Congratulations, Papa, you've got a fine-looking son!"

Jake beamed so hard the room seemed lit by his happiness. "Can I see him—and my wife?" he asked, his body straining for the bedroom.

"The doctor's cleaning them up, Jake," Laura replied gently, pulling away from Si to envelop Jake in a maternal hug. "Wait just a moment—he'll call you."

Everyone buzzed happily, congratulating Jake and asking Laura how things had gone. They almost didn't hear the doctor's cry over their happy news-sharing.

"Mrs. Klaassen! Come here, quickly! I need you!"

Laura shot Si a panicked look before disappearing once more into the bedroom and closing the door firmly behind her. Everyone seemed petrified, not a soul moving or even breathing. Behind the door they could hear the sounds of Liz's moaning, a baby's weak cry, and hushed, frantic voices.

Si reached his arms wide to gather his family near. "Jake, Adam," he said in an emotion-filled voice, "come. Josie, Frances, you too. Come close. We should pray."

They stood in a tight circle, heads bowed and almost touching. They clutched hands and squeezed tightly, willing everything well behind the closed door. Samantha, unfamiliar with praying, wasn't sure what to do, but she found her thoughts begging to an unknown Someone. *Oh, please, please let Liz be okay! And the little baby, too. Keep 'em both safe for Jake—he loves 'em and needs 'em so much!*

It seemed hours passed before a creaking announced the opening of the bedroom door. All heads raised and all eyes turned to the sound. The doctor stepped out and sighed once. He pulled a wrinkled handkerchief out of his pocket and wiped his face. Jake crossed to him quickly.

"Dr. Newton, Liz—is she…?" He couldn't complete the thought.

Dr. Newton reached out and put a hand on Jake's broad shoulder. "Liz is fine, Jake. She had a rough time of it—the baby was breech. She'll be down for awhile, but she'll be fine."

Jake's shoulders slumped with relief momentarily, but then his head raised sharply. "The baby!" he exclaimed. "My son…?"

The doctor shook his head. "That wife of yours is sure one for surprises, Jake."

Everyone looked puzzled by his odd response.

The doctor expelled a huff of tired laughter. "Go on in and see her now. I think she should be the one to share the news." And he headed for the door, still shaking his head in disbelief.

Confusion marring his handsome face, Jake stepped into the bedroom and crossed quickly to the bed. When he sat, his broad back blocked Liz from the view of the others crowded in the doorway. But what they couldn't see, they could hear. Jake's shout nearly raised the rafters. "Why, Liz Stoesz! No *wonder* you were as big as a house!"

Liz's tinkling laughter was heard before she shushed her husband weakly. "No shouting, please, Jake. You'll wake them."

Them!? The group at the door could no longer be restrained. Si broke through first to rush to Laura's side. Adam and Josie followed quickly, stopping at the foot of the bed. Samantha came more slowly, afraid of intruding but unable to resist. She stood close to Josie and gaped, as shocked as the others were.

In the bed, snuggled securely in Liz's arms, were two tiny bundles. Liz looked pale and weak, but undeniably happy. "Can you believe it, Mother?" Liz asked, shaking her head in wonderment. "Twins!"

Jake looked up at Si proudly, "Two sons, Si! Can you believe what she's done? Liz has given me *two sons!*"

Si held Laura tightly against his side as he beamed down at his daughter. "They're just beautiful, Liz," he said. His voice sounded thick with tears.

Liz nodded tiredly. "Yes, they are, Papa. The most beautiful babies ever."

Samantha thought they were about as pretty as baby birds, but wisely kept that thought to herself. Besides, it didn't seem to matter much what they looked like. They were fine, and Liz was fine. Her heart thumped thankfully in her chest. *Someone had heard their prayers!*

"We do have a small problem, though," Liz said, adjusting the blanket more snugly around the baby boy on her right.

Jake's eyebrows raised. "A problem? How on earth can we have a problem?"

"Well," Liz explained, a hint of teasing in her weak voice. "I know this one"—and she touched the fuzzy dark hair on the head of the baby on her left—"is Jacob Andrew. He was born first, so should be given the name we chose. But we can't name his brother Amanda Joy, now can we?"

Jake laughed and stroked the cheek of the unnamed baby. The baby puckered up his tiny mouth and twisted his head within the confines of the blanket. "No," Jake said seriously, "I suppose we can't."

"So we have a problem," Liz reiterated.

"Not much of one," was Jake's response. He turned to Adam and asked, "Uncle Adam, how would you feel about having a little namesake?"

Adam's eyes grew wide. "A—a namesake?" he stammered. "Why, I—I—"

Liz touched Jake's hand. "Perhaps Adam would like to save that for his own little boy someday, Jake," she said gently.

But Adam shook his head madly. "No, Liz! I mean, yes, maybe someday I'll have a son, but I never considered naming him after myself. I'd be honored to have the baby given my name."

Jake turned back to Liz and suggested, "How about Adam James? Little Jacob Andrew was named for my pa and me; Adam James can be named for your brother and father." Si's full name was Simon James. Si puffed up at the suggestion.

"I'd like that very much," Liz responded.

The new mother yawned widely behind her hand. Laura took the hint and began shooing everyone from the room. "Come on, now, everyone out. Liz has labored harder today than ever before, and she needs her rest." She leaned over the bed to kiss first Liz, then the heads of each of her new grandsons.

"*Schlop Die gesunt, kleine mudder,*" Laura whispered, and Liz released a contented sigh before letting her eyelids drop.

Everyone tip-toed out of the room, Adam lingering to gaze in wonder at the tiny baby boy named Adam James. It was something, having a baby named in your honor! He felt proud and responsible, and determined to always be the kind of example his little namesake could look up to.

Samantha followed Adam's gaze, and she thought she knew what he was thinking. She felt a funny swelling in her chest. Adam was so unlike the men she'd known before. He could be moved by the coming of a baby, and wasn't ashamed to show it. In her eyes, he was more manly than any of the tough, hard-nosed men in her past.

They closed the bedroom door once more to give Liz some quiet, and Si and Laura gave Jake a final hug before Si asked Adam to get the horses hitched up. "We need to be heading home," he said, "to share the good news with the others."

"Ma," Josie asked, pleading, "can I stay, just for tonight? I can help Frances, and I'd like to hold one of the babies yet before I go home."

Si and Laura looked at Jake. "Is it okay with you?" Laura asked.

Jake nodded, looking as though his feet couldn't touch the floor. "That's fine. She can bunk in with Frances, and— oh, no!" He slapped a palm to his forehead.

Everyone started in alarm. "What's wrong?" Adam exclaimed.

Jake looked at everyone blankly. "I just realized—I'm going to need another cradle!"

Chapter Ten

Days slipped by one by one. Samantha settled into a routine as comfortably as a man settles into a pair of old slippers. Her days were filled with household chores and garden work that she found to be most enjoyable. Liz's time was spent taking care of the two small boys who grew more plump and attractive each day. They looked so much alike that nearly everyone who came in contact with them couldn't decide which was Andy and which was A.J., as Jake had come to call them. Liz had no problem with that, though, and could even determine which one was fussing before she climbed the stairs to their bedroom when a pathetic, hiccuping wail that had not yet grown to be annoying was heard.

Samantha grew, too, during the last days of summer. She grew in contentment and self-confidence as she successfully handled the responsibility bestowed on her. She certainly earned her four dollars a week! She had never canned vegetables before, but with Liz in her rocker handing out instructions—in a patient voice that reminded her so much of Laura—Samantha put up quart jars of green beans, tomatoes, carrots, corn, and even pickled beets. She baked bread for the family's consumption, washed loads and loads of little flannel diapers and gowns, gathered eggs, kept the house clean…. It seemed the workload was neverending, but not once did she complain. When she dropped into bed at night, exhausted, it was a happy exhaustion that she'd not known a person could feel. It was so wonderful to be needed, and to be appreciated.

One thing was bothering her, though. It was living a lie. Samantha admired Liz and Jake and the whole Klaassen family so much, and she wanted to be honest with them and confess that she wasn't Frances Welch at all. At first it had been somewhat funny to fool them, but as she'd gotten to know them and be accepted into their loving family unit, her conscience pricked each time one of them called her Frances. Part of her wanted to 'fess up and let them know who she really was, but one thing always stopped her: Pa. If they knew her real name, then the sheriff would send her name down the line, and sooner or later Pa would arrive to take her back home.

Home. Already this place was home more than the house she grew up in had ever been. Not even when Gran was alive had it truly been a *home* in the sense that the people who resided within the walls loved and respected one another. Gran being there had made it bearable, but it stopped short of being a real *home.* Whenever her conscience bothered her, she got busy to keep from thinking about it. She wasn't willing to give up what she had now—not just yet.

Harvest had begun the last week of August, as well as school opening. Samantha watched children walking by the road early in the morning, heading to school, swinging their tin lunch pails and carrying books and tablets. In a way, she envied them. Josie stopped by many afternoons for a visit with her nephews, sometimes accompanied by Becky or Sarah, who was sprouting two large front teeth and was losing her lisp. Josie told tales of the days in school, and Samantha had to wonder what it would be like to go.

She had attended school before, and had been a better-than-average student. But with the home life she'd had, she was always a misfit and hadn't made friends. Samantha wondered if things would be different here, going with Josie, Arn, and the others. Then she remembered Priscilla Koehn, and thought, *Well, maybe not.* Still, she wouldn't be needed here with Liz once harvest was over, which was only another four weeks or so. It was time to think about what she would do, and where she would go after that.

Harvest was Adam's favorite time of year. Being outside in the fields, smelling the scent of fresh-cut grain, bantering with the men whose spirits were as high as his, working hard and sweating much. Farming was in Adam's blood, and he'd been quite young when the decision had been made to stay near the family homestead and farm with his father, taking over when Si decided he was too old to continue. Adam had helped with harvests since he had turned thirteen, staying out of school the first weeks until the work was done. It had never bothered him to work rather than attend the start of school. He always caught up and never felt disadvantaged by it—his education was in the fields.

Arn, however, didn't seem to share Adam's enthusiasm for farming. Adam had caught the younger boy looking off toward the schoolhouse longingly. At fifteen, Arn was expected to help with harvest, but wasn't required to enjoy it. Although Arn was fast developing the husky build of his farm-loving brothers Adam and Frank, he didn't possess the farmer's heart, and Adam figured when Arn was grown his vocation would be closer to Daniel's than Si's. Another man might feel threatened by the realization that his son didn't want to follow in his footsteps, but Adam knew Si would support Arn's decision in whatever job choice he made, as long as Arn was happy with it.

As Adam scraped the fallen stalks of wheat together with a long, wooden rake, he found his thoughts wandering to Liz and Jake and their twins. A smile crossed his face as he remembered holding little Adam James for the first time. The baby had fit snugly in the crook of his arm, a warm and soft bundle. When he had touched a finger to the baby's palm, A.J. had curled his tiny hand around Adam's work-roughened finger. Liz had explained it was a reflex reaction, but Adam's heart had thrilled, feeling as if A.J. was accepting him as his uncle.

He remembered something else about that time—when he'd looked up, he'd caught Frances watching him with a soft, strange expression on her face. When he'd met her gaze, she had colored prettily and looked away, fussing with her overall straps in a peculiar way. He wondered, *Why was she embarrassed? And what did that soft look mean?*

Frances had changed so much in the weeks spent with Liz. Adam never had thanked Liz for working that change, either. He needed to do that. The sullen, defensive girl was gone, replaced by a young lady who, although never overtly outgoing, could offer a warm smile and engage in a conversation. He recalled the morning in the strawberry patch, when she'd even managed to tease a little bit. He had to admit, she was an uncommonly pretty girl with that wild mane of hair and unusual pale blue eyes. If that warmer, more open side of her could be expanded, he could even imagine being attracted to her.

That thought brought Adam up short, and he stopped his raking. Attractive? Well, yes, she was. But could he think of her *that way*? Again, he remembered the shy way she behaved when he spotted her observing him with the baby. Could it be that *she* was thinking of *him* that way…?

"Adam!"

His father's voice cut into his thoughts. He turned his head to locate Si.

"It's not lunch time yet, son, keep at it!"

Adam nodded, and began raking in earnest. He'd have to give that thought some serious consideration when the work was done.

"Frances, starting tomorrow, you're in for it," Jake announced at the supper table on Wednesday.

Samantha looked up from cutting her chicken and raised an eyebrow. "What do you mean?" she asked in a squeaky voice. Her face said, *Have I done something wrong?*

Jake laughed at her. "Don't look so worried, goofy, I'm not planning to burn you at the stake. But after the next few days, that might look pretty good, just to get out of the work! No, tomorrow the harvest crew will begin in my fields. That means you and Liz will be responsible for fixing them breakfast, lunch, and two snacks during the day. It's a heap of cooking, and Liz is still pretty tied down with Andy and A.J., so the majority of the job will fall to you."

Samantha swallowed hard. "I'm okay at cooking for *us*, I guess," she said, gesturing to the meal on the table. The fried chicken was crisp and tasty, the boiled potatoes and gravy passable, and the green beans had been flavored up with some chopped onion. Even her bread was as good as Liz's had ever been. "But I'm not too sure I can cook okay for that many people."

Liz reached across Andy, who was nearly dozing at her breast, to pat Samantha's arm soothingly. "Now, Frances, one thing you need to keep in mind: when those men come in, they're so hungry you could feed them boot leather and they wouldn't complain, as long as you provided salt and pepper to season it! You're a fine cook, and I'll help you judge amounts so we're sure to have enough. I cooked for the last two harvest crews, and I wasn't any older than you the first time. You'll do fine."

Samantha still looked uncertain. "Well, if you'll help, I guess so," she said. Andy had fallen asleep, his little mouth drooping open as he relaxed. "Here," Samantha offered, "Give me Andy, and I'll carry him up to his cradle so you can eat your supper without dribblin' on him."

Liz laughed softly and willingly relinquished her bundle. "Thank you, Frances," she said gratefully, "it would be nice to eat without having to lean across a little body!"

Samantha cuddled Andy close as she mounted the stairs. It felt good, holding a little one. At first she'd been nervous to even touch the babies, but Liz had assured her they wouldn't break, and soon she was learning the pleasantries of caring for them. Of course, Liz took care of most of their needs, but there were times, like now, when an extra pair of hands came in very useful.

Useful. Samantha savored that word. Before coming here, she'd felt more useless than anything. As she tucked Andy into his cradle (borrowed from Jake's brother's attic), Samantha hummed softly. She rubbed Andy's tiny back until she was sure he was sound asleep. Smiling gently, she leaned down to place a kiss on the neck of the slumbering infant, then she turned to the other cradle. Baby A.J. lay on his side, his nearly transparent eyelids quivering. As Samantha watched, he stretched one arm upward towards his nose, curled his hand into a tiny fist, then let it relax again, bringing the arm back down. His rosebud mouth puckered and he made a soft sucking sound.

Uh-oh. He was waking, and no doubt would squall to be fed. To be sure he wouldn't disturb his sleeping brother, Samantha gently scooped him up and tip-toed out of the room. She paused at the top of the stairs, holding the baby nearly beneath her chin, breathing in the scent of him. Andy and A.J. looked alike—two peas in a pod, Si would laughingly call them—but Samantha was learning which was which by observing them.

A.J. wasn't quite as demanding as his brother, and seemed to enjoy snuggling more than Andy. When Andy wanted something, you'd better get it quick or prepare for a storm! But A.J. was more relaxed, easier to placate. Although she felt the stirrings of love for both little boys—in their helplessness, it was hard not to—she had to admit to herself that A.J. was the favored one in her eyes.

As she walked slowly downstairs with the now awake baby who peered up at her curiously, touching her cheek with a dimpled hand, she admitted that he certainly had been named correctly. He seemed to have inherited his uncle Adam's mild disposition and loving spirit.

"Oh, is he ready to eat now?" Liz asked when Samantha sat down at the table, still holding little A.J.

"He was waking up, so I brought him down in case he decided to howl," Samantha answered, turning her face slightly to better feel the baby's touch. She was learning the pleasure of touching and being touched by the tiniest of teachers. "I'll hold him while you finish up, long as he stays quiet."

But Jake spoke up, "Oh, let me have him, Frances. I've not been around enough during the day lately to really enjoy my boys. I'll hold him while you get the clean up started."

Reluctantly, Samantha rose and handed little A.J. to his papa. As she turned away, Jake added, "You'll want to turn in early tonight. We're going to work you extra hard until the harvesting is done here!"

Samantha nodded. That's what she was here for, she knew. But when the harvesting was finished, what then?

Samantha woke promptly at five o'clock the following morning, the crowing of the rooster signaling the arrival of the sun, and she yawned widely, snuggling into her pillow for an extra few minutes of rest. Then she remembered that today was the start of harvest in Jake's fields. Without further delay, she hooked her heels over the edge of the bed and pulled herself out from under the sheet. She stood, giving an all-over stretch to wake herself up, squinting into the murky darkness. It was then she spotted something hanging on the back of the door, and curiosity overcame her. She crossed to it quickly.

Hooked on a nail hung a dress. Samantha took it down, fingering the collar questioningly. Where had it come from? She checked it over carefully. It wasn't new—it must be a hand-me-down of Liz's. She glanced to the overalls and flannel shirt draped over the small chair in the corner, thinking of how hot she had been in those bulky clothes. Without another thought she slipped out of her nightgown and into the dress. It buttoned up the front, and as she fastened the buttons she realized it would fit loosely, but already it felt infinitely more comfortable than the overalls had.

She put on her stockings and boots then tip-toed down the stairs, wincing at the one that squeaked. Liz was already at the stove, measuring coffee into a tall blue enamel pot. She turned from her task when she heard Samantha enter. She smiled.

"You found the dress," she whispered cheerfully. "Do you like it?"

Samantha smoothed the skirt in a self-conscious gesture. "Yes, but—"

Liz cut in, "It's just one of my old ones. I hope you don't mind wearing a dress that's too big as you're much smaller than I ever remember being! But it's got to feel better than your hot clothing."

Samantha nodded, but she still didn't understand one thing: why now? She'd been here for almost three weeks already, shuffling around in her makeshift clothing. Why did Liz suddenly provide her with something else to wear?

Liz seemed to sense Samantha's puzzlement, for she cleared her throat in a nervous manner and said, "Frances, I'd like to tell you something, but I don't want to hurt your feelings."

Samantha shrugged, frowning a bit. "Well, what?" she asked.

Liz took a deep breath and dove in. "Jake is rather old-fashioned, and while he likes you very much, he doesn't exactly approve of your mode of dress." Liz fiddled with a loose thread on her dress pocket, unable to meet Samantha's eyes. This was so awkward! It was a hard subject to approach, and she wished Jake had brought it up himself days ago.

Samantha bristled defensively. "Well, those clothes are all I've got. I've been so busy I haven't had time for dress-sewing!"

Liz reached out for Samantha, but didn't quite touch her. "Oh, I know that, Frances! And I'm sorry—we *have* kept you awfully busy, and neither of us are faulting you for the clothes you wear. It's just that—well, with the harvest crew here and all, Jake was hoping I might be able to persuade you to wear one of my dresses." In a rush, Liz finished, "Some of the men might poke fun at you, and we'd feel a lot better if you were in a dress. There!"

Samantha stared at Liz in amazement. Not once had she ever imagined that Jake didn't approve of her overalls! Granted, they were hot and uncomfortable, but they were the only article of clothing she owned. So she wore them. And while she had been wishing she had something else to wear, Jake had been secretly wishing she did, too!

Suddenly, her defensiveness gave way to amusement, and she released a tiny bubble of laughter.

Liz lost her worried look and grinned, too. "Are you mad?" Liz asked.

Samantha shook her head. "No, I'm not mad. I'm feelin' relieved I won't have to drag myself around in those darn overalls one more day!"

With an air of deliverance, Liz threw an arm around Samantha's shoulders and gave her a quick squeeze. "I'm glad, too." And both women shared a laugh.

Samantha scooped up the bucket beside the kitchen stove and headed outside to the pump. The sun was just rising against the horizon, flooding the fields with a shimmer of gold. Samantha smiled. *A golden day*, she thought. *It'll be a golden day, for sure.*

Promptly at six, as Liz had predicted, the stomping of many feet was heard on the front stoop. Jake, adjusting his suspenders, threw open the door and immediately shushed the men's greetings with a finger placed against his lips. He pointed to the staircase, whispering, "The babies are still sleeping!" Nodding in understanding, the men entered, walking as if on eggshells to avoid making any noise.

Samantha had to turn her back quickly so they wouldn't see her amused grin. They all looked so funny, grown men tip-toeing with shoulders hunched and lips pursed tight! They wasted no time seating themselves. Normally only four chairs surrounded the round table, but Jake had hauled in some old nail kegs and wooden boxes from the barn to create make-shift seating. Eight men crowded around the table, looking out of place with their elbows pressed together awkwardly. The rest caught a seat wherever they could and balanced their plates on their laps.

Liz and Samantha had done their duty—they provided fried eggs, fried potatoes, pancakes, *zwieback*, and coffee. Liz stayed beside the stove, frying more pancakes as needed, while Samantha made the rounds, refilling coffee cups, holding out a jar of strawberry preserves for sweetening the *zwieback*, and carrying plates back and forth between the stove and the men needing "just a couple more o' those pancakes" or "a good-size spoon of potatoes, please." Samantha was too busy to feel self-conscious in her borrowed dress that really was a size larger than her slender frame. She would have liked to have paid some extra attention to Si, Frank, Adam and Arn—and to ask after Laura, Josie, Becky and the little kids—but there just wasn't the time.

As the last pancake was being flipped onto Si's plate, one of the babies upstairs began to tune up. Liz looked upward and uttered, "Uh-oh," before quickly wiping her hands on her apron and heading for the stairs, handing Si's plate to Samantha to deliver to him.

Si was grinning from ear to ear. "I was hoping they'd wake up before we headed out. Haven't seen those little guys in over a week!"

Since it was now unnecessary to be quiet, a big-boned man named Elmer Harms boomed out, "I betcha they're growin' like weeds, huh, Jake?"

"Oh, sure," Jake answered proudly. "We'll have them out milking cows in another week or so."

The men laughed appreciatively, all eyes turned toward the stairway as Liz descended, a baby on each arm.

Samantha stood back and watched the group of men *ooh* and *aah* over the babies, reaching out thick fingers to poke at tiny tummies and ruffle downy hair. Andy and A.J. took it all in with big, curious eyes for about two minutes before deciding being wet and hungry outweighed being cute and entertaining. First Andy opened his mouth to yell, and A.J., not to be outdone, joined in. Reluctantly the men backed off, and Liz shut herself in the bedroom with the babies to change their diapers and give them their breakfast.

The men began filing out the door, dropping their empty plates on the dry sink as they went. Adam was the last to leave, and he turned back with an apologetic face.

"I guess you're the clean-up crew, huh?" he asked Samantha.

Samantha shrugged. "I guess so," she agreed. Hands on hips, she surveyed the pile of dishes, forks, cups, and skillets.

"I'd stay and give you a hand, but—" and he gestured toward the barn where the others were waiting impatiently for him.

Samantha waved two hands at him in dismissal. "Oh, go do your work and let me do mine!" she exclaimed. He might have thought she was disgruntled had it not been for the teasing glint in her eyes.

He grinned. "Yes, ma'am," he drawled, and started out the door. But just before he stepped through, he looked back over his shoulder and said, "By the way, you look right nice in that dress, Miss Frances."

He paused just long enough to see her lift her fingers to touch the collar of the cotton dress fussily. Then, feeling gratified, he joined the men.

Chapter Eleven

The men needed a mid-morning snack, but it took too much time for them to come in for it. Consequently, Samantha was delegated the task of riding Tess, Liz's gentle mare, to the fields to deliver their snack of sandwiches and deviled eggs. Although she was not adverse to riding a horse, she refused to ride side-saddle, so she donned her overalls before climbing astride Tess's broad back. When she caught up with the workers, the conversation she'd had with Liz that morning still was fresh in her mind, and she felt a bit conspicuous.

But Samantha was practiced at hiding her feelings. She looked quite sure of herself as she hopped down from the horse and untied the burlap sack full of food which she had hung on the saddle horn.

Jake whistled the men in, and all gathered around as she handed out the snack. She noticed Adam sending her a strange look, but she was too busy making certain everyone got his fair share to worry too much about it. Besides, Jake's younger brother Lucas was paying an awful lot of attention to her, so her mind was occupied trying to come up with clever responses to his overt flirting. She'd never engaged in idle chit-chat with young men before, but she discovered it could be quite enjoyable. It gave her a lighthearted, pleasantly female feeling that was fun to explore. It wasn't until lunch time, when the men had come in, that she remembered Adam's odd look and wondered about it.

Liz and Samantha had set up a makeshift table outside, putting several long planks over a pair of wooden sawhorses. Samantha had hauled all the chairs, boxes, and kegs outside, too, and the men gathered around the humble picnic table for their lunch of stewed chicken, corn-on-the-cob, mashed potatoes, *zwieback*, coffee, and apple pie that Samantha had baked only that morning. There hadn't been time to change back into Liz's dress when she had returned from delivering the men's snack, so Samantha tripped around the table in her ungainly overalls.

Unlike breakfast's silence, the men now chatted boisterously, telling wild stories about hunting trips and other harvests, and ribbing Frank Klaassen about having to spend so much time away from courting Anna. Frank took it well, though his ears glowed red. His temperament wasn't quite as even as Adam's, so the men had a good time trying to rile him.

"Yeah, yeah, Frank," one of the men—Samantha thought his name was Ed—hollered in a gravely voice, "you can't be away from 'em too long, or they lose interest. Gotta keep plyin' 'em with sweet talk and posies. Can't do much o' that when you're workin' mornin' to evenin.'"

"Reckon not," Frank countered smoothly, barely giving the older man a glance.

Another took up that tack. "'Course that Anna, she's still a schoolgirl. Got her days pretty well filled up with book-learnin'. The mornin's shouldn't be much of a problem—he just needs to worry 'bout the evenin's."

"Uh-huh." Ed apparently enjoyed being in the middle of things, as he jumped in again, watching Frank closely for his reaction. "I heard the new school teacher's not too bad to look at, an' not a whole lot older'n Frank here. Anna bein' free these days might look like a mighty good prospect to that young man!"

Frank shot him a sharp look, but Adam cut in, keeping him from answering. "I'm sure Frank and Anna have things pretty well arranged between them."

Ed poked his neighbor and teased, "How 'bout you, Adam? You got things 'arranged' with some special young lady?"

Jake's brother Lucas called from across the table, "Adam may not have much to do with it, but that pretty little Priscilla Koehn seems to be workin' on arrangin' somethin' with him. She sure was eye-ballin' you at church Sunday, Adam! You were talkin' to her, Frances," he suddenly called out, trying to involve her in their rivalry. "Did she say anything to you about likin' Adam there?"

Samantha gave Adam a quick glance, trying to decide whether or not to play along. Finally she answered noncommittally, "Maybe she did and maybe she didn't. A lady wouldn't be tellin' secrets, so just let me out of it."

The men laughed, and one of them nudged Lucas and said loudly, "Not many females 'round who won't spread a good piece of gossip. Reckon we got ourselves a real special one here. 'Course, it's hard to tell if she's a lady or not, since she's covered head to toe in a pair of men's pants!"

Most of the men roared at that, and Samantha pursed her lips tightly. They could just leave her and her britches alone! But the conversation switched quickly back to Adam.

Ed's neighbor whistled, and leaned toward Adam, saying, "You could do a lot worse than Priscilla Koehn, Adam, boy. Priscilla's a mighty lovely little lady. She'd look right smart on your arm."

Samantha bristled at the thought. Josie was right—Adam had more sense than to get himself involved with a shallow little flirt like Priscilla! She cocked an ear to catch his reply to their badgering.

"You fellows oughtta concentrate a little harder on your plates before those of us who are more interested in eating than yapping finish it all and you end up without second helpings."

While the others seemed to consider that prospect, Adam motioned to Samantha. "Frances, I sure would appreciate another piece of pie. It's every bit as good as Mother's."

Samantha hurried to his side, pie pan and server in hand. As she scooped a sizable wedge onto his plate, he said softly, "I liked the dress, but I suppose it would be hard to ride Tess in it."

She gave him a slight scowl. So *that* was what the strange look was all about! Did he think she'd changed clothes because of the compliment he'd paid her earlier? Did he really think she was that bull-headed? Suddenly she got a mental picture of the dainty Priscilla with her perfect curls and impeccable clothing. She was sure Priscilla wouldn't be caught *dead* wearing a pair of men's over-sized overalls! She felt a rush of jealousy as she imagined Adam and Priscilla walking arm in arm. She felt stung by the implication that she'd changed back into her grubby clothes just to aggravate him.

Tartly, she hissed directly into his shapely ear, "My britches are better suited to a lot of things, horse riding included."

And she turned on a bare heel and thumped back into the kitchen haughtily, nose in the air. Adam watched her go, amazed. He had only been trying to reassure her after the crazy crack Russ made about her overalls. Why in thunder had she gotten so riled?

Once inside, Samantha felt her anger deflate. She placed her hands on her warm cheeks and berated herself. Of all the foolish ways to behave! Why had she responded like that? He'd complimented her on how she looked in the dress, then complimented her pies. And she'd returned the favor by being fractious. Why had she seen his comment as a way of upbraiding her? By now she knew Adam well enough to realize he wouldn't intentionally belittle her. It was her own insecurities that read a criticism into his words.

You addlepated fool, she scolded herself, *you're always repayin' a kindness with a fit of impatience! When will you ever learn to think before you speak?*

But maybe she could fix it. Quickly, before she could change her mind, she dashed up to her room and changed back into the dress Liz had loaned her. She took an additional few minutes to brush her willful hair into a thick tail and tied it with a piece of yellow yarn. Back down she ran, only to step into an empty yard, save Liz who was cleaning up.

Samantha's heart sagged. She had wanted Adam to see that she could be a lady. It was as close to an apology as she could make herself give. But she was too late. He, along with the others, had already headed back to the fields. *Some golden day this has turned out to be!* she thought, disheartened and upset. With a sigh, she moved to the table and began to stack dirty dishes. And if she carried Adam's plate a little tighter than the others, it was no one's business but her own.

The harvest crew spent five days in Jake's fields before all the wheat was cut, raked, and stacked into sheaths to be transported to the railroad when completely dry. The days passed in a blur for Samantha, who kept so busy she almost felt as if she walked in her sleep at times. She'd worn Liz's dress continually after the first day, but Adam hadn't made any comment about it, and she found herself growing angry with him for not noticing and herself for worrying so much about it.

Sunday arrived, and Liz, Jake, the twins, and Samantha were invited to have dinner with Laura and Si. Samantha made noises about wanting to stay at the house rather than go to church, but Liz had taken her aside to plead, "Oh, Frances, I could really use you there. It's Jake's turn to lead the singing, so I'll be left holding both babies. Please come along and help me with the boys?"

Samantha had grudgingly agreed, and it wasn't until mid-service, as she cuddled little A.J. (who slept, snoring contentedly through the whole service), that she realized Laura could have sat with Liz and held one of her grandsons while Jake was at the front of the church. Obviously, her church attendance was important enough to Liz for her to use a bit of wiles to get Samantha there. It made her wonder what was so all-fired special, and she tried to focus on what the minister was saying.

Samantha's previous church experiences had taken place when she was quite young, so she didn't have many memories. But she did seem to recall the preacher at Gran's place of worship had done a lot of Bible-thumping and raised his voice quite a bit. Reverend Goertzen was quite the opposite— he was so soft-spoken, one had to strain to catch his words.

This morning he was assuring his congregation of God's all-powerful love for each of them. Samantha found herself enthralled as the minister read from the book of John, "'Greater love hath no man than this, that he lay his life down for his friends.' This, then, is what our Lord and Saviour did for us—He gave up His own life, that we might see redemption for our sins. He claimed us as His friends, even before He knew us. How humbling to think that this perfect Person, God's holy Son, could love us enough to die for us."

Samantha shifted A.J. a bit lower in her arms and thought sadly, *Humbling is right. There's no way the preacher could be meaning me—I sit here in church the biggest liar there ever was! I sure don't deserve the love of God.*

The minister might have been reading her thoughts, as he continued, "We wonder, how can we deserve that kind of love? And, people, I can tell you, none of us *deserve* it. We can't earn it by doing kind deeds, or dropping hundreds of dollars into the offering plate on Sunday morning. No matter how we try, we can't live a perfect life and work our way into God's favor. We're sinners—we were born sinful, and we do so many wrong things.... But yet He loved us. He loved us enough to die for us."

Samantha found herself wondering why the perfect Son of God would go to all that bother, and she leaned forward a bit, trying to understand.

"And the reason is simple. He loved us because He created us. He saw in each one of us the potential to be like Him. But He knew that sin would drag us down and keep us from being what we could be. So how do we get past that sin? How can He look past it?"

Reverend Goertzen let his eyes rove over the congregation, and Samantha thought he had compassionate eyes, as if he really cared about each of the people listening to him. When his eyes met hers, she almost gasped, wondering if he could see into her soul to the sins that were hiding there.

"Each of us are more deserving of punishment than Jesus Christ was. He had done no wrong, but *we* had. So, in His infinite love for us, He took our place. He died so that we could call upon His blood and be forgiven of our sins." He quoted again, "'Greater love hath no man than this…' I wonder how many of us would be willing to bear the punishment for our brother's sin. Or our neighbor's wrongdoing. Yet, we claim to love our brothers and our neighbors, don't we? But we don't love them with Christ's love. Not until we have Christ living in our heart can we love one another with Christ's love."

Christ living in our heart? Samantha frowned. What did he mean by that?

"Brothers and sisters," Reverend Goertzen spoke earnestly, leaning forward against the homemade wooden podium that held his Bible, "we can go to church, we can tithe our income, we can help our neighbors, but until we accept Christ's gift of love and receive Him into our hearts, all that goodness is for nothing. It's just vanity. Until Christ's love is inside of you, you remain apart from Him. And His death was in vain."

Strong words, but spoken so softy and sincerely that the harshness was removed and only the need for acceptance remained. Samantha braved a glance at Laura who was seated on the other side of Liz. *She's got that love in her heart,* she thought. *An' so do Liz an' Jake an' Adam an' Josie… They've got that love, an' that's what makes 'em different from the folks at home. That's what makes 'em able to be loving to me even when I tried to steal.* The realization swept across her, and her heart thumped wildly in her chest. Another strong desire caught her: *I wish I could be like them.…*

The minister had concluded his sermon by encouraging his congregation to take the love of Jesus with them and share it with everyone they knew, so that Jesus' death would have meaning. Jake went up to lead the worshippers in a final hymn, and then everyone filed out.

Samantha was hardly aware of Si taking A.J. from her arms. She followed Liz automatically, nodding when spoken to, but unaware of what anyone said. There were too many things to ponder.

Josie linked arms with Samantha outside the church and invited, "Ride in the wagon with us instead of going with Liz, Frances. I haven't talked to you in ages!" When no response was forthcoming, Josie nudged her and said laughingly, "Where are you, Frances? You sure aren't here!"

Samantha gave herself a shake and forced herself to turn her attention to Josie. "I guess I was daydreaming," she said sheepishly.

"I guess so!" Josie agreed. She repeated her invitation, "Do you want to ride home with us? It'll give us a chance to catch up on things. You won't *believe* what Priscilla pulled at school last week!"

Once they were bouncing along toward home, Josie poked Becky and encouraged, "Tell Frances what Priscilla did last Thursday." She leaned over to Samantha and said, shaking her head, "Wait 'til you hear this."

Becky, glad to be included in the older girls' gossip, scooted closer and giggled. "Oh," she announced dramatically, keeping her voice low and secretive, "that Priscilla was in such trouble with Mr. Reimer! He made her stand with her nose in the corner for fifteen minutes! She was so mad, she was almost spitting!"

"Never mind that," Josie cut her off, glancing at the others in the wagon to be sure they weren't being overheard, "tell us what *she* did."

Becky's dark eyes sparkled as she related the tale in a whisper. "*Well*, last Thursday Mr. Reimer gave us an assignment to write an essay about what our future plans were. We all took that to mean jobs and such. But Priscilla wrote this lovey-dovey poem about how she was"—Becky's eyes fluttered upward and she placed her folded hands beneath her chin as she quoted—"'going to be a farmer's wife and live with Adam all my life.'"

She dropped her simpering pose and continued, "It went on and on, and she even drew *pictures* to go along with it of a man and woman in wedding finery, with the words 'I do, forever and ever' written underneath the picture. Over the man's head, she put Adam's name, and her own name over the woman's head."

Josie took over now. "Mr. Reimer was really angry. He said school time wasn't to be wasted on such foolishness. He gave her a failing grade for the assignment and made her stand in the corner like a six year old. It was so funny!"

Samantha joined in laughter with Josie and Becky, even though thinking of Priscilla and Adam together gave her a funny feeling. That Priscilla was so sure of herself! What if she managed to convince Adam that he should give her another look? Samantha looked over at Adam, who was whispering to Sarah as she sat in his lap with her arms looped around his neck. Just then he glanced up and caught her gaze. He smiled. She looked away, flustered.

She hadn't spoken to him much after that encounter over her clothing. He'd been at the house every day of the harvest, but she had kept her distance, too embarrassed to face him. And he hadn't sought her out, either, which had gotten her dander up. Her feelings were so confused where Adam was concerned! If he felt bad about being hissed at, he sure didn't act like it. Maybe she shouldn't feel guilty about it, either. She had enough other things to feel guilty about without worrying about stepping on Adam Klaassen's toes!

As the wagon pulled into the yard, she remembered how the minister had said if people let sin go on unforgiven, it was if saying Jesus had died in vain. If it was true that Jesus had died for everyone, then that included Samantha O'Brien, and she was guilty of more than just fibbing about her name or trying to steal some groceries. She was guilty of letting Jesus die for a person who wouldn't repent. Although the concept of Someone loving her enough to die for her was new, it was sending down roots in Samantha's heart. She had seen firsthand the difference Jesus could make in someone's life. *I reckon from the way that ol' Priscilla behaves, Jesus died in vain for her. I sure don't want that on my conscience. But now, what do I do about it?*

Her thoughts came to an abrupt standstill as someone tapped her on the shoulder. She looked up to see Adam standing outside the wagon bed, his hand held out to her.

"Want a help down?" he asked.

Without a word, Samantha nodded, and placed her small hand gingerly in his much larger, work-roughened palm. With her other hand, she braced herself on the wooden side of the wagon bed, and hopped out carefully, quickly adjusting her skirts when her feet touched the ground.

"Thank you," she said quietly, and made as if to pull her hand away. But Adam closed his fingers around hers and wouldn't let her go.

"Frances," he said, his dark eyes serious as they met her pale, uncertain ones, "I feel I owe you an apology."

Samantha wished she could yank her hand away and run, but she felt impaled to the spot. "W-What for?" she managed to stutter.

Adam squeezed her hand gently. "I'm afraid I hurt your feelings when I commented about your overalls." His gaze was so sincere it was hard for Samantha to meet. "I didn't mean to make you uncomfortable, but I think that's what I did, and I'm sorry for that."

Samantha looked down, fidgeting. She owed him a bigger apology, but her tongue felt as if it was swollen and she wasn't sure she could talk.

Adam kind of bounced her hand and ducked down to try and look eye to eye with her again. "Will you please forgive me? So we can be friends again?"

Samantha felt foolish. *He said we were friends.... Say something!* she commanded herself. Finally she raised her head slightly, looking at him through her eyelashes. He had the hint of a smile on his tanned face, and she noticed how the sun had already put little crinkles around his eyes from squinting. He was almost too pretty to be a man, she thought, and it was so hard to talk to him! But his sincerity tore at her heart, and she had to put him at ease.

"There ain't—there's not anything to forgive, Adam," she finally said in a soft little voice. "You didn't say anything wrong. But I did." She swallowed, looking down at her feet again. "I'm sorry I yelled in your ear. I was just feeling kind of unladylike, wearing my overalls, so I *acted* unladylike. I'm sorry, too."

Adam released a breath and sighed, relieved, "Whew!"

She looked up at him, startled.

He was grinning. "Well, I feel better!" he said, placing his other hand on top of hers, sandwiching her hand between his palms. "Do you?"

Her mouth pulled up slightly at the corners, as if she was trying to keep from smiling. She was biting the inside of her cheeks, too—he could tell. She nodded.

"Good!" he said, then released her hand, abruptly changing topics. "I'd better get these horses taken care of, and you'd better catch up with the others or there won't be any dinner left."

With another nod, she turned to go. But she took only three steps before stopping and turning back. "Adam?"

He stopped messing with the harness and looked up queryingly.

She took a deep breath, gathering courage, then finally managed to say the words she'd thought of saying for weeks. "That day I was trying to steal from your uncle's store—and we...tussled...." Her glance skittered away briefly and she blushed. She turned her eyes back to his and continued bravely, "I called you a durn honyocker." She paused, biting her lower lip. "I feel bad about that, too. You're not a durn honyocker. You're a really nice person, and I shouldn't 've called you that."

Adam felt his ears turn warm. "Oh, shoot, Frances, I would've expected to be called something worse than that for sitting on you like I did. Let's just call it even, okay?"

She almost glowed as a smile burst across her face. The release was heavenly! Suddenly shy, she lifted a hand to wave, then picked up her skirts and ran to the house.

Adam, watching her go, shook his head in wonder. He'd been right all along. A smile *could* transform a person.

Chapter Twelve

A cold lunch of *zwieback*, sausage, cheeses, and pie was the noon meal. It was customary to eat a cold meal on Sunday so the ladies wouldn't spend hours cooking. The meal was simple to put out and clean up, and Samantha found she enjoyed the extra time it left for visiting. Several times during the dinner, she looked up from talking with Josie or the younger girls to find Adam watching her. Each time he would smile briefly, then turn his attention elsewhere. But then when she'd look, he'd have his gaze on her again. It gave her a funny feeling down low in her belly—a light, quivery lifting that seemed to rise up and push at her heart, a not unpleasant feminine feeling.

When the meal was finished and the dishes were neatly scraped and stacked to be washed later, the family congregated in the parlor—the women to coo over the babies and the men to talk harvest and the war in Europe. Samantha looked on from the doorway briefly before wandering outside and heading to her favorite spot, the porch swing near the lilac bushes. It was there that Adam and Teddy stumbled upon her on their way back from visiting a new batch of barn kittens. Teddy still cuddled one yellow and white furball which he promptly dropped into Samantha's lap when she exclaimed, "Oh, he's so sweet!"

"Wanna keep that one?" Teddy asked her as she stroked the tiny head and the kitten set up a loud purr in response. "There's four more I can go play with, so you can keep that one here, if you want."

"Oh, yes!" Samantha exclaimed. "I do."

So Teddy trotted off to the barn, leaving Adam and Samantha sharing the wide porch swing.

Samantha focused her full attention on the little kitten in her lap. That fluttery feeling was back, having Adam so near. Never having experienced these feelings before, she felt a bit uncomfortable in his presence, so instead of looking at him she turned the baby kitty onto its back and teased it with one finger.

Adam set them into gentle motion, keeping one foot planted on the porch floor and rocking the swing slowly up and back, up and back. He reached out to poke at the kitten, and the kitty squirmed around, ignoring Samantha's finger to curl tiny paws around Adam's forefinger and bite down sharply on the tip.

"Ouch!" Adam yelped and jerked his hand back.

Samantha laughed, and rubbed her hand against the kitten's tummy. "Shame on you, baby," she scolded the cat, "picking on Adam that way. Why don't you find someone your own size to take on?"

Adam snorted. "Hmph! Size has nothing to do with it," he retorted, "when you've got teeth like razors! Why, I was just trying to play, and he went for blood!"

Samantha just laughed again. The kitten yawned, showing off a little pink tongue and minuscule teeth, before curling himself into a ball on Samantha's lap and drifting off to sleep.

Neither of the swing's occupants said anything for a long time. Through the window came the muffled sound of voices; from the barn drifted the occasional snort of a horse or low-pitched voice of a cow. In the distance, whippoorwills called and mockingbirds answered. Adam's foot scraped against the painted porch floor, and the chain squeaked softly as they swung. The scents of cut wheat, marigolds, and lilacs mingled, creating a heady perfume. The September sun shone brightly, sending golden shafts of light through the porch railings, creating a series of shadows across the porch floor and across Samantha's lap where a little yellow and white kitten continued to nap.

Adam sighed contentedly, and Samantha sneaked a peek at him. He was relaxed, his eyes half-closed and his lips tipped into that familiar hint of a smile. Samantha felt a pang of remorse for misleading him into believing she was someone she was not. She wondered how quickly his stance would change if she was to open her mouth and confess that her name was really Samantha O'Brien and not Frances Welch, as he believed. She wondered, too, what was worse. Living a lie wasn't easy—it pricked her conscience sorely, especially now that she was growing to love this wonderful family. But would it be better to spill the truth and be sent back to Pa because of it? Having gotten a taste of happiness, she was more than reluctant to lose it. Besides, she reasoned with herself, it wouldn't be long and harvest would be finished. Jake would be back home days, and Samantha's help wouldn't be needed any longer. She'd be free to move on. She could head down the road, and the Klaassens would never know they'd been deceived.

For some reason, that thought wasn't as much of a comfort as it should have been. Moving on, she realized, wouldn't be any easier than keeping her secret had been.

Adam suddenly yawned widely, and raised his arms to stretch, his hands balled into fists. He swiveled his gaze to grin at Samantha. "Think maybe I'll go in and help myself to another piece of rhubarb pie. Want to come?" he invited.

But Samantha shook her head, pointing to the kitten still sleeping peacefully in her lap. "No, I think I'll just stay put for awhile, at least 'til this little one wakes up."

"Okay," Adam agreed. He stood up, sending the swing sideways. The kitten jerked awake, blinking its little eyes and flexing its paws. Adam gestured. "I guess I disturbed your guest," he said. "Since he's awake, why don't we walk him back to the barn to his mama, and you can come have a piece of pie after all."

Samantha scooped the little kitty against her chest as she stood. "All right," she agreed. "But instead of rhubarb, can I have apple pie? I've never cared much for rhubarb."

Adam put his hands on his hips and shook his head. "Don't care for rhubarb?" he exclaimed in mock dismay. "Why, how did you manage to get this far through life without developing a taste for rhubarb?"

Samantha shot back over her shoulder as she stepped off the porch, "I'd rather eat straw than eat rhubarb."

Adam laughed as he caught up with her. "Well, then, you're in luck," he announced, "because right this way is a very large supply of straw and you can just eat to your heart's content!"

She grinned.

He grinned.

Samantha thought, *I wish harvest could last forever, so I could stay on working here forever....*

And he thought, *She has the prettiest smile, when she chooses to use it. And those eyes.... I could look into those blue eyes every day. It's a shame when harvest ends, she'll leave this place. Unless....*

The wheels in his head were already turning.

After supper, Liz, Jake and Samantha loaded Andy and A.J. into baskets softened with quilts and climbed into Jake's buckboard to head back home. As the wagon rattled along, Liz sent her husband an inquisitive look. "What were you and Frank discussing so seriously in the corner of the kitchen?" she asked.

Samantha looked up from tucking A.J.'s blanket a little more securely around his chin as Jake answered. The concern in his voice made her concerned, too.

"We were talking about Thomas Enns, Henry's oldest boy. He ran off and joined the army." Liz reached to curl an arm around Jake's forearm and lean against him. "I guess Henry's pretty well beside himself. Thomas is eighteen, though, and doesn't need permission to go."

Samantha hadn't thought much about the war in Europe. She'd picked up bits and pieces of conversations here and there—she knew that wheat prices were higher than they'd ever been, and that farmers were exempt from the draft since they were needed to produce the wheat. But hearing of someone she knew—although only slightly—going off to fight gave her a tight feeling in her chest. She patted A.J.'s tummy absently as she listened to Jake and Liz.

"Has Henry spoken with Reverend Goertzen?" Liz wondered. "Maybe he could help."

"In what way?" Jake demanded in a tone Samantha had never heard him use before. "I don't see how talking to the minister would help anything. The boy is gone, he's going to be holding a gun—and somebody will be shooting back! Henry's worried sick, and no amount of talking will eliminate that worry."

Liz squeezed Jake's arm comfortingly as Jake went on, more calmly this time. "I can't imagine having a child fighting somewhere. Before we had the twins, I never gave much thought to such things. Being a father myself makes me understand Henry's anguish. I never want to feel the pain of seeing one of my boys march off to war."

There wasn't much Liz could say to that. Instead, she laid her forehead against his shoulder. He placed his free hand on her knee and squeezed. She laid her hand over it, interlacing her fingers with his. Watching them, Samantha felt a lump in her throat. She wondered how it must feel to love and be loved by someone. Even though they were sharing feelings of pain, Samantha thought it was beautiful to behold, and she wondered if she would ever have that beauty for herself.

Her thoughts skittered back to the minutes she and Adam and shared, side by side on the porch swing in the quiet afternoon. Other images flashed through her mind—Adam ardently arguing with his uncle on her behalf; Adam holding tiny A.J., a soft expression on his face; Adam teasingly offering a strawberry, then laughing with his head thrown back; Adam comforting Sarah when she stubbed a toe; Adam redirecting the conversation of the men trying to rile his brother....

She bit her lower lip and wished fervently her situation could be different—that she belonged here, that she wasn't living a lie, that she was worthy of the love of someone as special as Adam. *I might as well be wishing I was the Queen of England!* she scolded herself. Samantha came from a world where wishes never came true.

Chapter Thirteen

*S*ummer melted away beneath an azure sky, replaced by a mellow Fall that pulled at Samantha's heartstrings with its earthen colors of mahogany red, pumpkin orange, and golden yellow. Many times she stood on the narrow stoop at Jake and Liz's front door and almost drank in the pleasant changes in nature. She'd never seen so many colors before. Fall arrived in the city, too, but it was somehow different in the country, with all the open spaces and towering trees and wild breezes that carried wondrous scents Samantha couldn't even recognize.

Although harvest on the Stoesz farm had ended a week ago, Samantha had stayed on. Liz insisted she simply couldn't do without her, it was so exhausting just keeping up with the needs of the twins. Could she help until Jake had finished harvest at all of the area farms and was home again? Samantha had agreed. She really didn't need much of an excuse to stick around. She had been in Mountain Lake for over a month now, with no sign of Pa. It gave her a security she hadn't known before, and made her much less than anxious to move on. Besides, she reasoned with herself, the longer she stayed, the more money she could put aside for her traveling later on.

One sunny Saturday afternoon in late September, the Klaassen wagon rumbled into the yard, spilling out half of the family. Laura was helped down from the high seat by Adam, but Teddy, Sarah, Becky, and Josie leaped out the back and nearly knocked the door down in their exuberance. Sarah was waving a brown paper-wrapped package, and all were clamoring so loudly that no one person could be understood.

When Laura and Adam stepped through the door, they both burst out laughing at the sight. Liz and Samantha stood, each holding a squalling baby, their faces a study of bewilderment as Josie and the younger children surrounded them, gesturing and talking excitedly.

Adam looked at Laura and raised his eyebrows in a silent question: *Should I?* Laura gave her assent with a quick nod, and Adam placed two fingers in his mouth and blew. The piercing whistle stopped the commotion instantly, even stilling the babies for one startled second. All gawked at him, open-mouthed.

"That's better!" he exclaimed, and strode across the room to take little A.J. from Samantha's arms before he could tune up again. "Mercy, it sounded like a gaggle of hungry geese in here! No wonder you were bawling." And he snuggled his tiny nephew, rocking him gently back and forth.

Liz allowed Laura to take Andy, then placed her hands on her hips and demanded of her younger siblings, "What on earth is all the racket about?"

"This! This!" Sarah exclaimed, waving the package around. Teddy put in, "It's a present—for Frances."

Samantha's eyes widened and fastened on the lumpy package. A hand came to rest on her chest, and she asked in an astonished voice, "For *me*?"

"Yes!" Becky answered, then demanded of her younger sister, "Hand it over, Sarah!"

With enthusiasm, Sarah did so, nearly thrusting the package clear through Samantha's stomach. Samantha took it gingerly, unsure of how to behave. She couldn't remember the last time she'd been given a present.

"But—but—" she stammered, clearly confused, "it's not my birthday, or Christmas, or anything. W-w-what's it for?"

Josie put an arm around her friend. "It's a thank you present."

Samantha shook her head as if to clear it. "Thank you? For what?" She let her gaze travel over the circle of smiling faces, finally settling on Laura's. "Thank you for what?" she repeated.

Laura answered gently, "It's a thank you for all the help you've given Liz. She tells us you've worked as much as two people these past weeks, and we're so grateful you were here for her and the twins. The gift is just a little extra something to show our gratitude."

Samantha felt a stinging at the back of her nose. She looked down at the crumpled brown paper, squeezing it hard with both hands. It was soft, with a funny bump in the middle. A thank you present to show their appreciation. She swallowed hard. They just didn't understand! Instead of them thanking her, *she* should be thanking *them*! They'd given her a place in their family, made her feel wanted and needed, had shown her more kindness than she'd ever known in her entire lifetime.... And now they were *thanking* her?

Samantha was overwhelmed by emotions she couldn't put into words. Instead she murmured stupidly, "Well, gee…"

Sarah jumped up and down, demanding, "Open it, Frances!"

"Yes, do," Josie encouraged.

Adam told his sisters softly, "Give Frances a minute to think, girls. I think we've caught her a bit off guard here."

Samantha lifted her eyes to his, and the gentle smile in his eyes above A.J.'s downy head seemed to say, *It's okay. Just relax and enjoy this.*

"Well—well," she said straight at Adam, her heart pounding in a funny way high in her chest, "let me sit down first."

Teddy quickly pulled out a straight-back chair from the table and Samantha seated herself. The youngest two Klaassens crowded close, getting their noses in the way. Samantha tugged the string off and laid it carefully on the table. She pulled back the brown paper slowly, savoring the anticipation. As she peeled the paper back, she got a brief glimpse of roses and vines on a pale yellow background. She held her breath. Opening the flaps completely, she found two neatly folded lengths of fabric—the rose-print calico on top, and another piece of sky blue gingham on the bottom. Sandwiched between them were two wooden spools of thread and a small wooden tube of sewing needles.

"Oh, my," Samantha breathed out slowly, running her hand across the roses, a finger tracing the pattern the vines made as they weaved between the blooms. "It's beautiful!"

Laura said, "I hope you don't mind that we picked out the fabric for you. We thought about taking you in and letting you choose your own, but that would have spoiled the surprise. If you don't care for either of them, we can certainly find something else."

"Oh, no! No!" Samantha exclaimed, her eyes still glued to the fabrics in her lap. "These are just perfect. But—but—" At last she looked up. "I've been paid for my work here. I don't understand why you got me this."

Becky shrugged, grinning so widely dimples appeared in her apple cheeks. "It's a bonus!" she laughed. "Besides, we figured you were tired of wearing Liz's old hand-me-overs. Now you'll have a Sunday dress, and a work dress all of your own."

Samantha pushed both palms onto the soft cotton fabrics, reveling in the crisp newness. Two dresses! One for Sunday and one for everyday! She couldn't wait to start cutting out pieces and threading the needle and turning these wonderful fabrics into clothes! Oh, she wanted this more than she'd ever wanted anything. But—

She looked up into the happy faces surrounding her, her own brow furrowed into a worried scowl. "This is—this is so wonderful. But I just don't know…." She bit her lower lip in confusion.

Laura reached out and put a hand on Samantha's shoulder. "What's troubling you, dear?"

Samantha swallowed. How could she tell them that they'd already given her much more than she ever expected to receive in life? Never having been given things, Samantha wasn't good at receiving. Unsure how to say what she was feeling, she simply said softly, "I don't want to take more'n I deserve."

Laura's only response to that was, "There's about as much chance of that happening as Sarah here suddenly sprouting a mustache." Humor was just what Samantha needed in that emotionally charged moment.

Samantha managed a nod, then raised her face to directly meet Laura's eyes. With all the sincerity she could muster, she said simply, "Thank you very much."

Laura's eyes crinkled up in a smile, and she gave Samantha a quick squeeze. And Samantha didn't pull away. She didn't return the embrace, but everyone in the room saw her lean slightly against Laura with eyes closed, seemingly savoring the brief contact. It made Adam's heart thump in a hard beat, and put a smile on the faces of all present.

"Now," Liz scolded, breaking the serious moment, "if you all will clear out of here, maybe Frances and I can restore order! Then I will gladly dish up gingerbread and whipped cream to anyone who would like some."

Immediately the kitchen cleared. The three youngest siblings dashed outside for a quick game of tag, Laura took both babies to their bedroom for naps, and Adam headed to the barn to say hello to Jake. Before he left, though, he noticed Samantha scoop up the folds of fabric and lift them to her nose briefly. He was touched more than he could understand by the simple gesture. As he watched her press the gift close to her heart to carry it upstairs, his own heart lifted and swelled, and he puzzled over his reaction. It made him happy, seeing her happy, he told himself as he left the room. That was all.

Samantha's dresses turned out beautifully. Every spare minute of the past two weeks had been spent holed up in her under-the-eaves bedroom, stitching feverishly. She had torn apart one of Liz's old dresses to use as a make-shift pattern, modifying some pieces to fit her slimmer frame. Now she stood proudly in front of the oval mirror above her washstand, wearing her favorite—the morning sunshine yellow one covered with delicate pink roses and trailing deep green vines.

She turned this way and that, trying to get a glimpse of the whole thing. She blew out an exasperated breath. The mirror was just too small! She reached out to shift its position, angling it sharply downward, then looked again.

A knock at the door interrupted her, and she spun to see Josie sticking her nose in.

"Oh, Frances!" Josie sighed, stepping into the room uninvited. "You did such a good job!"

Samantha beamed. "I just love it," she admitted. "Does it look okay? I can't see!"

Josie fingered the tiny clerical collar which Samantha had embellished with a bit of white lace she had purchased with her own earned money. "Yes, it fits beautifully!" Josie manipulated Samantha like a large doll, turning her in circles as she examined the perfect button holes, the even gathers in the skirt, and the puff at the shoulder of the sleeves. "You look like an angel, Frances!"

Samantha felt herself blush. She wasn't used to such flattery! But she had to admit, it felt good.

"Come downstairs," Josie tugged at her wrist. "*Tante* Hulda is down with Mother and Liz, putting her stamp of approval on the twins. Come show off your creation."

Samantha held back, suddenly self-conscious. "I don't wanna show off," she argued weakly.

But Josie just laughed at her. "Oh, don't be silly! Mother will adore this dress, and even *Tante* Hulda will be impressed."

So Samantha allowed herself to be led to the kitchen, where she was the recipient of many more compliments.

"That's a lovely dress, Frances," the girls' aunt, Hulda, said in her thick, husky voice. "The colors make you look healthy." Aside, to Laura, she whispered loudly, "That girl is too thin!" Then she waved a pudgy hand at Samantha and demanded, "Come closer, child. Let me check your stitching."

Reluctantly Samantha obeyed the older, somewhat intimidating woman, allowing her to scrutinize her handiwork. Hulda muttered "Mm-hm," and "Ah," under her breath as she did so. At last she settled back in the rocking chair, crossed her heavy arms across her ample bust and peered up at Samantha from over the round lenses of her spectacles which sat precariously at the end of her pugged nose.

"Well, Miss Frances, you've done a commendable job," was the verdict. "You've obviously sewn before."

Samantha nodded hesitantly, backing up a bit now that the inspection was over.

"Yes, ma'am. I was taught to sew a long time ago, by my great-grandmother."

"She taught you well," Hulda approved. "I don't suppose you would be interested in sewing for profit?"

Confused, Samantha turned to Laura for support.

Laura smilingly explained, "Would you be interested in sewing for other people, who would pay you?"

"Pay me to sew?" Samantha thought that ludicrous. Why, sewing was so easy!

Hulda put in, "Many of the women in town do not enjoy sewing, or do not feel adequate in their ability."

Laura added, "They either buy custom-made"—Hulda interrupted with a snort and a wave of her dimpled hand in a gesture of derision—"or hire someone to sew for them."

Samantha still looked incredulous. "I sew for myself, but I don't know if I'm good enough to sew for others," she said.

Hulda stated emphatically, "No doubt you are good enough. It's a matter of whether you want to or not. I could put a sign up at our store by the dress goods, offering your services. It would help to hang a sample garment—" Samantha placed her hands protectively against the skirt of her dress. Hulda, noticing, softened in understanding. "But I suppose we could do without. Just wear that dress to church on Sunday, and we shall have business! Mark my words!"

Samantha looked from Josie to Laura to Hulda. All waited expectantly for her response. Finally she sighed.

"I would love to have the chance to make a little more money, but I'm not sure that Mr. Klaassen would approve of me working out of your store. After all—" and she ducked her head in embarrassment—"I did try to steal from there...."

"Nonsense," was Hulda's proclamation. "Water under the bridge! Hiram wouldn't hold a grudge, especially when the venture will prove profitable to him as well." Her eyes sparkled with mischief. "We do have the fabrics available for sale, and, even after paying you to sew, the ladies will spend less than they would on a ready-made dress. Anyone can see the advantages there. No, Hiram will not argue. He will bank on it!"

Samantha thought about having access to the many fabrics and laces at the store, cutting and stitching until a finished dress emerged where once only assorted shapes of material lay. She thought of earning extra money that would keep her far away from her pa. She thought of being able to stay in Mountain Lake, close to the Klaassens. Close to Adam....

She smiled at Hulda and said, "If you think it will be okay, I'll try it."

"Wonderful!" Josie exclaimed, and hugged Samantha impulsively.

"Now sit down here by me," Hulda ordered, "and have some gingerbread with us to celebrate our new business venture."

Still basking in the warmth of their confidence in her, Samantha eagerly joined the others for cake and chatter. As she daintily smoothed the skirt of her fine new dress across her knees, she wondered with a spark of unfamiliar vanity, *What will Adam think when he sees me in this?*

Chapter Fourteen

Samantha turned the heads of many a young man the following Sunday morning, Adam's included. He watched with an improper rush of jealousy as Lucas Stoesz hot-footed it across the church yard to help Samantha out of Jake's buggy. The trim-fitting dress and perky flowered bonnet added a maturity to her appearance that made Adam feel as if someone had socked him hard in the midsection. The feeling was much less than brotherly, he had to admit, and he carefully guarded his expression as he followed his family into the church and settled himself on his familiar bench.

Lucas deposited Samantha next to Liz, leaning down to whisper something in her ear before straightening. Adam watched with interest as Samantha, pink-cheeked, lifted her bashful gaze to Lucas's brazen one and nodded slightly. A huge grin split Lucas's face, and he unabashedly winked at Samantha before moving down the short aisle to sit with his father.

That Lucas is just a little too sure of himself, Adam decided, his brows pinched together in displeasure. He reasoned with himself that his young friend didn't have a father or other family member around to look out for her, and she certainly would be out of her league with Lucas! It was his duty—as her benefactor, so to speak—to provide protection when needed. He disliked the thought that protection from his brother-in-law's sibling would be necessary, but he knew Lucas well enough to be concerned. Lucas had always been just a bit more reckless than was wise.

Reverend Goertzen stepped up to the pulpit, and Adam forced his attention to the front of the church. He wondered about the somber expression on the minister's face.

"Brothers and sisters," Reverend Goertzen began, his voice low and solemn, "I must begin our service this morning with some distressing news. I have just come from the Enns farm. Henry and Marta received a telegram yesterday, informing them that their son, Thomas, was killed in a training accident."

Gasps were heard across the small congregation, and a woman in the back began sobbing quietly.

Reverend Goertzen continued, "This morning, I would like our prayers focused on the Enns family. They are understandably distressed, and much in need of comfort. Shall we pray?"

The remainder of the service was a blur to Samantha. The morning had started out with such promise! Her new dress had gotten just the reaction she and Hulda Klaassen had hoped for; she had noticed Adam watching her with an expression of interest; and Lucas Stoezs, who was admittedly handsome, had out and out flirted with her and asked to walk her home after the service. She had sat down on this bench feeling happy and accepted, but the news of Thomas had tarnished the brightness of the morning.

She didn't know Thomas well—she'd only seen him in the churchyard with the other young men—but that didn't really matter. He'd been young and healthy and full of life, and now he was gone. It wasn't fair!

After the service, which was brief, Si and Laura sent the children home in their wagon and rode with several other couples to the Enns farm to spend the afternoon with Henry and Marta. Jake and Liz decided to follow Liz's siblings to their home rather than heading to their own farm to be alone. At this time of sorrow, they needed one another.

It was a quiet bunch that sat around the table in Laura's neat kitchen, mostly pushing food around on green enamel plates instead of eating. Sarah and Teddy couldn't really understand the impact of what had happened, but they absorbed the tense currents and reflected the somber moods of the older people around them. When lunch was finished, Liz sent the two youngsters out to the barn to entertain the kittens, and she supervised the little clean up that was needed. The afternoon stretched before them endlessly.

Adam had been in the parlor with Frank, Arn, and Jake, but restlessness drove him to the yard. He needed to think. He needed to do something. He decided to take a walk to clear his head. But he really didn't want to be alone. Spotting Samantha and Josie on the porch swing, he crossed the yard with long strides and paused at the foot of the porch steps.

"I'm going for a walk. Want to come along?" he asked the girls.

Josie shook her head. "I'll stay around in case Liz needs help with the twins. Why don't you go ahead, Frances? You've been pulling extra duty lately. A walk would do you good."

Samantha looked from Josie to Adam, indecision marring her face.

Adam clinched it. "I'd like the company," he said simply.

Without a word she stood and found herself walking side by side with Adam.

"The north pasture is cut," Adam said, looking down at the top of Samantha's head, noting the red glints in her hair from the touch of the sun. "It will be easier to walk there. Shall we go that way?"

Samantha shrugged. "That's fine."

So they headed in that direction. Neither said much. Instead, they absorbed the early Fall sunshine which was kept from being too warm by the slight breezes that whirled leaves across their path and gently clacked the tips of empty branches together. Adam seemed to be lost in thought, and Samantha was certain he was thinking of his friend. Unsure of the right words, she chose not to speak at all. Adam didn't seem to mind.

Occasionally her shoulder would brush against his upper arm, sending prickles of awareness down her arm. Once she nearly stumbled, her shoe catching in her wind-tossed skirts, and Adam reached out a steadying hand to her. But as soon as she was right again, he released her arm. She found herself wondering what he would do if she suddenly put her hand in his. *Probably push it away and ask what in tarnation was wrong with me!* she decided, annoyed with herself for thinking such a thing. Adam was in turmoil—the last thing he needed was some idiotic female pushing herself on him. Determinedly, she turned her attention away from her companion and focused on her surroundings.

Her eyes settled on something strange in the distance. It looked like the front of a shack, but there wasn't any back. It seemed to be swallowed by a hill. Curiosity got the best of her, and she broke the silence to point and ask, "Adam, what is that?"

Adam startled and came to a stop. "What?" he asked.

"That, over there," she said, stabbing her finger in the direction of the funny little house. "That building with dirt around it."

Adam shaded his eyes with a hand for a moment, looking, then dropped his hand and grinned at her. "That's Grandpa Klaassen's dugout," he said.

"Dugout?" she asked, puzzled.

Adam nodded, and started walking towards it. "It's the first house built on our land. When Grandpa and Grandma settled here, he didn't have time to build a proper house before winter hit, so he just dug into the side of a hill, making a house in the hole. I haven't been out there for years. Let's go take a peek."

Samantha had to trot to keep up with him. As they drew near, she could make out the log construction of the simple dwelling. He was right, she realized—it was a house dug right in the side of a hill! Samantha had never heard of such a thing.

Adam had to push hard on the door to open it. The inside of the dugout was dark and musty, smelling of earth and neglect. Samantha was less than enthused about stepping into the murky depths, but Adam seemed eager to explore, so she followed reluctantly. Adam waved his arms, breaking down cobwebs and scattering dust everywhere. Samantha sneezed.

Adam sent her a sympathetic look. "Not too clean, is it? Dark, too. Maybe I can open the shutters."

The oiled paper windows had long since rotted away, but sturdy wooden shutters still stood in the openings. Adam forced them outward, and a minimal amount of light entered, followed by the sweet fall breeze. He stood in the shaft of light from the window, looking. A scarred table still remained along one wall, and a pile of old clothing, mouse-eaten and filthy, lay discarded in a corner. Samantha kicked at it, sending up a puff of dust. She covered her nose and moved near the door where the air was fresher.

"Josie and Liz used to play house out here," Adam told her. "I came out here a lot, too, as a kid. I thought it was a neat hide-out. It doesn't look like anyone's been around for a long time, though."

Now that her eyes were adjusting, Samantha could make out the smooth dirt walls and the overhead beams of the ceiling. Shelves had been wedged into the back wall of the dugout, and a row of grimy glass jars still rested on one. It wasn't a large area, but had ample room for a bed, table, and a couple of chairs. To her delight, she even discovered a fireplace centering one wall. Examining it closely, she realized it had been made of mud and grass, formed into bricks. Samantha had to admire the ingenuity it took to design such a structure.

As she turned in a circle, surveying the entire area minutely, her eyes met Adam's. He stood in the slice of light, tiny particles of dust dancing around him like glittering bits of sunshine. His sandy hair had turned to burnished gold, and his brown eyes sparkled with some emotion she couldn't recognize. She froze for a moment as a feeling as real as the dirt floor beneath her feet coursed through her, catching her breath and causing her heart to miss a beat.

An image flashed through her mind, of herself tending a fire and Adam returning home to her, belonging to her in the way that Jake belonged to Liz or Si belonged to Laura. It lasted only a moment—a wonderful, heartfelt moment—and then it was gone, replaced by the realization that it was only a dream. A dream that couldn't—*couldn't*—come true.

She averted her gaze quickly, pretending to swish dust from her skirts, collecting her thoughts. To cover her unsettledness, she forced a casual tone and inquired, "Your grandparents lived here?" She took up moving slowly around the room, pretending to examine every nook and cranny.

"Yeah," Adam replied, grinning. "Grandma called it her badger's den. She teased that when she'd married Grandpa, he had been worried about his penniless state, but she had assured him she could be happy living in a hole in the ground, as long as he was in it with her. So Grandpa put her word to the test!"

Samantha laughed appreciatively, her momentary lapse camouflaged. "Your grandma must be fun."

Adam nodded, his eyes crinkling up in a way Samantha found appealing. "Yes, both of my grandparents are wonderful. I miss them, now that they're gone."

"Are they—?" Samantha wasn't sure how to ask. Adam understood.

"Both alive and well," he told her, "and living in Minneapolis. My oldest brother, Daniel, lives near them in the city, and keeps an eye on them. They always visit at Christmas time. Maybe you'll meet them then."

Samantha's heart thumped at the implication. "So did your parents live here, too?"

"Oh, no," Adam answered. "Grandpa built the house we live in before Pa or Uncle Hiram were born. Then, when Grandpa had a stroke and couldn't farm anymore, he split the land between Pa and Uncle Hiram and took Grandma to the city. Uncle Hiram wasn't interested in farming, so he sold Pa his half of the farm and opened up his mercantile."

Samantha found this all interesting. The family had been on the land for quite a long time! It held a fascination for her.

"Will you stay on the farm like your pa has done?" she asked Adam now.

Adam didn't need to think about that. "Sure, I will," he responded with certainty. "Pa has already told me this north pasture and the east field will be mine, and the other side will go to Frank. There's enough land to support more than one family here, and I have no desire for city life. Daniel and Arn are welcome to that."

Samantha nodded, pleased by his response. In her mind, farming took strength of body and spirit—being at one with the land. Adam possessed the necessary traits to be a farmer. She admired the fact that he knew what he wanted and wasn't afraid to work for it. She felt a twinge of envy for the legacy he'd been given. Not only the land, but the knowledge and commitment of the people who'd gone before him. He'd been given a good, solid base to build on, both physically and spiritually.

She thought of her own family—Pa with his drunkenness, and David who had left and never returned. She thought of her crazy, unstable home life. Such a contrast between Adam's world and her own! She wondered if he knew how lucky he was.

Adam knew well how lucky he was. Standing in the dugout brought back many memories of childhood and listening to his grandparents' stories. He came from a God-fearing family, and he was proud to be a part of it. Watching Samantha move around the small space, poking her nose into corners and swiping at the dust motes in the air, he had to wonder what her background was—who her people were, where she had come from. Time had passed, but none of them were any more enlightened than they had been the first day she arrived and refused to give her name.

Curiosity got the best of him. He might not get an answer, but he had to ask.

"Frances, do you have grandparents?"

The question caught her off guard. He could tell by the way she stiffened and sucked in her lower lip. There was a long silence during which she stared hard at the shelves on the wall. Then slowly she turned, glanced at him briefly, and answered, eyes on the dirt floor, "No, not anymore."

Adam asked quietly, "Parents, then?"

Samantha's expression closed as completely as the cover of a book. Her eyes skittered to the doorway, and, instead of answering his question, she said stiffly, "I think I'll wait for you outside."

He felt guilty and small for making her uncomfortable when she had been enjoying herself. To end her uneasiness, he crossed back to the windows and pulled the shutters closed. "We'd better be heading back to the house now," he said, "or they'll send a search party out after us. Ready?"

Samantha nodded, feeling bad about her secretiveness. She wished she could be as open with him as he had been with her. But how could she? It was better for everyone if she continued to be Frances Welch, homeless and alone. With a sinking heart, she realized that the day would come when answers would be expected. Adam's question today was proof of that.

As she watched Adam secure the shutters of the little dugout, she came to a sad realization: she did not belong here. She was not his kind, and she never could be. Her foolish heart was planting ideas in her head that could never come true. It was time to move on—now, before her heart was so firmly planted that it could not be uprooted.

She would talk to Liz. Soon.

Chapter Fifteen

$\mathcal{B}$y the time Adam and Samantha had returned to the house, Laura and Si were already home, dropped off by a neighbor. Soon afterward, Liz and Jake bundled up the twins and headed back to their own home, Samantha in tow. Samantha had decided the sooner she broke the news of her leaving, the easier it would be. Supper was over and little Andy and A.J. were tucked safely into their cradles. Jake had gone out to see to the evening chores. Liz was settled in the kitchen rocker, mending a pair of Jake's socks.

Now, Samantha told herself.

Samantha put the last of the dishes away on their shelf, then pulled out a chair from the table and sat down, fingering the table edge nervously. Liz glanced up at her and sent a tired smile.

"It's been a long day, hasn't it?" Liz asked.

Samantha nodded. "Yep, and not an easy one for you folks. I sure am sorry about Thomas Enns."

Liz sighed. "It's going to be terribly hard for Henry and Marta. Thomas was their oldest, and his going away was awful enough without having to face the fact that he's never coming home again."

Samantha nodded in silence. *Never coming home again....* She could understand that feeling all too well! A lump rose in her throat, making it difficult to talk. But she swallowed resolutely and brought up the subject she knew she had to face. "Liz, I think it's time I be on my way."

Liz's head came up sharply, her darning forgotten. "Oh, Frances, no! Why, what on earth would I do without you?"

Samantha smiled at that. It was nice to be needed. "You'd do just fine and you know it," she responded gently, determined not to be swayed. "The twins are sleeping through the night now, and there's just the Voth's wheat to be finished harvesting and Jake will be here days again. I appreciate the job I've had here and all, but I just think it's time for me to go."

Liz stared, eyes wide and distressed. It was hard for Samantha to meet her gaze. Abruptly Liz asked, "Have I done something to offend you, Frances?"

"No, nothing like that," Samantha rushed to assure her, feeling guiltier by the minute. "But when I took this job, it was for harvest. Well, now harvest is over."

Liz argued, "But what about the deal you made with *Tante* Hulda? I thought she'd already gotten requests from two ladies for dresses. Will you fill those orders?"

In all honesty, Samantha had forgotten. She wasn't sure how she would handle that situation. So she responded with a shrug. "I don't know. I'll have to talk to Mrs. Klaassen about that yet. I just wanted to let you know as soon as I made up my mind."

Liz rocked herself, looking at Samantha speculatively. She had been happy here, Liz knew, so something had happened. Something that had scared her. She thought back over the afternoon, remembering seeing her walk off towards the north pasture with Adam. Maybe Adam could shed some light on the subject. She fully intended to talk to him, but she needed to keep the girl here until then.

"When were you wanting to leave?" Liz asked now.

Samantha dropped her gaze to the table top. "Now. Before the cold weather hits. I need to be settled somewhere before the snow flies."

"Where will you go?" Liz wanted to know.

Samantha bit her lower lip, a sure sign of nervousness. "I'm not sure yet. The city, probably. Maybe Minneapolis. I'm sure I can get work there." *And Adam's grandparents and brother live there, so maybe I'd run into him someday....*

Liz watched the expression of wistfulness cross her young friend's face. No more questions tonight, she decided. But tomorrow, she would definitely talk to Adam!

Adam's response to Liz's news was an emphatic, "But she *can't* go!"

Liz was surprised by Adam's vehemence. His strong reaction proved to Liz that his feelings for the girl went deeper than friendship. She phrased her next words carefully. "I don't want her to leave, either, Adam, for strictly selfish reasons—she's such a help! But what are your reasons for keeping her here?"

Adam swallowed. How could he answer that? What *were* his feelings for Frances Welch? Sympathy for her aloneness? Brotherly caring? Simple Christian concern for a fellow human being? Or did it go beyond any of those? Was it possible that he actually loved the girl? That thought brought him up short. Had he ever really defined his feelings for Frances?

"Liz, I...." Adam stared helplessly at his sister. Liz's eyes were filled with compassion, as if she already knew the answer and understood the conflict involved. Adam, as a Christian man, would not become seriously involved with a non-Christian no matter how much his heart might wish him to. With a sad smile, Liz opened her arms to her little brother, and he moved against her gratefully. After a long hug, he pulled back and took Liz's face in his hands.

"Sis, I don't want her to go. If she has no family, she needs us more than you have needed her. I can't let her know how I feel—and we can't pressure her. She'll run like a scared rabbit." Adam dropped his hands and turned away, running a hand through his hair distractedly. "I think I know why she wants to go. She's scared—*I* scared her."

Liz reached out a hand and placed it on Adam's shoulder, asking, "How?"

Adam shook his head, angry with himself at the realization. "Yesterday Frances and I went walking, and ended up at the dugout. We got to talking about Grandpa and Grandma, and I asked her about her own grandparents."

Liz could almost guess the girl's reaction, remembering her response to questions about her background in the past. "She refused to answer?"

"Oh, she answered. I think she said, 'Not anymore,' but then she closed her mouth and wouldn't even look at me." Adam slammed his hands down on the tabletop. "After all my intentions to go easy with her, to let her come to me! I wanted her to trust me, and then I had to go and open my big mouth!"

Liz rushed to reassure her brother. "Adam, one question could hardly be considered applying pressure. And it seems to me the conversation moved naturally in that direction. We have a right to ask questions occasionally. If that makes her lack faith in you, then I think the problem lies with her, not you."

Adam appreciated his sister's attempt to absolve him of blame, but he couldn't accept it. "No, I frightened her, and I need to set it right. I'll talk to her."

"Do you think you should?" Liz asked worriedly. "Maybe it would be best just to—"

"To let her go?" Adam demanded, interrupting. Then he softened. "No, Liz, right or wrong, I can't just let her go."

And Liz's heart sank. She understood.

Adam, determined to speak with Samantha that evening, hitched up the team after the supper hour was completed and the evening chores attended to. The ride to Liz and Jake's was a chilly one; October had arrived and with it a hint of winter in the air. He pulled the collar of his heavy jacket tighter around his jaw and wished he'd grabbed his gloves. By the time he arrived on Jake's property, the moon was high and stars were peppering the sky.

Liz answered Adam's brief knock, gesturing him in with a wave of her hand. Jake looked up from the table where he was working some figures on a lined pad of paper.

"Hey, Adam! What brings you here at this hour?" Jake greeted, grinning broadly. "I hope it's a game of checkers."

Adam smiled but shook his head. "Not tonight, Jake. I came to see Frances."

Jake's eyebrows shot up. His gaze went to Liz, but she refused to meet it. *So that's how it is,* Jake thought.

"Well, I think she's in her room," Jake said, looking back at Adam. "I'll give her a holler." And he moved to the bottom of the staircase, calling, "Frances? Company!"

Adam stayed beside the door, watching as Samantha descended. When she saw who was there, her steps slowed somewhat and a look of pleased surprise crossed her face. Then she carefully wiped her face clean of all expression and came all the way down.

"Hi, Frances," Adam said quietly.

"Adam," she returned. She stayed a good five feet away from him, twisting a strand of hair that fell across her shoulder. She was wearing her blue gingham dress and looked very young and vulnerable. Her wary blue eyes avoided meeting his.

Adam cleared his throat, painfully aware of his audience. "I was wondering if you'd like to take a little walk to the corral. The night sky's real pretty."

Samantha looked at Liz, puzzled. Liz just shrugged and pointed toward the hooks on the wall near the door. "If you go out," she advised, "take a shawl. It's chilly tonight."

Adam lifted down a shawl and draped it across Samantha's shoulders, taking care not to touch her as he did so. He opened the door, and with a final solemn wink at Liz, followed Samantha outside. They walked silently across the yard, the dry grass crunching beneath her feet. The air was crisp, the sky was bright. It was a beautiful fall night, but both of them were too tense to fully appreciate it.

They stopped by the corral fence. Samantha clutched the shawl tightly with two fists and rested her elbows on the top rail. Adam turned to lean against the fence backwards, one foot propped up on a low rail. Both examined the sky for a few moments.

Adam broke the silence. "Liz tells me you're leaving," he said in a conversational tone.

Samantha shot him a sharp look. "Yes," was all she said.

Her single-word answer rankled. It reminded him of the days when she had first arrived, tight-lipped and sullen. He thought she had progressed beyond that, and he expected more from her now. But if she wanted to be difficult, two could play that game.

"Why?" he demanded gently.

She turned her gaze back to the stars. Her voice was taut as she replied, "I really don't understand why it concerns you, but if you must know, I feel it's time. Liz doesn't need me like she did at first, and I need to be looking for a job."

Adam chose to ignore her assumption that it didn't concern him. Instead, he argued the next point. "You have a job here in Mountain Lake—sewing for the mercantile customers."

Why did he have to make this so hard? Samantha sighed impatiently. "I need a job where I can support myself. I can't make enough sewing dresses now and then to pay for lodging and food and all of my other needs. So I need to move on."

"You *need* to," Adam pressed, "or you just *want* to? There's a difference, Frances." He paused, but she remained stubbornly silent, refusing to look at him. He went on, "I suspect your leaving has less to do with needing a job than simply running away."

Samantha dropped her arms and gaped at him, open-mouthed. "Running away?" she queried, her tone defensive. "Running away from what?"

Adam let his foot fall and he shifted to face her. They were nearly nose to nose, and their breath hung heavy in the cool night air as they faced off. "That's what I would like to know," he said quietly, his brown eyes locked on her pale blue ones. His voice was gentle as he asked, "What are you trying to escape, Frances?"

She set her jaw and glared at him, drawing on anger to keep from giving in to his kindness. "Just what are you saying, Adam?"

"I'm saying," he said evenly, meeting her glare with his own steady look, "that something happened to scare you into leaving. I'm saying that you're running like a frightened rabbit instead of sticking things out."

Brown eyes met blue, and sparks flew from both factions.

She dropped her gaze first. "I'm not running away," she lied firmly.

"Oh, no? Then why this talk of leaving all of a sudden, when I know you were perfectly happy here. You have a place to stay, a job, people who care about you. Why do you want to leave? What are you trying to get away from, Frances?" Adam's tone, though not brusque, was certainly firmer than he had used before with her.

It took all the self-control she possessed to keep from crying out, *You! I need to get away from you and the feelings I have for you! Because I don't deserve someone like you and it's tearing me apart inside!* Instead, she flared defiantly, "You are really making me mad, Adam. Just because you helped me out a little bit when I needed it doesn't give you the right to question me and tell me what to do!"

Her obstinant attitude was irritating, bringing a rush of temper. It was on the tip of Adam's tongue to shout that loving her gave him every right to question her and expect a straight answer. But he couldn't shout something like that in anger. And now wasn't the time to be admitting he loved her, anyway. Instead he told her with clenched teeth, "Well, *someone* needs to tell you what to do. You're not thinking straight, girl!"

His words cut her to the quick. How dare he insinuate that she wasn't smart enough to think for herself! Her blood boiled. *Nobody tells me I'm dumb anymore! Nobody!*

She pushed off from the railing with a vicious shove of her palms. Her tone was harsh, meant to convey that the subject was closed. "I've already overstayed my welcome here. I'm thankful for all your family's done for me, but the job is finished and it's time to move on."

Adam forcibly calmed himself, remembering her reaction to his questions about her family. His voice took on a pleading quality as he headed in another direction, trying to placate her. "Frances, the other day at the dugout—"

Samantha cut him off with a shrill laugh. "You think *you're* responsible for my leave-taking? You think you did something when you were alone with me that makes me want to leave?" She knew she was being intentionally cruel but knew no other way to make him see how wrong it was for her to remain in Mountain Lake. She forced her voice to assume a cynical edge as she finished, "You think too highly of yourself, Adam. This decision is my own, and no one else helped it along."

The look on Adam's face said clearly that he didn't believe her. There was a glint of anger in his eyes as well. Her chest felt tight, and all she wanted to do was get into her bed and pull the covers over her head. She must leave—she *must*—before Adam guessed what was on her heart. She pulled the shawl even tighter, crossing her arms, and she turned to go back to the house. "Good night, Adam," she said firmly.

"You sure are a stubborn little thing," Adam muttered under his breath. As she took a step toward the house, he reached out to catch her arm, intending to make her stay put and talk this thing out. The moment Adam's hand closed on her forearm, Samantha reacted instinctively. She jerked away, her arms flying upward to curl around her head as she dropped into a crouch, pressing her face against her knees.

Adam stared in shocked silence. For a moment he couldn't move, just stood motionless, his eyes riveted on her protective pose. Moonlight bathed her, making her fingers glow white as she clutched the back of her neck tightly. The incongruity of the moment—the beautiful, starlit night and her frozen, fear-filled reaction—struck him. Compassion filled him, his anger dissolving as quickly as it had flared, and he dropped to his knees beside her, reaching out a tentative hand to gently stroke her tense back—once, then again. He could feel her muscles quivering; he swallowed hard.

"Frances?" he said, his voice soft, almost begging. "Hey, Frances, look at me."

Instead of raising her face, she pulled tighter into her cocoon. He could imagine her folding into herself both physically and emotionally.

Adam stroked her back again, his fingers brushing as softly as a butterfly's touch. He moved gently. Persuasively. Heartbreakingly. His voice was whisper-soft, tender as his touch. "Frances, please listen to me. I wasn't going to hurt you. This is Adam, remember? I'd never hurt you, Frances." His voice caught in his throat. *Oh, Lord, what have I done to her?* He continued soothingly, "I was kind of mad, but I wouldn't hurt you. You believe me, don't you, Frances?"

Slowly his words registered in Samantha's terrified mind. It was Adam, not Pa. Adam...*Adam.* Ever so slowly she brought down her arms, and she peered at him sideways through a veil of hair. He was crouched so close she could see the green flecks in his eyes. Those eyes were looking at her now with such concern and regret that it hurt her to meet them. But Adam would never have guessed that from the hollow expression on her face.

"Here," Adam was saying, rising and reaching out a hand to draw her with him. "Come on now, Frances, stand up. It's okay now."

She jerked back from his offered hand, standing quickly and stiffly. She moved several feet away, still watching him with a stoic yet wary expression. Her hands grasped convulsively at the shawl. "I want to go in now," she said in an emotionless voice. As if it took great concentration, she began walking toward the house, her steps measured and stilted. Adam stood in place, watching her go.

As she entered the house, closing the door without a backwards glance, Adam felt a lump rising in his throat. Now he fully understood her reluctance to talk about her past, to share anything of her upbringing. Horror seized his gut as he pictured her, hunkering into that pose that said clearly what she expected to happen next. He forced his fingers through the hair above his ears, squeezing the strands with his fists, frustrated and angry with himself. He spun, dug his fingers into the wooden rail of the corral fence, and raised his face to the heavens. *What a horrible life she must have led. And I reminded her of it. I made her think I would hurt her, that I could treat her like that!*

In time he calmed. But he couldn't face his sister right now. He crossed with heavy steps to his wagon, leaped in, scooped up the reins and slapped them down hard on the horses' rumps, startling them into motion. "Gee-up!" he cried in a hoarse, tear-choked voice. Aloud, he whispered, "Good-bye, Frances." For he was sure that he had lost her now.

By the time Samantha reached her room, the numbing shock had worn off to be replaced with humiliation. Her reaction had been pure instinct, her body acting without a thought. When Adam had grabbed her arm, there hadn't been room for reasoning. Her brain had screamed for her to protect herself, and her body had obeyed.

What must he think of me now? she railed against herself, curled into a ball on the straw-filled mattress. *He knows now. He knows what my Pa's done to me. How can I ever face him again?… I can't wait now. Tomorrow I must go. Tomorrow I will go.*

Her throat ached with the need to cry, but her eyes remained dry. Samantha didn't cry. Her thoughts begged,

Oh, Gran, please help me now. Give me the courage to do what I must do. Give me the courage to leave this place and this man. Please, please!

She lay in her bed, dry-eyed and hurting, huddled tightly in the fetal position, wishing.... Wishing for what could never be.

Chapter Sixteen

*S*amantha sat on the hard wooden bench on the train depot porch, shivering. She wasn't sure if it was cold or fear that made her tremble, but she tugged her woven shawl more snugly around her shoulders, trying to hunch down inside of it as best she could.

She had purchased a ticket for Minneapolis and now held it tightly in her fist beneath the shawl, waiting for the train to come and carry her away from Mountain Lake and the family who meant as much to her as her Gran had meant.

She felt guilty about sneaking out the way she had. But she knew there would have been an argument—or at least a series of questions she couldn't answer—if she had waited to speak to Liz and Jake. So she had lain awake until she was certain they both were asleep before creeping down the stairs and beginning the long walk into town. In the moments when she had hovered over little A.J. and Andy's cradles to bestow a goodbye kiss, she had almost relented. The little boys smelled so sweet and tugged at her heartstrings in a peculiar way. It was *so* hard to leave....

But she had to leave. She knew that. Particularly after the disagreement she'd had with Adam. She closed her eyes, picturing his stricken face, his eyes sorrowful and sympathetic. She could only imagine what he'd been thinking as she'd cowered that way. Well, before anymore of her secrets were revealed and Adam realized how he'd been fooled, she'd go. She couldn't bear to look into Adam's eyes and see that expression of pain again.

She shifted on the bench. She was so tired. The long walk on no sleep was taking its toll. She checked the clock hanging above the ticket window. The train wasn't due for another hour or so. Maybe she'd close her eyes for just a bit. She twisted her body sideways and scootched down on the bench, resting her head against the lapped siding of the depot wall. A short nap, and then she'd be gone.

"Jake!" Liz was running across the hard ground, apron flying. Jake met her in the doorway of the barn. "Jake, she's gone! I just went to her room, and she's gone!"

"Now, settle down, honey," Jake soothed, his hands on his wife's shoulders. "I'm sure she can't have gone far. I'll find her, don't worry."

Liz shook her head, tears springing into her eyes. "No, Jake, she won't let you find her." She covered her face with both hands, fighting the urge to bawl. "She was so upset last night when she came in—I could see that. I should have gone up and talked to her. I should have—"

Jake gave her a little shake. "Liz, don't you start blaming yourself for Frances's disappearance. She made it clear she was ready to go, and she went. I'm willing to go look for her if that's what you want, but not if it's only because of some misguided sense of guilt."

Liz shook her head, swiping at her tears with shaking fingers. "No, it's not guilt, Jake. I just can't let things go at this. She was upset...." Liz took Jake's hands. "Jake, please, go get Adam. Adam will know what to do."

Jake gave his wife a quick kiss on the forehead before turning to release Samson from his stall. "Don't worry, honey," he said, pausing to give his wife a confident smile, "we'll find her, and everything will be just fine."

Liz watched Samson gallop down the lane, Jake hunched over the horse's broad back. She said a quick prayer that Jake was right.

Adam's brow was furrowed into a worried scowl as he straddled Bet and encouraged her to move a little faster. He should have guessed she'd pull a stunt like this after the way he'd left her. What else could she do but run? She was no doubt scared to death of him now! He should never have grabbed her like that. He should never have lost his temper. It wasn't like him, to get angry like that, but when faced with losing her....

He had to find her. He had to! He needed to set things right. He needed to assure her that he was nothing like the person who had mistreated her in her past. As he bounced along toward town, the horse's warm hide against his legs, his thoughts drifted backwards, and he made sense of Samantha's odd behavior. Having been abused, of course she would be leery and insecure. Of course she would be reluctant to talk about her past. What they had seen as sullenness had really been a protective shell—a necessary means to cope.

He pressed his heels into Bet's side to force her into a run. *Oh, Lord, please let me find her and help her understand that she doesn't need to be afraid anymore! Give me a chance to show her how much I care.*

The shrill blast of a train's whistle jolted Samantha out of a sound sleep. She jerked awake, wincing as stiff muscles were strained. Slowly she pulled herself into a sitting position, rotating her neck. She could see the train now, and her heart started to pound. In a few minutes she would be gone, off to a new city and a new life. *I should be excited!* she told herself firmly. *I'm doing the right thing. Everyone will be better off with me gone. And I can start over again somewhere else, free from Pa and the feelings of guilt that being here have created.*

The train chugged into the depot, then screeched to a noisy stop. Samantha stood, scooping up her bundle of clothing. She stepped up to the suited railroad man who stood blocking the opening to the passenger car.

The man looked her up and down once before inquiring solemnly, "Ticket?"

"Yes, sir," she replied, reaching for her dress pocket. *The ticket!* "Oh, no!" she cried in alarm. Her pocket was empty! She patted her skirts, looking around frantically. "My ticket! It's gone!"

The man watched impassively as she searched through her belongings. "Oh, it's not here," she despaired. She dashed back over to the bench to crawl around, still hunting for her ticket. As Samantha knelt beside the bench, peering beneath it, a cluster of travelers descended the train steps, including a scruffy-looking man who poked at the ticket-taker and asked in a raspy voice, "Where's the sheriff's office?"

The ticket man simply pointed out the direction, his nose held high, and the older man shuffled off around the depot and out of sight.

Samantha plunked herself down on the bench, completely frustrated. Her ticket was nowhere to be found! It must have blown away while she slept, she reasoned in frustration. She could buy another one, but then she'd have very little money left for the rest of her journey. She thumped her fists against her skirt in helpless fury. She didn't know what to do!

"Frances!" burst a loud voice, and she spun on her seat, her palms pressed hard against the wooden bench.

Adam! Oh, no! He stood at the corner of the wooden platform, his dear face wearing an expression of concern and sorrow. She stared at him and a hand flew to cover her mouth in a gesture of alarm. Then without answering him, she raced to the ticket window and cried in a desperately shrill voice, "Please, I need another ticket!"

Adam clumped across the boardwalk and reached out a hand, but stopped short of touching her. "Frances, I'd like to talk to you." His voice was pleading.

She shot him a frantic glance, then immediately turned her attention back to the station worker. "A ticket, please!"

"Frances?" Adam tried again.

She froze, her fingers digging into the wooden counter. She bit her lower lip. *Why did he have to come now? I was so close....*

"Frances, Liz was worried," Adam said gently, even though she still wouldn't look at him. He didn't add how much he'd been worried. "Why'd you take off like that?"

Samantha gave one last pleading look to the ticket master before stepping aside and turning her back on Adam.

He stepped behind her shoulder. "Frances, can we go somewhere and talk, please?"

Tiredness, frustration, and desperation rolled over Samantha like an ocean wave. She didn't know what to do, what to say. It was all too much to bear. She felt the lump rise from her chest to her throat and it couldn't be contained a moment longer. To the surprise of Adam—and herself—she suddenly burst into loud, heart-wrenching tears. Abashed, she brought both hands up to cover her face, but she couldn't hide her weeping. Once started, it struck like a gale force. Her shoulders shook with racking sobs, and tears crept between her fingers to rain downward.

Adam looked back over his shoulder to see a small gathering of people staring curiously from the boardwalk in front of the depot. Realizing this breakdown would be all the more humiliating for her if it took place out in the open, his eyes searched for a private place to take her. *Ah, yes.* Throwing an arm around her waist, he guided her quickly behind the depot building and into a small storage shed.

When he slammed the door, he shut them completely in darkness. It took only a few moments for his eyes to adjust to the murkiness, but it seemed a lifetime passed as he stood, listening to Samantha's painful sobbing. He placed his hands on her shoulders and pushed her over to a nail keg, helping her sit. She doubled up immediately, placing her face in her lap as she cried. Adam found another keg and pulled it close to her, seating himself with his knees nearly touching hers.

Years of comforting crying little brothers and sisters made Adam long to reach out and hold his distraught friend and end her suffering. But he sensed that these tears were needed to purge herself of too-long held hurts, so he sat with his hands tightly cupping his knees, silent and still, breathing in the musty odors of grease, dirt, and mold, just listening, his heart aching for the pain that was being expressed so violently.

Gradually the wild crying softened. He sensed it changing from harsh to healing. Eventually, after what seemed an eternity, it finally faded to weak hiccups as the tears slowed. And, with a series of shuddering sighs, the sobs died out.

Slowly she sat up, taking in one long, ragged breath. Adam reached into his back pocket and withdrew a handkerchief which he pressed into her lap. She took it gratefully to mop at her face and blow her nose noisily once, then again. With shaking fingers she explored her sore, swollen eyelids, and sighed loudly.

"Oh, my, I haven't cried like that since I was six years old." Her voice was hollow and raw. Her head ached and her eyes stung.

Adam said sensibly, "Then I think it was about time."

She twisted the soggy handkerchief in her hands, staring downward. She went on as if he hadn't spoken. "Yeah, the last time I cried like that was when I was six. When Gran died." She paused, lifting her face to look past him pensively. "Have I ever told you about Gran?"

Adam shook his head, afraid to speak. She'd never told him about anything, as she well knew!

Samantha began speaking in an emotionless, even tone that was somehow more chilling than her wild crying had been. "You see, my mama died birthing me. Pa wanted to take me out and drown me like some unwanted kitten, but Gran wouldn't let him. She moved in and took over. She cared for me and Pa and my brother David just like it was nothing. It was really something, though. She was past seventy when I was born, but she ran that household as well as any woman half her age. Wasn't easy, either, with Pa…"

She paused a moment, seemingly lost in thought. Adam held his breath, wanting to ask questions, but afraid of frightening her into permanent silence. In time, she continued: "Gran was…Gran was a lot like your mother. Always smiling and kind, never fault-finding or fractious. She had this soft lap just right for snuggling up in. She used to hold me after Pa would—after he'd…." She swallowed, unable to say the words.

The image of her huddled into a ball in the moonlight flashed through Adam's mind, and he reached out to squeeze her hands. The comforting pressure told her as clearly as words that she didn't need to say any more. He knew. She pulled in another shuddering breath before going on. "Anyway, she'd always hold me and comfort me, and tell me not to believe the things he said, that I *was* special, that I *was* good. When Gran told me that, I could almost believe it." Her tone had turned wistful.

Still holding her hands, Adam prompted softly, "Your Gran died when you were six?"

Samantha nodded. "Yes. She was Pa's grandmother. You'd think he'd've been sad, but I don't think he was. I think he was angry, because then there wasn't anybody to wait on him, except me and Davey, and we couldn't do it good enough." She added earnestly, looking into his eyes for the first time since they'd entered the shed, "We tried, though! We really did. But it was never good enough. Davey stuck around for awhile—about three years, I guess, after Gran died. But then he said he had to git. Told me to wait for him, told me he'd be back for me. He *promised*." She snorted bitterly and shook her head. "That promise wasn't worth much. I haven't seen him since."

Adam struggled with how to respond to that. She'd lost so much!

"A person shouldn't make a promise he might not be able to keep," she said, her voice small and pathetic. "I waited every night for seven years, hoping he'd come back and rescue me. Took me a long time to figure out no one was going to rescue me but *me*. So I made my own plans to leave. I ran off, but I didn't get far. Pa always caught up with me...."

So she was a runaway, just as the sheriff said, Adam thought.

Samantha went on, as if telling a story. "'Til this time. I decided if I was going to get away, I'd have to be somebody else. So I stole some clothes out of a trunk in the cellar to make me look like a boy, and when Pa was sleepin' off a drink, I lit out. I just wanted to get away from Pa, like Davey had. I just wanted to escape. I didn't mean to—"

Her chin shot upward, and Adam could see her throat convulsing.

"Frances, what is it?" he asked in the gentlest of tones. "You didn't mean what?"

Instead of answering his question she began babbling nonsensically, tears at the surface again. "Oh, Adam, I'm so sorry. At first I thought it was smart and funny, fooling you into thinking I was somebody else. But then I got to know all of you and I knew it was wrong, and I wanted to tell you. Honest, I wanted to! I didn't mean to lie to you! But I had to or you could send me home! That's why I *had* to lie! Oh, please, can't you understand?"

Adam was thoroughly confused. It had been obvious early on that she wasn't a boy. "I'm sorry," he said, "I *don't* understand, Frances. What—?"

She shook her head impatiently and confessed at last, "That's just it! I'm not Frances. I'm Samantha."

Adam sat back as if pole-axed. Samantha? Her name was *Samantha*?!

She swallowed the tears gathering in her throat again as she hastened to explain, to apologize, to somehow make him understand that she'd had no choice. "At first I was Frances to fool you and keep from having to go home. But the longer I was Frances, the easier it was to *be* Frances, and after awhile

I almost believed it myself. I hated it—lying to you—you all were so nice to me. But if I told you the truth, you could find out where I came from. And—and I'd have to leave. I'd have to go back. Adam, I didn't want to go back!"

Adam's world was spinning. Not Frances, but Samantha. All this time…. And she *had* been running, but from her own family, not Adam.

She was crying again, the tears rolling endlessly downward as she spoke pleadingly, one hand wrapped around his forearm with a strength he wouldn't have thought possible from such a small person. "I don't expect you to forgive me. I couldn't expect that. But can't you please try to understand? You and your folks were nicer to me than anybody ever was—except for Gran, and maybe Davey. I couldn't tell you the truth. Not without you being able to send me home. And I couldn't go home! I just couldn't!"

Adam understood. He sat there, silently comparing her childhood to his. He balanced his secure home against her unstable one, his knowledge of being loved against her feelings of unworth. He had so many warm, wonderful memories of family and home and acceptance. He almost felt guilty for having been born into his family when Samantha had been thrust into an abusive, angry environment.

He could understand. And he could comfort her now. He reached out to smooth her tangled hair from her tear-stained face. He ran his thumbs beneath her eyes, whisking away the tears, finding the skin there sleek with moisture. He spoke her name—her true name—for the first time. "Samantha, it's all right. I understand." Then followed the words she needed so much to hear, "And I forgive you."

Her face crumpled, but she held the tears at bay, looking at him for a long moment, an expression of rapt gratitude shining in her swollen eyes. Then she threw herself at him, wrapping her arms around his neck and clinging hard. He returned the embrace, cupping the back of her head to hold her closely against his shoulder.

How good it feels to hold her, he thought, closing his eyes and tilting his head slightly to feel her warm hair firm against his cheek.

How wonderful and secure I feel right now, she thought, breathing in the unique scent that was Adam. *If only I could stay here until all the pain goes away....*

In time they separated, a bit self-consciously perhaps, smiling weakly at one another and then letting their gazes skitter elsewhere.

Samantha wiped her face once again, then queried shakily, "Want to hear something funny?"

Adam couldn't imagine finding amusement in this situation, but he offered a small nod, his gentle smile encouraging her.

"Gran believed like you do—that there's a God who loves us and watches out for us. I used to say my bedtime prayers when I was little—you know, God bless everybody. Gran would listen to my prayers, then tuck me in. Like Laura does with Teddy and Sarah."

Adam was grateful for this small memory. At least there was some pleasantness in her fractured past.

Her voice lost its blithesome undertone as she continued, "When Gran would leave the room, I'd tell God that I really didn't mean God bless Pa, and I'd ask would He please make Pa go away. But instead of taking Pa away, He took Gran, and then Davey...."

"Adam," she asked in a small, anguished voice, "do you think God took Gran and David away to punish me for those prayers?"

Adam captured her hands, bringing them briefly to his lips before replying earnestly, "No, Samantha! God loves you!

You were just a hurting little girl. He would never hold you responsible for those prayers."

"Then why did Gran die? And Davey never come back for me?" she insisted. "I loved them both so much, and they left me."

Her little-girl voice, so full of wounded bitterness, pierced Adam's heart, and he prayed inwardly for the right words to ease her pain at last. "Listen to me, Samantha. Your Gran was old. She was doing much more than she had the strength for, but she wanted to do it, because she loved you. You weren't responsible for her death. And David had reasons of his own for leaving. He wasn't leaving to get away from you, but the circumstances he was in. I don't know why he didn't come back for you as he promised, but I know it was his choice. You can't blame yourself for that, either."

"But Pa said—" Samantha started, only to be interrupted.

"Your pa is a bitter, unhappy man. Maybe your mother dying so early made him bitter, maybe he was just always that way. Some people seem to enjoy being unhappy. The only way they can make themselves feel better is to make everyone around them feel bad, too. Instead of hating him, we should feel sorry for him. He must be very miserable to act the way he has. And by his actions he lost a son—and a very special daughter."

Samantha looked at him doubtfully. "Me? Special?"

"Yes, you," Adam answered emphatically, determined to convince her of the truth of his statement. "Why, with all the people in my family, you'd think we'd never need anyone else! But we did, and there you were. You've been such a help to Liz and Jake and the twins. You're a good friend to Josie, and Sarah adores you. Samantha, you are loved by every member of my family!" *Especially me,* his thoughts continued, but the time wasn't right to tell her. She needed time to heal. He squeezed her hands again as he said, "And as much as *we* love you, *God* loves you even more."

Samantha's chin quivered. Oh, how she wanted to believe Adam was right! Wistfully she told him, "I want to believe I'm somebody special, and worthy of love but—"

Adam cut in, "Then just do it! What's stopping you?"

Tears were threatening again. "I lied to you! I pretended to be somebody I wasn't! And before that, I tried to—"

Adam placed two fingers very gently over her lips to silence her. "And you think that makes you unworthy?" he asked. Her face told him clearly that yes, that's exactly what she thought. "Samantha, the Bible tells us that 'while we were yet sinners, Christ died for us.' You can't have any greater love than that. God didn't wait around for us to become perfect, then love us. He just loves us where we are—imperfect and floundering and needy. All we have to do is accept that love, and the whole world changes."

"You believe in that love, don't you?" Samantha asked. "I can tell by the way you are with other people. All of you— you're always kind and giving. I've never seen your mother or father lose their tempers, or say hateful things. They act like how I think God must be."

"That's because we have accepted the love of God and asked Him to live inside our hearts," Adam explained, his own heart beating hard enough to move his shirt front. "When Christ's spirit is a part of you, you begin to be bent to His nature. 'Old things are passed away; behold, all things are made new.' And here's a promise you can keep—'I will never leave you nor forsake you.' Christ will be with you every day, helping you become the person you ought to be."

Samantha sat in thoughtful silence for several long minutes. Adam waited patiently for his words to be absorbed. From the brief glance he'd been given of her childhood, he couldn't help but marvel at her resilience. The years of abuse had taken their toll on her emotionally, but he knew with God all things were possible, and her feelings of unworthiness could be changed with God's help. He prayed that he could get through to her, to help her realize that what she saw in his family could be hers—if only she would ask.

Samantha replayed words she'd heard the minister speak in church. She remembered evidence of God's power she'd seen in the lives of the people around her. More than she'd ever wanted anything, she wanted the peace and happiness that Adam and his family had. And all she had to do was *ask*! It seemed almost too simple to be true. But Adam had said if she'd just believe, it could be hers, too.

I believe. I do believe!

"Adam?" came her small voice. "Will you please pray with me?"

Adam immediately dropped onto his knees beside the nail keg, and Samantha joined him. Right there, in a musty storage shed behind the train depot, Samantha asked Jesus to live in her heart. And the journey toward recovery was begun.

When they had finished, Adam stood up, holding out a hand to help draw her to her feet. They stood in the gloom of the shed, staring into one another's eyes, the merest hint of a smile lighting two faces.

"Come on, Samantha," Adam said. "Let's go home."

Chapter Seventeen

*A*dam swung himself onto Bet's broad back, then reached a hand down for Samantha. She hesitated only a moment before placing her hand in his and allowing him to pull her up in front of him. She supposed from all appearances she was sitting in his lap and questioned the propriety of such a position, but the secure feeling it gave her to be cradled there made her toss propriety to the wind and just enjoy the ride.

It was warm against Adam's woolly jacket, and the gentle swaying motion of the plodding horse soon lulled Samantha into dreamland. She slept, her head resting on Adam's shoulder. Occasionally he would glance down at her peaceful face, smile to himself, and think, *Samantha*. The name suited her far better than Frances. Samantha of the russet hair and cornflower eyes.

He shifted his arm a bit, pulling her closer. The significance of what had occurred in the storage shed behind the depot brought a lightness to his heart. Samantha now knew the Lord. The barrier that had kept him from admitting his love for her was removed. His heart thrummed happily. Now he could—. With a jolt he realized he didn't even know how old she was! Was she old enough to be betrothed?

Let's see, he made his mind count backwards. *Her Gran died when she was six, her brother had been gone for seven or eight years after staying home for—what? Two or three years after Gran's death? That would make her seventeen or so. Josie's age....*

He studied her relaxed face. She looked younger—especially in sleep. Her age mattered not a whit. If she was too young now, he'd just wait. He certainly wasn't so old he had to be married right away! And she was worth waiting for. He experienced a rush of feeling for the young woman who lay so trustingly in his embrace. She was a beautiful person with well-placed features. And that hair! It flew everywhere in wild disarray, but he loved it. It was perfect for her—free and flying and uninhibited. But more than her physical beauty, there was her inner beauty. Oh, she could be stubborn at times, but he'd seen her sweet, giving spirit. The stubbornness, he was convinced now, was just a cover for the insecurity she felt.

Compassion filled him—what an unhappy life she'd had before coming here! Somehow he would make it up to her. He would spend the rest of his life spoiling her with tenderness, giving her every happiness, if only she would accept him. If only she returned his feelings....

The farm was in sight. He called softly to Bet, "Whoa there, girl." He wanted to wake Samantha before entering the yard. Gently he shook her shoulders. "Samantha? Samantha, you need to wake up, honey."

The endearment filtered into Samantha's tired mind, and she smiled sleepily before opening her eyes and meeting Adam's tender gaze.

She blushed prettily and asked sheepishly, "Not much company, was I?"

"I should say not," Adam teased quietly, "and did you know you snore?"

Samantha jerked upright and retorted, "Snore?! I do not!"

Adam laughed at her. "Of course you don't," he said, grinning. "What say we get down and walk the rest of the way?"

Samantha realized how much more appropriate that would look to his waiting family, so readily agreed. He helped her slide off before hopping down beside her. They shared one last lingering look before Adam tugged at Bet's harness and they headed for the house.

As they entered the yard, Samantha pointed to an unfamiliar buggy beside the barn. "Looks like you've got a visitor," she said.

"Reckon so," Adam replied.

He recognized the rig as one belonging to John Jenkins, the town blacksmith. Sometimes he rented it out, and Adam wondered who might be calling in a rented rig.

"Go on up to the house," Adam suggested, "while I take care of Bet. I'll be there in a few minutes."

Samantha suddenly felt shy about approaching his family. She was sure they all knew how she'd taken off in the middle of the night, and she wasn't quite ready to face them. She looked hopefully at Adam, "Can't I just come with you? Then we could go in together." Her cornflower eyes were childishly wide and filled with apprehension.

Adam smiled in understanding, and nodded his head. "Come on," he invited.

Samantha watched as Adam brushed Bet down with a wide, short bristled brush, speaking gentle words of small-talk as he worked. She listened, a small smile on her face. She so appreciated Adam's tenderness with all creatures.

A barn cat rubbed against her leg, and she scooped it up, scratching its chin and enjoying its happy purr. She found herself murmuring silly things to the cat, and when she looked up Adam was watching her, a soft expression in his eyes. She blushed.

"Guess it's kind of silly, talking to a cat," she said, placing the animal back on the floor.

Adam just shrugged. "No sillier than talking to a horse," was his response, and she gave a small chuckle.

"Then we're both silly," she said, peeking at him coyly from beneath heavy lashes.

"Two of a kind," Adam agreed lightly, "that's us."

They stood silently in the barn, oblivious to the purring cat and Bet's snorts of contentment. Nothing existed but Adam and Samantha. A question crossed Adam's mind: *Should I?* In silent answer, he very slowly stepped forward, crossing the hard-packed dirt floor, scuffing up bits of hay as he came.

Samantha held her breath as he advanced, her eyes locked on his. *Would he? Would he really?...*

When he stood mere inches in front of her, he stopped, bringing up his hands to chafe her upper arms gently. Her gaze flittered from his eyes to his lips, then to his eyes again. He had watched the course her blue eyes had taken, and one side of his mouth tipped up sweetly before he leaned his head forward and placed his lips softly—so softly she almost thought she imagined it—on her slightly parted lips.

When he pulled back, she released in one *whoosh* the breath she'd been holding. Adam was still smiling with his eyes as he dropped his hands and stepped back. She knew she was blushing, but she couldn't avert her gaze. He had kissed her! Not a lover's kiss—more like a brotherly kiss—but a kiss just the same. Her heart pounded.

"I'm finished out here," he said now, his voice low, making her wonder fleetingly if he was talking about her or Bet. "Let's go see the folks now."

Samantha nodded. Then Adam held out his hand, and, after a moment of shy hesitation, she placed hers into it. And then they were holding hands loosely, ambling to the big house together, both content and relaxed with one another.

Adam pulled the screened porch door open and gestured for Samantha to enter first. She did, but stopped immediately inside the doorway. He heard her sharp intake of breath. Adam peeked over her shoulder to see Sheriff Barnes and a man he'd didn't know seated at the kitchen table with Si and Laura, sipping at cups of coffee.

As the door squeaked shut, all four looked up.

The stranger grinned, showing yellowed, crooked teeth. "Well, hello, girlie. Betcha yore surprised to see me here, huh?"

Samantha had gone pale and seemed unable to move. Adam applied gentle pressure to her back, and she moved stiffly into the room.

Laura stood up. "Adam, this is Burt O'Brien, from Milwaukee, Wisconsin. He's come to pick up his daughter."

Adam looked worriedly at Samantha's stricken face. *Oh, not now. Why did he have to come now? And why did I stop her from boarding that train...?*

Sheriff Barnes stood. He crossed the room to stand beside Samantha, asking, "Is this your father, young lady?" His tone was brusque, but his eyes looked sad.

Samantha nodded woodenly; her tongue felt swollen, too thick to form words. She was frozen in place, staring at the disreputable looking man at the table, and Adam could only guess at what she was thinking. The moment hung suspended, somehow dreamlike.

Adam spoke up, trying to bring some reality to the moment. "Ma, Pa, I found Samantha at the train station. She agreed to come back home with me. We—"

The raspy-voiced man croaked rudely, "*Home*, huh? I hate to tell ya, sonny, but this ain't her home. She'll be *goin'* home, though. Right now. With me." And he grasped Samantha's arm just above her elbow with grime-encrusted fingers and started to push her out the door.

"Wait a minute!" Adam cried. This was all happening too fast—he couldn't think.

"Wait fer what?" Burt demanded in a harsh, grating voice. "S'pose yore wantin' me to thank ya fer keepin' track o' my gal. Wal, okay, thank ya. 'Preciate your hospitality." He spat the words out, his taunting grin making a mockery of the words. "Now jus' step aside an' let me pass. I'm takin' my girlie home."

Laura and Si came quickly to Adam's side as Burt pushed Samantha out the door. He stomped in a blundering gait across the yard, Samantha stumbling along beside him as if in shock. Adam trotted behind them, wanting to stop him but afraid to intervene. He knew now that Burt O'Brien was a violent man, and he didn't want to create a scene in which Samantha could be hurt. With a mighty shove, Burt forced her into the buggy and climbed up awkwardly behind her. Adam ran around to the opposite side of the rig, reaching up to clasp Samantha's hand. It was icy.

"Samantha, I—" But what could he say? *I'll come for you?* Only an hour ago she had told him tearfully that people shouldn't make promises they couldn't keep. He wouldn't add another broken promise to all those that had been made before. So he squeezed her cold hand and tried to tell her with his eyes what was on his heart.

She managed to give him a reassuring smile. She whispered, "Adam, don't worry. I'll be okay. I have Someone stronger than me on my side now. I'll be fine."

Her bravado tugged at his heart painfully. He could see the fear in her cornflower blue eyes. *Oh, Lord, how can I help her now?*

Suddenly Adam pulled back. "Wait, please, just wait a minute! Don't leave!" he begged, and he took off at a run for the house.

Si and Laura hovered near the buggy, unsure of what to do. Laura spoke up, trying to postpone their leave-taking. "Mr. O'Brien, Samantha has been working for our daughter, helping out with household chores and caring for her babies."

"Oh, yeah?" Burt replied, shooting his daughter a speculative glance. "Good to hear she's been makin' herself useful."

"Yes," Laura rushed on, "and we were hoping that maybe—"

"No," Burt said firmly, cutting her off rudely. He spat over the edge of the buggy, his brown-tinged spittle landing near Si's booted foot. "She ain't stayin' here. She's got her own house to tend, an' she's gonna tend it. Now you folks jus' step back so we can git to the train station afore the train goes without us." And he raised his hands as if to slap the reins down against the horse's back.

Adam came bounding out of the house, waving something in his hand, calling, "Mr. O'Brien! Wait! Please wait!"

He slid to a halt next to the buggy, panting hard. He leaned across the foul-smelling man to press something into Samantha's lap, telling her, "Here are promises you can count on, Samantha." *They will keep you until I can make my own promises to you,* his eyes continued.

She looked down, and tears blurred her vision as she recognized the little black book. It was Adam's Bible. She clutched it tightly and nodded through her tears.

"Hi-yup!" Burt yelled, bringing the reins down on the horse's back, sending the startled animal into a trot. He didn't give anyone a chance for goodbyes.

Adam watched as Samantha turned in her seat to look back at him, her face pinched and pale. But to reassure him, she forced a brave, tremulous smile, lifting her hand to wave. Adam took two steps forward, wanting to chase down the buggy and bring her back, but Laura stopped him with a hand on his arm.

"Let her go, son," Laura said softly. "We have to let her go."

"But, Ma, that man—" Adam's voice broke. "He'll hurt her, Ma, I know he will."

Laura squeezed Adam's arm, her own heart breaking at Adam's distress. She spoke soothingly. "We have to let her go, Adam, and trust the Lord to watch out for her."

Adam looked to Sheriff Barnes for help, but the big man simply shook his head, an expression of regret creasing his face as well. "I'm sorry, Adam. She's under-age—not old enough to be on her own, legally. I had to send her home."

The buggy rounded the bend, carrying Samantha away. Adam pressed his hands hard into his jacket pockets, his jaw clenched. He'd only just gotten her—she'd only just become his. And now she was gone. It wasn't fair. *Oh, God, it isn't fair!* He looked down into his mother's empathetic face. "Ma," he choked out, and could say no more. Lowering his head, he wept.

Chapter Eighteen

October passed, bleak and dismal with overcast skies and biting winds that matched Adam's somber mood. The first snowfall, usually an event of celebration, cheered Adam not in the least. Samantha's abrupt departure from his life—as sudden and unexpected as her entrance had been—left a hollow void that Adam found impossible to fill. His days were full and busy, yet empty. The joy was gone. And he didn't know how to recapture it.

He haunted the post office, hoping and praying for some word from Samantha that would let him know how she was. But nothing came, and gradually he came to accept that she wouldn't—or couldn't—write to him. The memories of their brief time together were no doubt as painful for her as they were for him. It was better to let go.

The day he overhead Sarah ask, "Mama, will Adam ever smile again?" he realized that he must somehow regain his old, cheerful spirit. But how?

He agonized, the image of Samantha cowering in fright after their brief argument haunting his dreams and creeping into his mind at odd times during the day. There were so many other images he could call on—Samantha in her overalls picking berries with her hair wild around her piquant face; Samantha smiling blissfully as she cradled little A.J.; Samantha happily exploring the dugout; Samantha rising from her knees in a storage shed, her face shining; Samantha relaxed in sleep against his arm....

Yet that horrible picture overwhelmed him. Was she being abused now? Was she lying somewhere, bruised and broken, waiting for a rescuer? Those thoughts tortured him until he wanted to scream at the heavens.

Adam needed a change. He needed a task so mind-consuming that all thoughts of Samantha would be erased. He thought of his friend Thomas Enns, and where he had gone. The thought of going off to fight, as Thomas had, filled him with dread, yet he knew if he went, he could rid his thoughts of Samantha. There were great risks involved, and his family would be in opposition to such a plan. Yet in his despondent state, the idea held merit.

He would do it, he decided. He would enlist in the army. Frank and Arn, with Teddy's help, could handle the farm work, he was sure, so he didn't need to feel guilty about leaving his father shorthanded. He would wait until after Thanksgiving. One last holiday with his family, and then he would go. The course of action decided, Adam made a determined effort to at least pretend to be his old, jocular self again. He wanted to leave his family with pleasant memories to recall while he was away. He didn't allow himself to dwell on the reason, but he knew it was just in case he didn't return....

Back in Milwaukee, Samantha settled back into her familiar routine. Household chores, caring for Pa's needs.... The days were as she remembered—strained and bleak and joyless. She had printed up a little sign and hung it in the post office, advertising that she would mend or construct garments for people. Before long, she had a steady business going, and she carefully hoarded away half of the money she earned. Pa took control of the other half, and most of it he squandered on drink. She read Adam's Bible daily, taking comfort in the words she found there. And as time passed, she discovered a peace of spirit within herself despite the outer turmoil in her life.

As she learned more about Jesus and His love for her, she began seeing her father in a different light. She understood that Jesus loved her pa, too, and if she wanted to be like Him, she must try to see her father through Christ's eyes. Instead of viewing him as hateful, she looked deep inside to a man so full of unhappiness that only hate could come out. Instead of reviling him, she began pitying him, and prayed for him daily, that he might come to know the peace she now felt in her heart.

On Sundays she walked to the little church she had attended with Gran all those years ago. A new, younger minister was serving there now, and his teachings were as gentle and mind-soothing as Reverend Goertzen's. Samantha drank in the words spoken by the light-haired man behind the pulpit, reflecting on those words through the week. The more she listened and learned, the easier it was for her to bear Pa's ranting and raving. She was maturing into a spiritual young woman, and the changes did not go unnoticed by the young minister. However, as attentive as Samantha was to his teaching, she remained aloof to any other attentions. Her heart still remained in Mountain Lake.

Her mind carried her back to Mountain Lake often. She wondered how big the twins were, how Liz was feeling, if Sarah's front teeth were clear in and how that might have changed her looks, whether Hulda Klaassen had found someone else to sew up those dresses she was supposed to have made....

But most often she thought of Adam, although she tried not to. She loved him more than she had ever thought possible, but the realization only brought heartache instead of the carefree joy she always imagined loving someone would bring. Some days she hoped she would find a letter from him, other days she was glad she didn't. This was her life now, and dreaming of other times and places served no useful purpose. So she immersed herself in her work, in her Bible-reading, and her attempts to change her father.

This day as Samantha sat in a rocker near the small four-pane kitchen window, putting the hem in a petticoat, David weighed on her mind. He would be twenty-four years old now. Old enough to be married, maybe even have children. What was David like now? She remembered him as a thin, pale youth—taller than Pa already at fifteen—with a headful of russet curls that refused to be tamed and her own pale blue eyes. Always somber, rarely smiling. Her brother.... Did David ever think of her? Ever wonder how she was doing? Ever think of returning for her?

She nipped the thread with her teeth and let the white cloth drop into her lap. It seemed sometimes that she had lost every person she'd loved. First Gran, then David. And Adam. That hurt most, losing Adam, because she'd had him for such a short time. It was like being wakened rudely from a happy dream. The old Samantha would have engrossed herself in self-pity, but the new Samantha saw each loss as a means to strengthen her. She reminded herself that her Book of promises gave the assurance that all things work together for good.

Adam had told her she could count on those promises. She held to that now. Her life held meaning now, and purpose. It was only a matter of time before all things became good.

The week before Thanksgiving Adam broke the news to his father about enlisting in the army. They were in the tack shed, rubbing soap into two new saddles, when Adam interrupted the comfortable silence to announce his intentions.

Si erupted. "You are going to do no such thing!"

Adam put the soap aside and leaned forward, resting his elbows on his knees.

"Pa, please, can't we talk about this?"

The normally mellow Si shook his head firmly and answered, "Absolutely not. I forbid you to do such a thing."

Adam hung his head. He spoke to the spot of ground between his boots. "Pa, I'm not asking for your permission. I'm just telling you what I intend to do."

Adam had never defied his father before. It made Adam's chest feel tight and angered Si beyond words. Si bolted to his feet, pacing back and forth twice in the small space. His breath came out in white puffs, his face set angrily. Adam thought he resembled a disgruntled dragon, but it wasn't a humorous thought. After a couple of minutes Si had calmed himself enough to speak reasonably, but his voice still carried a hint of exasperation as he faced his son.

"Adam, don't think I can't figure out why you think you need to go. It's the girl, isn't it? It's because of Samantha."

Adam kept his head down, closing his eyes momentarily to mask the stab of pain the mention of Samantha had brought.

Si pressed gruffly, demanding a response, "Isn't it!"

Adam raised his head and answered defensively, "Yes, it is! She's in my heart, Pa, and I can't get her out. I need to get away from here—I need to get my mind so wrapped up in something else that no thought of Samantha can intrude. I just can't go on like this anymore, Pa!" Angry tears glinted in Adam's eyes, and he set his jaw firmly to keep them at bay. He would not humiliate himself by breaking down now!

"Listen to me, boy," Si said, pulling up a sawhorse and seating himself close to his son. "It's one thing to mope, but it's another to throw your life away. I understand that you have feelings for the girl. I understand that you're worried about her. But I don't understand how you can think making a foolhardy move like joining the army will fix anything!"

Si sighed and wiped a hand across his face tiredly, drawing his skin downward. He suddenly looked old to Adam, and it scared him. Si slapped his hands down on his knees.

"You're twenty years old now, and I reckon I can't tell you what to do," Si said in a sad, resigned voice. "If you mean to go, I can't stand in your way. But I can tell you to use the brain God gave you and think! And I want you to think long and hard on this before you go traipsing off: You accused Samantha of running away…" He paused for effect before asking, "Just what do you call what you're doing?"

Adam couldn't answer. There wasn't much to say when he knew, deep down, that his father was right. But he also knew, right or wrong, that he would go. Because he could think of no other way to rid his mind—and heart—of Samantha O'Brien.

Si stomped to the house, still seething from his encounter with Adam. Fool boy! Foolish, heartbroken boy! Thinking he can solve his problems by taking up a weapon and facing an enemy bigger than his own mind. Si knew Adam's worst enemy right now was himself, and he also knew that in time Adam would realize that and come to his senses. But how to keep him here until that realization came—ah, that was the problem.

Adam was normally a level-headed young man. He'd always been reasonable and logical, thinking before acting. Si couldn't believe that Adam was the one threatening to go marching off—he would've expected such rash behavior from Frank, who'd always been more inclined to act impulsively and regret it later. If it weren't for that girl....

Oh, Si didn't begrudge Adam his feelings. He understood, more than Adam might believe he did. One didn't choose to love—it simply happened. And Adam could no more choose to turn off his love for Samantha than he had chosen to have it grow. But understanding was one thing; agreeing to let him drown his sorrows with the horrors of battle was quite another. Although Si had admitted he couldn't stand in Adam's way if he was determined to go, he could try to change his mind. And he resolved to do that.

Si felt tired. No one said raising children was easy—and it sure didn't improve with age! Suddenly he just wanted to sit quietly with Laura. Her calming presence was always a balm. Yes, he'd find Laura. And together they would put Adam and this dilemma in the Lord's hands. Si felt a sense of relief. There was no better place to go.

The day after Thanksgiving, Adam stood on the wooden platform in front of the tiny depot building. His family gathered close, bestowing their goodbyes in voices loud enough to be heard over the raucous rumbling of the engine waiting to depart. He was leaving, but not to Europe. His parents had convinced him that if he needed to get away, a visit to his brother and grandparents in Minneapolis would be much less drastic than enlisting to fight. Adam wasn't so headstrong that he couldn't change his mind. He had wanted the chance to get away and busy himself elsewhere—he admitted that going to

Minneapolis might be a good idea. Spending a few weeks keeping up with Grandpa and Grandma Klaassen might be just what he needed to clear his Samantha-filled head.

"Give Daniel and Rose our love," Laura hollered next to Adam's ear, "and kiss little Christina and Katrina for me."

"I will," Adam promised.

Josie grabbed his arm, her mouth opened to speak. He turned to her with a smirk and cut her off, "And I'll give them the doll clothes you made the minute I arrive!" She'd only reminded him seven times already! How could he forget?

Josie punched at his arm playfully. She hugged him hard, her arms curled around his neck. "Take care, Adam," she said.

He squeezed her back, and planted a quick kiss on her cheek. "You, too—and stay away from Stephen Koehn until I get back!"

Adam laughed as she blushed and turned away. It hardly seemed that Josie could be old enough for young men to come courting, but she must be, for it was happening. But then, she was the same age as Samantha, and she—

He cut those thoughts off quickly. The purpose of this trip was to forget about Samantha.

Now Sarah tugged at Adam's coat sleeve, demanding to be lifted up for a hug. She gave him a noisy smack on the cheek before he lowered her to the ground and reached for Teddy, rubbing his little hat over his head affectionately. "Be good," Adam told the two youngest. They nodded, both teary-eyed. Next came Becky, then Arn who stood as tall as Adam now and insisted on simply shaking hands. His hug from Liz was longer and harder than the others, and he returned it with equal pressure. She pressed her nose against his, smiling into his eyes.

"Come back happy," she told him. He didn't hear her, as the train was too loud, but he could read her lips—and her eyes. He nodded.

Frank stood close, an arm curved around Anna. Yesterday at the height of celebration they had announced their intention to marry in February. Adam placed a gloved hand on Frank's shoulder, giving him a warm squeeze. "Take care of each other. I'll see you soon," he told the smiling couple.

Last was Si. The father and son clasped gloved hands, snowflakes flying wildly around their heads and cold air lifting their hair. They stood, a mere twelve inches separating them, for several long seconds before Adam lurched forward and found himself being held firmly in his father's strong embrace. Si was still not happy about Adam's decision to leave, but at least he wasn't heading to Europe. A visit with Daniel and Rose was certainly preferable to that! And he'd be back for Christmas—hopefully back to himself again.

The two men pulled apart as the conductor bawled, "Bo-o-oard!"

Arn grabbed up Adam's carpet bag and the whole family accompanied Adam to the steps that led to the railroad car. One more hug from little Sarah, and Adam hopped up into the car. He turned back for a last smile and wave before disappearing inside the long box.

Laura suggested, "Let's watch for him in the windows!" And all eyes scanned the side of the car, watching anxiously. At last Becky spotted him, and hollered, "There he is! 'Bye, Adam! 'Bye!" She waved wildly.

Adam used his sleeve to clear a peek-hole on the frosted glass, then pressed his nose to the open spot, waving. As the train started its chugging motion, Teddy ran down the boardwalk beside it, leaping off the end, continuing to holler and wave until Si called him back. Si placed an arm around Laura's waist, pulling her close against his side.

"Come, mother, " he said, "let's take this brood home."

Thanksgiving was just as Samantha expected. She had hoped that maybe—*maybe*—this year would be different. But she should have known better, she decided with a flash of cynicism.

She had prepared a fine meal, using some of her saved sewing money to purchase a goose, and making a savory sage dressing. She had fixed three different vegetables and baked bread, even stirred up a sweet potato pie in a flaky crust. But by the time Pa had staggered in, reeking of whiskey and mumbling belligerently, the food was cold. Some Thanksgiving it had been…. Samantha could not remember a holiday, ever, that had not been spoiled by her father's drinking.

As she put the last of the dishes back on the warped shelving above the dry sink, she sighed. She had so hoped this Thanksgiving would be different. All the prayers, all the changes she'd made within herself came for nothing. She rested her hands on the sharp edge of the dry sink and let her head drop low. Pa would never change. What was the use?

Suddenly an image of a family seated around a long trestle table popped into her mind. She could see their smiling faces, hear their laughing voices, and she was hit with a wave of melancholy so powerful tears spurted into her eyes. Oh, she missed the Klaassens and Mountain Lake! She missed them *so much*….

She crossed the dim room to light an oil lamp and curl up in her familiar rocker, the old rocker in which Gran used to sit. She remembered well the security of cuddling up in Gran's soft lap and being rocked. She remembered, too, being cradled in Adam's arms that one time as they had ridden back to his house on Bet's strong back. What she wouldn't give to have one of them here to hold her now.

The front door rattled, startling Samantha out of her reverie. She heard a grumbled curse, and the sounds of the doorknob being violently twisted broke through the room.

Pa was home. Samantha rose and hurried to the door to open it for him.

As Burt lurched through the open doorway, the stench of stale whiskey and cigar smoke drifted past Samantha's nose causing her to wince. He gave her a bleary glare.

"Whatsamatter, girlie?" he drawled, "Ain'tcha glad to see yore ol' man? Huh?"

And he laughed horribly, the stench of his breath making Samantha take a backward step.

"Come, Pa," Samantha said sensibly, "come sit down and I'll get you some coffee." She guided him to the small table and helped him into a chair. He slouched drunkenly, watching Samantha through watery, red-rimmed eyes as she poured a cup of coffee and ladled out a bowl of vegetable soup. When Samantha placed the cup and bowl in front of him, he reached out with strength belying his drunkenness to grasp her wrist.

A strange light shone in his blood-shot eyes, and his grin seemed somehow evil. Samantha looked at him in alarm.

"W-what is it, Pa?" she stammered, an unnamed fear claiming her.

Burt tightened his grip on her wrist, and lifted his other hand to pinch a strand of her hair between two dirty fingers. "Jus' quite the li'l homemaker, ain'tcha? All growed up an' knowin' how to take keer of a man…."

His implication was clear to Samantha. She twisted her arm, trying to pull away. "Pa, no," she croaked frantically.

As suddenly as it had begun, his strangeness ended. Throwing her wrist away, he ordered thickly, "Oh, git away from me, girl. Git me some o' that bread to sop up this soup. Y'know I can't eat soup without bread, girl!"

Her heart thudding, she skittered to obey.

Chapter Nineteen

dam stood outside a large store in downtown Minneapolis, admiring the variety of toys in the window. He smiled, imagining his little nieces, Katrina and Christina, cuddling the dolls that were dressed in satins and lace. There was a tin train that ran around a metal track, too. Wouldn't A.J. and Andy love watching that?

He had been in Minneapolis for three weeks now. He had thoroughly enjoyed the time spent with Daniel and Rose and getting acquainted with his two small nieces. The girls were sweet and loving, dimpled and curly-haired, and Adam found them irresistible. His grandparents were as pert and lively as ever, and many pleasant evenings were spent in their company. He had gone with Daniel to his law office several times, and developed a respect for Daniel and his work.

But as much as he enjoyed his visit, he hadn't accomplished what he had come for—he hadn't managed to forget Samantha.

The idea was ludicrous. How could he forget? But although she still hovered on the fringes of his mind, he no longer felt the stabbing pain of remembrance. Instead, thoughts of her brought a gratefulness that she had entered his life, and that they had been able to touch one another in a special way. He prayed for her daily, that the Lord would keep her in His capable care, and he trusted that wherever Samantha was, she was at peace with herself.

Now he turned his attention back to the store window display. He reached down into his pocket, pulling out a crumpled wad of bills. Counting it quickly, he decided there was enough for two of the big, golden-haired dolls and the train. Maybe he could even get a doll for Sarah and a painted top for Teddy, as well as gifts for his other family members.

He stepped inside the warm store, glad to be out of the biting December wind. Minnesota certainly wasn't known for its mild winters! He purchased the toys, asking the gray-haired man behind the wooden counter to wrap each gift. Smilingly the man agreed, and began pulling out patterned paper and bright colored ribbons from beneath the counter.

"I'm going to look around a bit while you wrap those," Adam told the man, and the man replied congenially, "Certainly, sir, go right ahead. Take your time."

Adam browsed casually, picking up a round polished rock paper weight, bouncing it in his hand once before deciding it would look nice on Daniel's work desk. He found a kaleidoscope for Becky, and spent a few cheerful minutes peeking into the brass tube, enjoying the varying designs that appeared as he turned the end.

On another table there were woolen scarves of every imaginable color, and he chose a blue one for Arn and a green one for Frank. For Si he selected thick, wool-lined gloves of brown suede.

He came across a glass-covered jewelry case. On black velvet rested brooches and necklaces, earrings and bracelets, each set with colored rhinestones. He chose a heart-shaped pin with a red center stone for Laura, and dainty necklaces of crystal teardrops on gold-plated chains for Josie, Anna, and Rose.

Moving on, he came to a large display of music boxes. He lifted the lid on the one closest to him, smiling as a tinkling melody spilled forth. A saleslady came up behind him.

"May I help you?" the smiling young woman asked.

Adam turned and found himself being appraised. He grinned, gesturing to the boxes. "These are sure pretty," he said.

"Yes, sir, they are," she agreed, smiling at him flirtatiously. "Any young lady would be pleased to receive one. Do you have a special young lady in mind?" Her tone held an interested question mark.

Samantha's face appeared before Adam's eyes. Yes, he had a special young lady in mind. But how would he get it to her? Buying one would be foolhardy, Adam knew, almost tempting fate. It was illogical, unreasonable, and probably even a waste of his hard-earned money. Adam found himself answering, "Yes, I do."

The saleslady seemed to deflate momentarily, but then she remembered herself, and inquired brightly, "Which one do you think she would prefer?"

Adam's eyes drifted across the selections. There were at least fifteen music boxes, each with a different picture inlaid on the tops with what appeared to be bits of shell. His eyes roved, and one jumped out at him. It had a gold filigreed edge, with a cream colored pearlized cover. Centered on it was a perfect opened rose, each petal set individually in varying shades of palest pink to deep burgundy. It brought to mind the dress Samantha had made, the one covered with roses and trailing vines.

He pointed. "I'll take that one," he said decisively, and the saleslady scooped it up and carried it to the counter.

Adam leaned against the wooden counter as the saleslady poked around somewhere below it, scouting for something. She finally stood, a scowl on her face. "I would like to wrap it in paper and put it in a box. It would be safer that way. But I can't find a box," she said in exasperation.

"Stay here," she directed. "I'll have our stockman look in the storage room. Surely there's something there that will hold your music box." And she moved away, her pointed-toed shoes clicking purposefully on the tiled floor.

Adam gathered up the toys he had purchased while he waited, stacking them carefully. He felt a bubble of happiness pressing against his heart, thinking of Samantha's hands holding that rose-covered music box. She would love it, he knew she would.

"We found one, sir!" the saleslady's voice intruded. He looked over his shoulder to see the saleslady approaching, followed by a tall, slender young man. The young man held a stack of boxes in his freckled arms. There was something vaguely familiar about him.

"Just put those under the counter, David," the saleslady instructed the stockman, and then she reached for Adam's music box. "We'll get you fixed up in no time, sir," she said cheerfully, and began wrapping the music box with plain brown paper.

Adam watched the stockman bend to place the supply of empty boxes below the counter, then straighten to leave. David, the woman had called him. Adam stared, trying to understand why the man seemed familiar. He was tall, his face freckled slightly, his head covered with auburn curls that seemed unable to behave. And his eyes were pale cornflower blue, just like—

Adam's jaw dropped. *David*.... Could this be Samantha's David? The brother who had run away? The stockman was heading to the back of the store. Adam said hurriedly, "Excuse me, I'll be right back," to the saleslady, and trotted after the man.

"David," Adam called.

The stockman turned around, his thin face attentive. "Yes?" he asked. "May I help you?"

Adam wasn't sure how to broach the subject. One couldn't just come out and ask if he had run away as a boy and left behind a sister! "I was wondering…" he said, pulling at his cheek with one hand. The man was watching him strangely. Adam laughed nervously. "This is really awkward," he admitted. "I need to ask you something, if I could."

The man called David didn't answer, just shrugged.

Adam plunged on. "Do you have a sister? A sister named Samantha?"

David's cornflower eyes narrowed, and his glance darted around the store as if seeking someone out. His eyes came back to Adam. "Why do you want to know?" he asked suspiciously.

Adam recognized in the tall young man the same defensiveness that Samantha possessed. It was uncanny, the physical resemblance and the familiar mannerisms.

"I'm a friend of Samantha's," Adam said. "She told me about a brother named David, whom she hasn't seen in several years. I just wondered if it might be you."

David stood still, staring off somewhere behind Adam, his face expressionless. For Adam it was eerie. It was as if seeing Samantha again, only not Samantha. Think how excited she would be if this was her brother!

"I'm sure there are dozens of Davids in the city," the man said now, his voice hollow. "I'm sorry, but I'm not the right one. I don't know anyone named Samantha."

And he turned and walked away quickly, disappearing through a swinging wooden door. Adam watched him go, frowning. He wasn't sure he believed what the man said. He couldn't be certain the man was Samantha's brother—it could be wishful thinking on Adam's part that made him see the similarities between the two—but he got the impression that David *was* Samantha's brother and was unwilling to admit it for some unknown reason. Whatever the reasons, Adam wouldn't press the issue now. He knew the name of the store, and he could come back. With that thought in mind, he gathered up his purchases and left.

Adam had no more than left the store, his arms laden with packages, than David emerged from the back area of the store and rushed to the front windows, watching as Adam headed down the snow-covered walkway. David sighed, pressing his forehead against the cold glass. He thought back to that night seven years ago, when he had kissed his little sister goodbye and sneaked away, promising to come back for her. She'd been only ten or so then, a skinny little waif with too much hair for her slender neck.

Seven years... Samantha would be grown now, a woman. The man had said he was a friend. The man was well-dressed, polite, obviously from a good family. How would Samantha have met someone like him, coming from their part of town? What was she like now? Was she still with Pa? So many questions... And that man could have answered them, had David summoned the courage to ask.

He pushed away from the window, heading back to his work area. He thought of Pa. Had Pa changed at all? For Samantha's sake, he hoped so. Life with him had been unbearable. David carried the emotional scars of his childhood yet.

There had been no choice about leaving—it had been a necessity. But guilt overwhelmed him as he remembered having to leave Samantha behind. He had wanted to bring her with him when he stole away, but how could he have? She was just a kid—she would've needed caring that he couldn't give, not on the run like he was. He couldn't have dragged her along. Did she understand how hard it had been for him to go without her?

He had worried so often over the years, wondering if Pa had taken out his anger at David's escape on the unwitting Samantha. The guilt had been horrible! Even now, it swept over him. He had promised to go back for her, and he had meant to. But as time passed and he settled into his new life here in the city, away from his father and the horrible memories of the past, it had been easy to neglect that promise. Going back for Samantha would have meant dredging up the past. And David had no interest in moving backward.

He wished he would have been able to ask that man about Samantha, if she was well, if she was happy. But how could he ask without giving himself away? And if Samantha knew where he was, then Pa would know. Thoughts of Pa could still frighten him, even now. If only he could see Samantha without having to see Pa, then maybe... No, it wouldn't work. Pa would know. Pa always found out about everything, somehow.

Well, he told himself now as he made himself get back to work, *if she has a friend in that young man, she must be doing okay. I don't need to worry about Samantha anymore.*

Still, it was hard not to be curious. His baby sister....

Adam deposited his purchases at the stately two-story home his brother and sister-in-law occupied. He had to spend a few moments fending off questions about the many ribboned packages from Christina before he could tell Rose he was going out again. He bundled up once more and caught a horse-drawn cab to ride to Daniel's law office.

"Daniel, I need your help," he burst out the minute he stepped through the door.

Daniel's eyebrows rose, but he set aside the papers he had been examining. "Professional or brotherly?" he inquired dryly.

Adam grinned. "Both, I guess. I was just at Smothers' Department Store, and I met a man…" Adam filled Daniel in, on how the man's name was David and how he resembled Samantha physically right down the spattering of freckles across the bridge of his nose. "I'm certain the man is Samantha's brother, but he denies it."

Daniel leaned back and rested his elbows on the armrests of his chair, making a steeple of his hands in front of his chest. "So what do you want me to?" he asked his younger brother.

Adam spoke earnestly, "I want you find out if he *is* who I think he is—if he is Samantha's brother David. Can you imagine what it would mean to Samantha, to have him back in her life? Why, she'd be beside herself with joy!"

Daniel rocked his chair a couple times, his head cocked. "Adam, it would be a simple matter to check at the store, find out this David's full name. If his last name is O'Brien, I think that would prove to be too much of a coincidence to over- look. Then I would say he is Samantha's missing brother. But, Adam, proving who is he, and reuniting him with Samantha are two different things. Have you considered why he might have told you he wasn't the man you were looking for? Have you considered that perhaps he has no interest in being reunited with Samantha?"

Adam shook his head, frustrated. It was beyond his com- prehension that a brother would refuse to reunite with a sister.

"I just figured maybe I caught him off guard. It must have been a shock! I tried to be discreet, but to have Samantha mentioned after being separated for all these years.... No, I'm sure if he really is Samantha's David, that he will want to see her."

"Well, then," Daniel continued, sounding less like a lawyer and more like a brother, "I think you need to consider something else. Samantha lost her brother a long time ago. From what you've said in the past, she feels abandoned by him. What will she think if she finds out he has been as near as a ten hour train ride all these years—and never made the effort to come for her? Are you sure that wouldn't be more hurtful to her?"

Adam wasn't sure how to respond to that. Yes, the old Samantha—the sullen, withdrawn girl that had arrived at the Klaassen farm—would certainly be angry and bitter at the knowledge that her brother had been this close, yet stayed away. But the new Samantha, he felt, would be willing to forgive. The new Samantha would at least make an effort to understand.

Adam decided, "We have to take that chance, Daniel. Her brother is all she has in the world. She needs him back in her life."

Daniel shrugged. "I hope you're right, little brother, because if I go poking my professional nose into this man's business—and he is who you think he is—I am going to be opening one big can of worms."

Adam smiled. "Big brother, open away."

Chapter Twenty

$\mathcal{S}$amantha had gathered evergreen boughs and tiny red holly berries. Carefully she draped the greenery along windowsills and shelf edges, dotting it with the bright berries. She had no tree, but this bit of decoration was almost as nice, she decided as she stepped back to survey her work. She placed two thick candles on the windowsill and swished a match along the underside of the sill, cupping the flame as she raised it to light the candles. *There,* she thought, smiling at the result, *that looks pretty.*

It was Christmas Eve. She would be leaving soon to go to the service at church. She had received a special invitation from the young minister, Reverend Johansen. It had taken her by surprise, but she had recovered quickly, managing to smile in a friendly manner and thank him without conveying any additional meaning. The blonde, blue-eyed man had acted a bit disappointed by her casual response, but hadn't pressed the issue. For Samantha, no one—not even a handsome, well-stationed man such as Reverend Thomas Johansen—could measure up to Adam Klaassen.

Burt was in his small bedroom, sleeping. He had staggered home almost two hours ago having spent most of the afternoon at his favorite tavern. Samantha had helped him into bed, and he'd been sleeping ever since. She could hear his snoring from out here. She checked the small wind-up clock on the table. Almost seven. She really should be going or she would be late. She tip-toed across the wooden floor and tapped lightly on Burt's door. No answer—just a snuffle and the squeak of the mattress as he apparently rolled over in his sleep.

Samantha cracked the door. "Pa?" she called softly. "Pa, I'm going to the church now."

Burt made a growling sound as he came awake. He sat up groggily, and turned his bleary gaze on Samantha, blinking as if to clear his vision.

"Wha—whaddaya wan'?" he asked belligerently. Samantha bit her lower lip. He was still pretty drunk. The nap hadn't done him much good. She stepped a bit further into the room.

"I'm going to the church now," she repeated, keeping her voice low. Burt couldn't abide loud noises when he was coming down off of a drunk. "Can I get something for you before I go?"

Her final word penetrated the fog of Burt's alcohol-laden brain, and he swung his feet over the edge of the bed, swaying and grabbing at his bedside table as he struggled to find his balance. "Go?" Burt exploded. "You ain't goin' no place, girlie!"

Samantha took a hesitant step backwards. "But, Pa," she said reasonably, "it's just to church. I'll be home in an hour, and we can have some cider together."

"I said, *no!*" he burst out. Burt swung his arm, knocking the china bowl and pitcher from the table beside his bed. The subsequent crash made him clutch his ears in agony. "Oooh!" he moaned. "My head! My head!"

Samantha rushed to his side. "Are you all right, Pa? Here, let me help you." She reached for him, but he slapped her hands away.

"No," he bellowed, making more noise than the breaking china had, "git away from me! Jus' leave—go on, git! Jus' go!"

Samantha hovered, uncertain and scared. He was so unpredictable!

"I—I'll clean up this mess," she gestured to the broken pieces of china scattered across the floor, "so you don't cut yourself." And she knelt, beginning to stack the larger pieces together.

Burt stared at her glassy-eyed, mumbling, "Yeah, yeah, you clean it up. Allus so worried 'bout 'er Pa. Allus takin' keer of 'er Pa. But she don' really keer. Not really. She don' really keer—nobody does, nobody…."

Samantha heard the ominous tone creep into her father's voice. She understood what was happening, having lived it hundreds of times before. *Oh, God, please, not again….*

Burt lurched to his feet. "You don' really keer," he roared, his face near hers, his breath hot and foul-smelling. His hand snaked out and he caught her by the arm, shaking her violently. "Ya left me! Jus' like yore ma, ya left me! Took off—you, an' Davey an' 'Livia. Ya don' keer! Yo're nothin' but a liar, S'mantha! A liar!"

Samantha screamed as he released her to swing his arm, the back of his hand striking her hard across the cheek. She tasted blood, and she tried desperately to duck away. He raised his hand again, continuing his verbal barrage with loud curses. The second blow caught her on the side of the head, making her ears ring. In defense, Samantha brought up her arms to protect her face. Her elbow caught him under the chin and he stumbled, falling heavily forward. He hit the table as he fell, taking it with him. Samantha scrambled sideways, crawling across the pile of the shattered china. Both of her knees and the palms of her hands were cut, but she paid little attention to the pain. Her focus was on escape.

Once she was out of her father's reach, she untangled her skirts from around her knees and rose clumsily to her feet. She looked back at her father. He had passed out and remained on the floor as he had fallen, the table lying beside him, one table leg broken and hanging crazily. She slumped against the doorway in relief. She was safe. For now.

Samantha remained in the doorway, breathing heavily. The inside of her mouth had been cut by her teeth and the sickening taste of blood filled her mouth. She touched her cheek. It felt swollen, and her fingers encountered a small amount of blood where he'd broken the skin on her cheekbone. *Some snow*, she thought, *I'll put some snow on it*. She staggered to the door, swinging it wide and breathing in the cold, clean air. She shivered, but stayed where she was, letting the cold air wash her clean of the horror of the last few moments. It had happened so quickly! Finally, she scooped up a handful of snow and placed it gingerly against her cheek. It stung, but she knew it would keep the swelling down.

Stepping back inside, she closed the door and leaned against it tiredly. The clump of snow began to melt in the warm room, and a trickle of wetness ran down her arm. Her palms and knees stung, her head ached, and she trembled weakly. She stumbled across the floor to wilt resignedly into her rocking chair. She set the chair in gentle motion. She would not be attending church this evening.

Laura leaned across a lapful of packages to whisper in Si's ear. "I think we have our Adam back."

Si simply smiled his reply, squeezing his wife's hand. He had to agree. Both of them watched Adam, who sat on the window seat, bouncing little A.J. in his lap and intoning, "Giddyap, horsie, go to town…" much to the delight of the chubby infant.

The time in Minneapolis had been beneficial. Adam had returned relaxed and happy, at peace with himself, his balance restored. He still missed Samantha, they knew that as surely as they knew she would always hold a special place in his heart. But he had been able to release her into the Lord's keeping, and subsequently could let loose of the bitterness her parting had incurred. Both of his parents were relieved and grateful.

As for Adam, it was good to be home. He had accomplished quite a bit in Minneapolis. Daniel had checked into the background of the man named David who worked at Smothers' Department Store. The man was known as David Bryant, and he clung to his story that he had no knowledge of a woman named Samantha O'Brien. Adam still didn't believe him, but, as Daniel had pointed out, it wasn't against the law to change your name or disown your relatives, so they had no way to force him into admitting the truth. Adam had left David Bryant his name and address in case he changed his mind, and all he could do now was hope for the best.

Coming home, he discovered, was bittersweet. Sweet to be among his dear family again, bitter because Samantha wasn't here to share in the homecoming. He hadn't placed the music box beneath the tree. It was hidden in his bedroom, under the bed behind the chamber pot. No one would look under there, he was sure! That gift was his promise to himself, to someday find Samantha. And when he had placed it in her hands, he wouldn't let anyone carry her away from him again.

"Adam, Adam, thank you!" Sarah exclaimed as she pulled from its wrappings the beautiful doll he had purchased in the city. "It's the prettiest one I've ever seen!"

Adam teased, "Are you sure you're not too big to play with dollies?"

"Never," Sarah sighed, staring in wonder at the china face complete with two tiny teeth, the perfectly curled ringlets, and the deep purple velvet dress.

"I'd rather have my kaleidoscope," announced tomboy Becky. "Thanks, Adam."

Adam grinned as one by one, his family opened the gifts he'd picked out for them.

It was a good feeling, making them happy. He realized how much his own unhappiness had affected them, and he made a decision to never again allow himself to become as despondent as he had been over Samantha's departure. No problem was worth distressing the people he loved. He needed to remember all of the lessons of his childhood—the most important one being, of course, that God is in control, and 'all things work together for good.'

At the Klaassen farm, Christmas day was bright with snow outside—and bright with happiness inside.

In Minneapolis, in cramped quarters above the department store where he was employed, David O'Brien—known to his fellow employees as David Bryant—sat on a worn sofa and sipped a cup of weak tea. He stared out the curtainless window at the falling snow. It seemed the whole world was white. White—colorless—matching David's mood.

On the battered table beside the sofa rested a folded piece of yellow paper. He reached out a slender hand and fingered it for the hundredth time. All it would take was a telegram to this Adam Klaassen and all of this soul-searching would be over. Should he? Should he open himself up to this stranger—this man who claimed to be a friend?

He dropped the paper and sighed. A tired sigh. He was so lonely. It seemed he'd been lonely his whole life long. As a child he didn't have friends—not the way other children were friends, visiting one another's homes and playing after school. He'd held himself away from the other children, ashamed of his tattered clothes (although Gran had made sure they were clean tatters) and ramshackle house…and his alcoholic father.

Especially his alcoholic father.

He'd tried to hide the fact that his father was a drunk, but everyone had known. He'd heard the titters of his classmates when his back was turned, calling his father Ol' Burpy Burt. A stupid name—should have even been funny. But it wasn't. It had hurt. It still hurt.

At least he'd had Gran, and there'd been his little sister, Samantha. He closed his eyes, sliding downward on the threadbare cushions and holding the now-cold mug two-handed against his stomach. He could remember the night Samantha was born. He had been quite young—only seven—but he remembered.

He remembered Mama crying out, and Pa stomping around the room with a white face, cursing in fear. He remembered a doctor emerging from the bedroom and announcing somberly, "I'm sorry. There was nothing I could do. She hemorrhaged. She's gone." David hadn't known what hemorrhage meant, but he knew what the doctor meant when he'd said his mama was gone. He remembered throwing himself into the corner, weeping inconsolably at the loss of his mother. He remembered Gran showing him a tiny, red-faced bundle and telling him he had a baby sister. He remembered thinking he'd rather just have his mama back.

He drew a hand through his hair. His opinion had changed in a hurry though. Oh, he'd still missed and wanted his mama back. But that Samantha.... He smiled, remembering. She'd been such a smiley baby. Pretty, too. She'd wrapped him around her little finger the first time she'd given him her spitty, toothless smile. As she'd gotten bigger, he'd thought of her as a friend. She'd followed him around endlessly, getting her nose in the way of everything he did and asking enough questions to drive a fellow to drink!

That expression sobered him in a hurry. What kind of a life might they have had if Burt O'Brien hadn't been driven to drink? Try as he might, he couldn't remember a time when his father hadn't turned to drink to drown his sorrows. His Gran had told him that Burt had once been a fine man, a good worker and provider for his wife and baby son. But he couldn't remember that. Other memories crowded it out.

David scowled, his memories carrying him backwards. The night his mother was laboring to deliver Samantha, Gran had begged Burt to fetch the doctor—Olivia was in trouble. But his Pa had complained that they couldn't afford a doctor. Gran had secretly sent little David after the old doctor against Burt's wishes. And it had been too late. By the time the doctor had arrived, Olivia had begun to hemorrhage—to bleed, David knew now—and there wasn't anything he could do. Is that why Burt had started drinking, David wondered now. Did he hold himself accountable for Olivia's premature death? Could that be why he kept himself in a drunken stupor? In an attempt to forget his guilt? It seemed he'd always blamed his children, but maybe....

David shook his head. *Stop thinking about it!* he commanded himself. *It doesn't accomplish anything, to dwell on the past! You can't change what's been....* He stood abruptly and crossed to his dry sink, dropping the mug into a pan of oily water. He stood there, staring into the pan of unwashed dishes. *This is your life,* he told himself glumly. *No better, really, than the life you had before. Do you really want to drag Samantha down with you a second time?*

But would he be dragging her down? He wondered. Maybe she was as lonely as he was. Maybe…. He remembered a tousle-haired little girl who had turned adoring eyes in his direction. Oh, how he'd loved her! She'd been the best thing in his life. And he'd walked away from her. Would she be able to forgive him for that? Would she be able to understand why he hadn't returned?

David stamped across the quiet room to grab up the slip of paper bearing Adam Klaassen's address. Crumpling it tightly in his fist, he turned to stare again at the falling snow. Great, fluffy flakes that coated everything, making the world clean and bright. Not colorless, as he'd thought before, but new and full of promise.

All right, then. He relaxed his fist, then smoothed the paper flat against his palm. The decision was made—he'd do it. He'd find out. If she wouldn't accept him, he'd be no worse off than he was right now. But he'd never know until he tried.

Chapter Twenty-one

The telegram arrived two days after Christmas. Hiram had his young assistant, Will Boehr, immediately saddle a horse and deliver the news to Adam. Adam read the stilted message—"Am Sam's brother. Would like contact. Please reply. David O'Brien"—and let out a whoop that startled the chickens into nervous flapping.

It took Adam the price of a month's worth of peppermint drops (and kept the telegraph lines buzzing) to finalize his plans with David to meet, but it was well worth the time and expense. The day before January 1, 1918, Adam was rattling across the country in a smoky train car, heading for Milwaukee. In his pack he had the address provided by David to locate Samantha's home—or at least the home she had lived in as a child. If she was no longer there, it would give him a starting point to begin his search. He also had the Christmas gift he had purchased for her, the rose-topped music box. And a heart that was beating out a message in time with the rocking rhythm of the train: *I'm coming, I'm coming. Wait for me, wait for me.*

David, he presumed, was on another train right now, traveling to Mountain Lake. The two men had decided it would be best for Adam to bring Samantha back to his own home for the reunion—a neutral territory, so to speak. David would stay in town above the cafe in one of the small rooms the owner let out for overnight visitors, and Frank would bring him to the farm when Adam returned with Samantha.

Only a few more hours, my Samantha, Adam thought, *and I'll have you close again.* And this time Adam had no intention of ever letting her go.

When Adam disembarked from the train at the Milwaukee station, he was pleased to see a line-up of cab drivers ready and waiting to transport travelers. He approached a short, white-haired man who tipped his felt hat and inquired, "Need a ride, sir?"

"Yes, I do," Adam replied cheerfully, "to Front Street." And he produced the address he'd written down.

The man scowled and rubbed his raspy chin with glove-covered fingers. "Wal, I reckon I c'n getcha there. Got any bags I c'n holp ya with?"

Adam indicated his single travel pouch by lifting it once. "Just this."

"Wal, then, let's go," the little man said.

Soon Adam was bouncing through busy city streets, peering out anxiously as the horse skittered around new-fangled automobiles.

"Here, now, Tootsie," the man called to the animal in a soothing voice, "you just keep yer attention where it belongs!"

Adam smiled. It sure was different in the city—noisier, busier… He noticed the sky was tinged with a gray smoke, no doubt from the factories that dotted the outskirts of the city. There were more buildings than trees, more people than cows, and more automobiles than he'd care to deal with on a daily basis!

"Look out!" he called to the driver as one turned a corner sharply and nearly ran the poor horse off the street.

"Crazy fool nincompoop!" the cab driver yelled, shaking his fist at the inconsiderate vehicle driver. Then he turned an apologetic smile on Adam and said, "Oh, pardon me, sir, but those young people and their autos! Nothin' but a menace, an' a waste o' road space, if ya ask me!"

Adam just grinned. He could imagine Si's reaction if Adam turned up in one of those things! Daniel and Rose were talking of purchasing an automobile, but Adam felt more comfortable with a horse. A horse was safer, softer, and more companionable!

It took almost a quarter of an hour to reach the area of town where David had said his old home was located. Adam hopped out of the curtained cab and held out a coin to the driver as he said, "Thanks for the ride!"

"An' thank you, sir!" the man replied jovially, pocketing the money eagerly.

"Good day," Adam called, and stayed beside the curb as the horse named Tootsie carried its driver away. He perused the area. It wasn't a fancy neighborhood—most of the houses looked more like shacks—but somewhere Samantha was waiting. He began to walk.

There were no people outside today. It was too cold. Adam had his collar turned up and the flaps of his hat pulled down as protection, but the chill wind still crept beneath the layers of clothing and made him shiver. He walked briskly, stamping his feet down firmly against the ground to warm them. He counted the houses on Front Street as he walked—two, four, six.... There—number nine. That was where David said he had lived as a youngster, with his sister and father. Adam's heart hammered in anticipation.

The house was much like the others on the street—small, squat, weather-worn. A stovepipe jutted from the narrowly sloped roof, emitting a steady series of coal-scented puffs. The windows bore bright calico curtains that were pulled to the side and tied with yellow ribbons. He wanted to peek in, but a layer of frost covered most of the pane. His heart caroming wildly in his chest, he stepped to the warped, planked door and knocked.

After only a few moments, the door squeaked open, and there she stood—*Samantha*. The inside of the house was dark, shielding her in shadows, but he could make out her expression of happy surprise as her eyes widened and she exclaimed, "Why, Adam! What—" Then as suddenly as she had brightened, her expression turned wary, and she peered around him nervously, asking, "W-what are you doing here?"

Adam's bright smile changed immediately to a frown of concern as he got a good look at her in the sunlight. There was a sickly yellowish-green mark on her cheekbone, and her hands were wrapped with strips of cloth bearing blood stains.

"Samantha, what has happened to you?" he demanded, taking her chin gently and turning her face up to his.

She pulled away. "Nothing, really—just a little accident. Adam, as wonderful as it is for me to see you, you can't stay. Pa will be home soon, and—"

"But, Samantha," Adam interrupted, sorely disappointed. This wasn't the reunion he had hoped for! "I've come all this way to see you, and to tell you—"

A third voice cut in harshly from behind Adam. "Wal, wal, wal.... What've we got here? Comp'ny, huh? S'mantha, girl, why di'n't ya tell me you was 'spectin' comp'ny?"

Adam turned to face the same man who had carted Samantha away from him only two short months ago. By the drawl in the voice and his defensive stance—arms slightly akimbo, neck angled forward and jaw jutting—Adam knew Burt O'Brien was in an ornery mood. He kept his own body angled to protect Samantha. Behind him, he could hear her shallow, frightened breathing.

"Hello, Mr. O'Brien," Adam greeted in a steely voice, speaking almost through clenched teeth. "My visit is a surprise. Samantha did not know I was coming."

"Yeah, yeah," Burt dismissed Adam's words with a wave of an ungloved, dirty hand. The man's coat hung open, revealing his grime-covered shirt. He wore no hat to fend away the cold, and his lank, gray hair stood up in the wind. He approached the pair who hovered in the doorway of the ramshackle house. His voice still bore a menacing undertone as he snorted, "I ain't s'prised to see ya, boy. Knew that girl'd have comp'ny when I was out. When the cat's away...." And he laughed evilly, baring his tobacco stained teeth. He pointed past Adam's shoulder to his daughter, who cowered there, her eyes wide with fright. "You entertainin', girl? You lookin' to treat this feller like yore man?" he rasped loudly.

"Now wait just a minute," Adam intervened, sickened by the man's implications. "You have no right—"

Burt poked at Adam's chest with one short, stubby finger. "I got all the rights!" he argued belligerently. Adam winced. Up close, the man's stench was overpowering. "I got all the rights 'cause I'm her pa. Don't be tellin' *me* I got no rights!"

Adam held up his hands as a sign of surrender. The man was completely unreasonable—no doubt hurting from a lack of alcohol in his system which made him worse than when he was rip-roarin' drunk. Best to try and calm him.

"I'm sorry, Mr. O'Brien. I just want you to understand that Samantha has done nothing wrong. I came here to bring her some news, and to deliver a Christmas gift." The mention of the Christmas gift suddenly reminded Adam that when he'd been delivered to Front Street, he'd been so anxious to get to Samantha that he had mistakenly left his bag on the cab. *The music box!*

He turned to Samantha and began to explain, "I brought you a gift, but I accidentally left it—"

When Adam turned his back to Burt, the older man was filled with anger. *Why, he's dismissin' me like I 'as nothin'!* his distorted mind told him. *Turnin' his back on me like I don' even matter.... I'll teach'im!* He stumbled forward two steps and took hold of Adam's coat sleeve, jerking him mightily.

Adam spun around, startled. Before he could recover, Burt planted his fist firmly into Adam's mid-section. Adam was surprised by the amount of strength behind the punch considering Burt's age and obvious poor health. He doubled over with a loud, "Hooph!"

"Pa, don't!" Samantha begged, trying to come between them, but Adam held out an arm to keep her back.

"Go back in the house, Samantha," Adam ordered softly, his eyes on Burt.

Burt laughed and waved at Samantha. "Yeah, girlie, go in the house. Let us men handle this'un." His voice held a warning that demanded obedience.

Reluctantly Samantha backed up, but remained in the doorway, watching with wide, fear-filled eyes.

"Mr. O'Brien, I don't want to fight you," Adam said calmly, his breath restored.

"No, you jus' wanna see my girl!" Burt responded, his face twisted in an ugly scowl. "Wal, ya can't, so jus' git on outta here! Git!"

When Adam didn't immediately turn tail and run, Burt cursed angrily and charged, fists flying. Adam fended off the older man's blows with difficulty. Burt was unsteady on his feet, weakened from the cold and the alcohol that had damaged his system, but he had the tenacity of a fire ant, Adam thought. The men tussled, Burt pursuing and Adam doing his best to deflect the blows rather than deliver any of his own. At one point they fell, rolled several times, and came back up again, their clothing coated with snow. They had worked their way nearly to the street.

"Pa, stop it! Please!" Samantha pleaded from the doorway. "Just let him go!"

Burt pulled away from Adam to glare at his daughter blearily. His breath came in heavy white puffs, and his chest heaved from the effort. He pointed at Samantha. "*You!*" he hollered in a grating voice, "You brung this on! You wan'ed 'im to come, din'cha?"

Samantha covered her mouth with both hands and shook her head. Her blue eyes were huge and shimmered with unshed tears.

"Liar!" Burt sneered. "Nothin' but a *liar*. Girl, I'm gonna—" He started for the house in his uneven gait. Adam reacted instantly. He couldn't let the man hurt Samantha again! Grabbing Burt by the arm, he pulled him backward, swinging him away from the house and toward the street.

"Why, you," Burt growled, and doubled up his fist.

Just then, Tootsie rounded the corner, her driver calling, "You there, sir, you left a package on board!"

To Samantha, watching from the doorway, the world suddenly took on an aura of unreality. Burt whirled to see who was coming and lost his balance, falling heavily into the street. Even as Samantha screamed, his hands came up in a useless attempt to protect himself as Tootsie reared, confused and frightened by the strange lump at her feet. Adam reached frantically to grab the horse's bridle, pulling her head down to keep her from stamping again. The driver jumped out of the cab, crying out, "Oh, good Lord in heaven, what've I done?"

The driver managed to back Tootsie away from Burt, but the damage was done. Adam could see the man's neck cocked at on odd angle as he lay in the snow. His arms were outflung, the dirty palms facing up, the fingers relaxed and unmoving. A thin trickle of blood ran from his ear. Adam knew he was dead.

Samantha's sobs cut through the air. Adam ran to her, pulling her tight against his chest. She clung, crying, repeating in a pathetic voice, "Oh, Pa…Pa…."

"Shhh," Adam soothed. "Shhh. He's not hurting. And he can't hurt you now." He was holding her—not the way he had intended, but he had her in his arms. He cradled her closely, protectively cupping her head with his hand. He could feel her warm tears soaking into his collar, could feel her shoulders shaking convulsively.

"He's dead, Adam!" she cried. "Oh, he's dead!"

Adam could just hold her, rock her, comfort her. He placed a kiss on the top of her head, on her russet waves that were as untamable as the wind, letting his lips rest there as she sobbed against his neck.

Neighbors came from their houses, and two men picked up Burt's lifeless body and placed it in the back of the cab which still stood near the curb. The driver approached, twisting his hat in his hands sorrowfully.

"I'm so sorry," he said. He touched Samantha's shoulder briefly. "If I can do anything…?"

Adam spoke over Samantha's head. "Could you take the body to the undertaker's? I'll make arrangements for burial later."

"Surely, sir, surely," the man agreed, nodding his head jerkily. "Will the little lady be all right?" he asked, his concern obvious.

Samantha had quieted, but still clung tenaciously to Adam's coat front.

Adam nodded, his arms tightening around her. "Yes, I'll see to her, thank you."

The man nodded, placed his hat on his head, and left. Adam suddenly realized they had been standing out in the cold. He guided Samantha into the house, shutting the door against the curious neighbors. He helped her into a rocking chair that sat near the stove, and knelt in front of her, holding her hands. She kept her head down, refusing to meet his eyes.

Adam felt as if an icy hand was clutching his heart at her downcast expression. *Oh, Samantha, can't we have some peace?*

"Samantha," he said gently, almost begging, "I am so sorry about your pa. I didn't want to hurt him, you know that, don't you?"

She nodded, fresh tears spurting into her eyes. "Yes, I know," she said in a pitiful little voice. "Pa, he…. He's always…." She sobbed once, harshly, then said, "It was just so awful…."

"I know, I know," Adam soothed, smoothing the hair away from her tear-stained face. He stood. "Let me get you something hot to drink, and a blanket." He looked around the small space searchingly.

She reached out and grasped his hand. He looked down, and she met his gaze steadily as she said, "No, I don't need anything but…. Please, Adam, just hold me?"

Without a moment's hesitation Adam reached for her and scooped her up into his arms. He seated himself in the rocker, cradling her in his lap. She nestled against him, and his arms curved around her to provide warmth and comfort.

They sat that way until the coals in the stove burned themselves out and the sun slipped over the horizon.

Four days later Samantha and Adam stepped off the train in Mountain Lake into Si and Laura's waiting arms. Samantha clung to Laura, and the tears that had plagued her constantly since her father's death came again. But she smiled through her tears as she said, "It's so good to be here."

Adam watched as Samantha moved from Laura to Si, then down the row of brothers and sisters assembled, hugging each in turn. To him it was nothing short of miraculous that she would go willingly into an embrace—she had changed so much!

He hadn't had a chance to tell her about David yet. She had been so distraught about Burt, and then their time was tied up planning a memorial service (which was attended sparsely by neighbors, mostly out of compassion for the daughter left behind), then making arrangement for storage of the body until Spring, as the ground was too hard to dig a grave. He had half expected David to turn up at the funeral, and that would have brought the separation to an end. He had telegraphed his parents to inform them of Burt's accident, so he was sure David was aware of his father's death and knew that Samantha would be returning to Mountain Lake. Samantha would need to be told about her brother soon.

"Samantha, do you want to come to our home," Liz was asking, her arm still around the younger woman, "or go on and stay with Mother?"

Samantha looked from Liz to Laura, then back again. "I—I'm not sure." She shook her head and laughed ruefully. "The simplest decisions just seem beyond me these days."

Laura reached over to cup Samantha's cold cheeks in her hands and assured her, "That's fine, Samantha. Why don't we all come to the farm for our evening meal, and then you can decide where to go from there."

"You are welcome at either place," Liz hastened to add.

She'll be staying close to me, Adam thought.

Soon everyone was snuggled down in soft hay in the back of Si's big wagon with mounds of quilts protecting them from the January cold. They chattered cheerfully all the way home, and Samantha found herself joining in despite herself. It was so wonderful to be carefree and laughing again! She felt a twinge of guilt for not feeling despondent about her father's untimely death. But most of the unhappiness she felt at his passing was regret for what could have been, but wasn't. She had missed out on a lot, not having a loving father, and she had prayed for him so hard…. Now he was gone, and the chance for a loving relationship was forever gone. That was her sorrow.

As they gathered around the table for the evening meal, Samantha looked around at her surrogate family, her heart full. How lucky she was to have them! *Gran, you surely answered my prayers,* she thought gratefully. *I have so many people to love, and who really love me back! And they've given me so much….*

Her gaze traveled sideways to Adam. He was seated on her right, as if afraid to let her out of his sight. His nearness made her feel protected and secure—yes, even loved. He had been her beacon of strength during these past, difficult days. She couldn't imagine what she would have done without him.

They held hands to pray, and when Si said, "And thank you, Lord, for bringing our Samantha safely here again," Adam squeezed her hand briefly. Samantha peeked at him, and they both smiled.

Ah, it was good to be home.

Chapter Twenty-two

Adam waited until breakfast was over, the clean up was complete, and the younger children had left for school before he approached Samantha. He had gone over in his mind a dozen different ways to tell her about David, but still wasn't quite sure how to bring up the subject. He knew she still possessed bitterness about the broken promise he had made to return for her. He hoped she could get past the hurt and move on to acceptance.

She was in the kitchen, laughing with Laura over something that Sarah had said at the breakfast table when he came up behind her and touched her lightly on the shoulder.

She turned, and the happy look of contentment on her face was enough to take his breath away. "Yes, Adam?" she asked, her head tipped in query.

"Could we go into the parlor and talk for a little while?" he asked, fiddling with the buttons on his flannel shirt. "There's something I need to discuss with you."

Samantha flashed a puzzled look at Laura, who simply smiled and turned back to her silverware sorting. She looked back at Adam and shrugged, "Okay."

Adam guided her with a hand on the small of her back, gesturing for her to sit in the upholstered settee. Once she was situated, he pulled a small parlor chair forward and seated himself, their knees almost touching. He ran a nervous hand through his hair once, then leaned forward, resting his elbows on his knees and clasping his hands in front of him.

Samantha watched his every move with growing unrest. His uncustomary nervousness made her uneasy, as well. Something was certainly pressing on him! A sudden fear clutched her heart: perhaps he wanted to send her away! He'd seen where she'd come from now—maybe he'd decided she wasn't the type of person he wanted in his life.

She asked in a quivering voice, "Adam, is there something wrong?"

"What?" He almost seemed startled, and after a moment of hesitation he reached out to pat her knee once before answering, "Oh, no, nothing's wrong. I just need to tell you something, and it's hard to know how to get started."

It was odd for her to be on the reassuring end, but she encouraged him gently, "You've never had any trouble talking to me before. Why not just get it out in the open? And we'll deal with it."

He liked her attitude, and his smile told her so. "Okay, then," he replied. He slapped his hands down hard on his thighs, took in one big breath, and announced, "Samantha, I have located your brother, David."

He might have just announced he was a foreign spy, judging by Samantha's reaction. She gasped, straightened and placed a hand on her heart which seemed suddenly incapable of beating. Her mouth dropped open, her eyes grew wide as a full moon, and she stammered, "*W-what* did you say?" She looked like she might suffer apoplexy. Had she heard him correctly? Had he truly said *I've found your brother*?

Adam immediately apologized, moving to sit beside her and fan her rapidly with one hand while patting her on the back with the other. "Oh, Samantha, I shouldn't have blurted it out like that! It's just that I knew you missed him, but you're still rather angry with him, and I wasn't sure the best way to say it, so I just *said* it. I wanted you to know right away because he's here in Mountain Lake, and he's so anxious to see you—and I'm sure you'll want to see him once you're over the shock, and—"

Samantha had recovered. She reached out to place a small hand over Adam's mouth. "Please stop talking," she said kindly, "and take me to my brother."

Adam fought a lump in his throat as he witnessed the reunion between David and Samantha. The tall, gangly man clung to the slender young woman, both of them alternately laughing and crying as they kept exclaiming over and over again, "I can't believe it's really you!"

When the initial excitement died down, David held his sister at arm's length and shook his head in astonishment. "I just can't believe this. You're all grown up! And you're so pretty, Sam. All these years I've pictured you as the little girl I left behind...."

He sobered and impulsively cupped her face with his long-fingered hands. "Oh, Sammy, I am so sorry I didn't come back for you. I am so, so sorry.... Can you ever forgive me?" His voice was anguished.

Samantha placed her hands over his, looking up into the cornflower blue eyes that matched her own. She answered sincerely, "There's nothing to forgive, Davey. I have you back again, and that's all that matters."

They hugged again, rocking slightly. Samantha's muffled voice came from somewhere in David's shirt front. "Davey? I love you, but I can't breathe in here."

David released a loud burst of laughter, startling himself. He couldn't remember the last time he'd laughed out loud. Only five minutes of having his sister back, and he was laughing aloud! It was wonderful.

Adam stepped in then. "I hate to break this up, but how about we take it out to the house? I know Mother and Father are anxious to see you two together. The kids'll be home from school before too much longer, and there will be no peace after that. If we want a quiet conversation, you'd better come now."

David released his fierce grip, but still kept Samantha close to his side with one arm curled around her waist. He said, "Yes. I would like to get to know the family that befriended Sam." He pulled his gaze away from Samantha and looked Adam full in the eyes. "Thank you, Adam, for being Sam's friend. I think you are probably the best thing that ever happened to her."

Adam stuck out his hand for a firm handshake, and stated without a qualm, "She is as good for me as I am for her."

Samantha's heart started thumping a joyous double-beat at his words. Did he mean that the way it sounded? Oh, she hoped....

The evening that followed was the happiest in either David or Samantha's memory. Laura prepared a homecoming feast fit for royalty, and afterward the entire family, including Frank's betrothed, Anna, gathered in the parlor to light a fire in the fireplace, pop popcorn and drink hot homemade apple cider spiced with cinnamon and cloves. Samantha and her brother could not be parted. They sat as close as two corn kernels on a cob, and their joy at being together once again was beautifully heartwrenching.

It was with reluctance that David said his goodbyes and readied himself for the ride back into town. Frank was driving Anna home and would drop David off at his boarding room on the way. David and Samantha hovered on the porch step, wrapped in a tight hug. David spoke against her hair.

"No more unfulfilled promises for either of us now, Sammy," he said. "This time, I'm in your life to stay."

She beamed up at him, tears shimmering on her eyelashes. "That's the only way I'll have it, David," she replied.

A quick kiss, and he hopped off the step and ran to climb into the wagon. The Klaassens called out, "Good night!" as the wagon lumbered out of the yard. Everyone headed back into the warm house for one more handful of popcorn before retiring to bed.

Liz came up behind Adam and whispered knowingly, "So when are you going to propose?"

Adam spun around, surprised. "You better just hush that up!" he exclaimed, hands on hips in a stern stance.

Liz just laughed. "Oh, nobody's listening—they're all having too much fun. So…. When?"

Adam played dumb. "When, what?"

She punched him on the shoulder. "You know what! It's as plain as the nose on your face. You love her. You're glowing, just having her back here. So when are you going to let her know?"

Adam scratched his chin thoughtfully, looking across the room at Samantha, who was surrounded by his family and obviously at home in their midst. "Soon, I hope," he admitted.

"But her life has been full of half-promises and uncertainties. I need to make sure that when I propose, I have more than just my name to offer her. When I promise to care for her, I need to have a home ready, I need—" He stopped because Liz was shaking her head in amused exasperation.

"Adam, you don't get it."

He wasn't playing at being dumb now. He had no idea what she was inferring.

"I don't get what?" he demanded, half insulted by her knowing smile.

"That Samantha is so head over heels in love with you, she needs nothing more than *you*." Liz leaned against him lightly with her shoulder, bumping him as if to say, *silly man*.

"That's all?" Adam asked, his left eyebrow cocked higher than the right. He clearly didn't believe her.

Liz laughed. "That's what I like about you, Adam. You really don't have a conceited bone in your body." She socked him again in sisterly fashion. "Yes, you silly goose!" She went on gaily, "If it will make you feel better, ready your home and do whatever else you think needs doing. But I'm telling you right now, all that will be more for your benefit than Samantha's. The offer of your name is all she needs."

Adam appreciated Liz's advice, but he wasn't quite convinced. He was the one who had listened to her pour out her hurts in the old shed behind the depot. He was the one who had helped dry her tears after her father's accident, understanding that her hurt was more for the loss of what could have been than losing him. She needed security and promises that would be kept. No, Liz might be right in some things, but this time she was most certainly wrong. He had a lot of things to work out before he could officially ask Samantha to be his wife. And he knew just where to get started.

The next three weeks, Adam was rarely at the house. The winter months were the slow months on a farm. Not having crops to attend, the men had a few hours of precious free time. So once morning chores were completed, Adam disappeared, returning briefly for his noon meal, then taking off again until it was time for milking in the evening. Although his family questioned him—Sarah nearly pestered the patience out of him!—he refused to tell anyone where he spent his time, or what he was doing.

The rest of the family had no secrets, though. Si and Frank spent most of their day in the barn, working on furniture for the small frame house that had been erected in a tree-laden area near the soybean fields to the west of the Klaassen's homestead. Frank and Anna's wedding was nearing, and Frank was readying the house like a mother robin readies her nest. Laura was busy finishing the quilting on a lovely double wedding ring quilt, the rings of which she had made from cutting up some of Frank's and Anna's old clothing. It was a beautiful quilt, the colorful patchwork rings showing crisply against the bleached muslin. But more beautiful than the pattern was the thought behind it. Bits and pieces of each of the couple's past, sewn together into a circle—a never-ending symbol of love. Samantha longed for the time when she, too, would·make preparations for a home and family. And those longings always centered around Adam.

Samantha had taken several dress orders and kept her hands busy stitching, but her mind was restless, wondering where Adam was, what he was doing, who he was with... The beautifully feminine Priscilla Koehn niggled at the back of her memory.

Could he be spending his time wooing her? Priscilla would certainly welcome the attention!

She sat in the parlor, sewing the hem on a new dress for a friend of Laura's, trying to reassure herself that certainly Adam wouldn't have come clear to Milwaukee for her if he didn't care for her. But on the other hand, Adam was such a caring person, he probably would have done it for just about anyone he thought was in trouble. Still, she had gotten that one kiss from him, and he had held her so tenderly after Pa died… But then, she had been horribly upset. Maybe he was just comforting her the way he'd comfort Sarah if she was hurting.

If only she knew how she stood with him! He'd been wonderfully kind to her, had treated her as if she mattered deeply, but he'd never come right out and said how he felt. Was it simply brotherly affection, special friendship, or did he love her? She wished she had the courage to just come out and ask—that is, if she could pin the man down long enough for a conversation these days!

Where was he keeping himself lately? What could he be doing that would consume so much time? Christmas was over—it couldn't be Christmas secrets. But a secret it was. One of the best kept secrets ever! It was driving her to distraction, trying to figure out what his disappearances and smug smiles and boyish winks could mean.

She thrust the wadded up dress aside, her tangled emotions more that she could deal with. David had started working at the mercantile with Hiram Klaassen. Maybe she could ride Bet over there and visit with him for awhile. Maybe he could help her sort out her thoughts.

"Yes, you may take Bet to town," Laura agreed when Samantha asked permission, "But bundle up warmly. There's a feeling of snow in the air. And try to be back well before dark. I don't want you caught out in the cold."

Samantha was warmed by Laura's motherly caring. She gave Laura a brief hug before answering, "Yes, ma'am. I won't be long. And thank you!"

Soon she was on Bet's back, snuggled up in Laura's wool coat, gloves, and a blanket. It was hard to balance with everything wrapped around her, but she appreciated the protection from the cold weather. Snow was bone-chilling, but she had to admit it sure was pretty. Like frosting on one of Laura's scripture cakes, it coated the ground with a thick layer of shimmering white. Fence posts wore little pointed hats of snow, and leafless tree branches were dressed up with a fine lining. A pair of cardinals flitted through the trees above her head, their brilliant red a beautiful contrast in the world of white.

"You sure created a wonderful world, God," Samantha spoke aloud into the quiet beauty, startling a small white rabbit into a zigzagged escape. She laughed at the rabbit's frantic reaction to her simple words, and prodded Bet with, "Come on, old girl. Let's get a move on."

Samantha hitched Bet to the wooden rail outside Klaassen's mercantile and gave her a brief rub on her nose before entering the store. At the clang of the cowbell, David exclaimed, "Sam! Did you ride in?" He came from behind the counter, hands outstretched.

"Yes, just to see you," Samantha replied gaily, returning David's squeeze.

"Brr, you're cold," David shivered, pulling away. "Come over by the stove and warm up."

Samantha did as she was bid, gladly. She hunkered near the pot-bellied stove that kept the store toasty warm, rubbing her hands together. She looked around. "Where's Mr. Klaassen?" she asked.

David puffed up proudly as he answered, "Gone for the afternoon. He left me in charge—books and all!" David squatted down next to Samantha, a look of wonder on his face. "Can you imagine someone trusting the son of Burt O'Brien to care for his property?" He shook his head, baffled but pleased.

Samantha reached out to pat his knee. "Davey, you are much more than just Burt O'Brien's son. The Klaassens know that, and so do you, I think."

David nodded introspectively. "Still, it's hard to imagine…." He brightened and asked, "So! What brings you into town on this nippy day?"

"You," she said, and they both stood and moved to seat themselves on barrels. "I was feeling restless, and decided I needed a chat with my big brother."

They both beamed, and both hearts thrilled that they could be together again. "Got a case of cabin fever?" David teased.

Samantha shook her head. "No, not that. Not that kind of restlessness. I just need to sort out some thoughts."

David sobered immediately. "What's the problem, Sammy?"

Frowning, Samantha responded thoughtfully, "I'm not sure there is a *problem*, really. It's more like an unanswered question." She paused, chewing on her lower lip thoughtfully, her delicate brows pulled into a puzzled frown. After a moment, she raised her head to look at David and ask in a small voice, "Davey, do you think I'm good enough for Adam?"

David reared back and said sternly, "What kind of a question is that?"

Samantha rushed on, "He's seen where I come from, and he knows how Pa…. Well, you know. If you put our family up against his, look at the difference! Sometimes I think he cares for me, but other times…." She bit her lip again. "I don't know what to think."

"Well, *I* do," David said emphatically. "None of the Klaassens look down their noses at you—and that goes doubly for Adam! It's like you said to me a little bit ago—there's a heap-sight more to you than just being Burt O'Brien's daughter. Adam sees that."

Samantha sighed. "I want to think so, David, really I do! But since I've come back here he's been so odd. He spends all his time away from the house—away from me!—and he won't say where he is or what he's doing. I get the feeling he's avoiding me for some reason. Do you think he knows how I feel about him, and he's staying away to keep from telling me he doesn't feel the same?"

Instead of answering, David posed a question: "How *do* you feel about him?"

Samantha looked her brother straight in the eyes as she responded honestly, "I love him. I love him *so much*.... When I was away from him, I felt incomplete. When I'm with him, I feel like I'm a better, bigger person than I was before. Somehow he makes me *more* than I've ever been." She lowered her head, laughing self-consciously. "I suppose that sounds funny."

David reached over and made her raise her face. "No, Sammy, it isn't funny. It's wonderful, and I'm so happy you've found someone like Adam. If I could have hand-picked someone for you, I think I would have chosen him. He's a good man."

"Yes, he is," Samantha agreed, warmed by David's approval. "I just wish I knew if he cared at all for me, too."

David grinned. "Stop wishing, Samantha. Adam's got feelings for you, have no doubt! Now, I don't know what he's doing off by himself, but I can almost guarantee it's not to avoid spending time with you. That wouldn't be Adam's way of handling things. He'd come right out and tell you if he thought there was problem between you."

Samantha had to agree. Adam was open and honest. Surely he wouldn't run from a conflict. "Then what—"

David cut in, "Has it crossed your mind, little sister, that he's planning a surprise for Frank and Anna? Their wedding is when—next Saturday?" She nodded. "Well, my guess is he's off doing some special fixings for his brother and future sister-in-law."

"That would make sense," Samantha admitted. "If I only knew for sure…."

David stood up, pulling Samantha with him. "Well, don't stew about it. The wedding is only a week away. I'll wager a bet that you'll know soon enough what Adam's up to! In the meantime, try not to turn those puppy dog eyes on him at every turn, or he may end up spilling the beans and spoil a good surprise."

She laughed. "David, it's so good to have you back! It's wonderful to have my big brother to talk to."

"I feel the same," he said, pulling her close and resting his chin on her hair. "Now can I give you one more piece of big brotherly advice?"

She pulled her head back to peer up at him. "What's that?"

He ordered with mock sternness, "Get on your horse and go home before the sun drops any further. And when you get there, drink a cup of hot tea to warm up your innards."

Samantha grinned and answered meekly, "Yes, sir."

David walked her outside and helped pull the blanket close around her after she'd swung up into Bet's saddle. "'Bye, baby sister," he said tenderly.

She smiled her reply, and headed off for home.

Chapter Twenty-three

The evening before the big wedding day, Grandpa and Grandma Klaassen, Daniel and Rose, and little Christina and Katrina arrived by train. The house was filled with people and chattering and laughter. It was a happy chaos, but chaos just the same, and Samantha drew a shawl around her shoulders and stepped out onto the railed porch to enjoy a few moments of quietness.

She was stargazing, seemingly lost in thought, when Adam came outside. If she was aware of his presence, she gave no indication of it. Her eyes remained riveted on the black velvet sky which wore a spattering of sparkling diamonds. Adam perched himself carefully on the porch railing, watching his young friend. He'd been so busy lately, gone so much, that her beauty almost caught him by surprise. Hers was a simple beauty enhanced by her modest nature and caring spirit. In his eyes, she was a perfect gemstone set in a moonlit mounting of gold. His heart swelled in anticipation as he thought of the preparations he'd been making. The time was nearing to tell her of his plans. But for now he enjoyed simply watching her as she gazed heavenward.

At last she let out a contented sigh and turned to meet his gaze. She smiled self-consciously. "Did you think you were being ignored?" she asked.

"Maybe. Just a little." He shifted his weight to lean more comfortably as she turned to perch gracefully on the railing.

"Probably the way all of us have felt here lately, by you," she hinted. But he just smiled, refusing to rise to the bait. So she turned her attention to the sky again. She released an airy sigh and admitted, "The night never fails to move me."

He raised an eyebrow and prompted softly, "How, Samantha?"

She searched the sky, her eyes roving over the millions of stars sparkling brightly. "It's just so beautiful!" she said, her eyes as bright as the North star. "The sky is so soft and black—like fine velvet—and the stars blink and shimmer…. Sometimes I think they're winking at me, sending me a message from heaven—maybe from Gran. And I feel so close to them, I could just reach out and put one in my pocket to save for a sad day when I need some beauty." She raised her hand, the fingers reaching skyward. Then she peeked at him in embarrassment and let the hand drop. "I sound foolish, I reckon."

"For wanting to put a star in your pocket?" Adam asked, and, at her nod, added, "Not at all. That's like carrying around a special wish and being able to take it out and hold it now and then, knowing that it's yours to keep forever."

Samantha looked at him in surprise. "You *do* understand!" she exclaimed.

"Well, sure." Adam straightened to eye her gravely. "I have wishes, too, Samantha. We all do. They might be different desires, but no one *never* makes a wish on a star."

He turned back and tipped his face upward. "If I could put one in my pocket, I'd choose that one." And he pointed to an exceptionally bright star that blinked almost blue.

Samantha followed his gaze and said, "Yes, that's a nice one, but I'd choose"—she pointed, too—"that one, because it's smaller and kind of by itself, and looks as if it could use someone to love it." *Just like me.* The words, unspoken, hovered in the air between them.

Adam and Samantha stared at the star for a long time before Adam finally found the courage to ask softly, "Do you sometimes feel like that star, Samantha?"

Samantha felt her cheeks grow warm despite the chill of the night air. She was glad of the shadows that hid her blushing face. She answered in a tremulous voice that caught at Adam's heart, "Maybe. Sometimes. I used to feel very alone. But now...." And she turned to look him full in the face as she finished boldly, "Now, I feel I have people who care. I feel that my wishes could come true."

Their eyes locked. They stood so close she could feel his warm breath brushing her cheek as he exhaled. So close, he could see the reflection of the stars in her cornflower blue eyes.

Adam's heart thrummed. *Yes, Samantha, I will make all your wishes come true. Just be patient with me, let me make things perfect for you.*

Samantha's heart begged, *Tell me, Adam. Tell me you care and that you will be the answer to all my wishes. Tell me....*

But neither voiced their thoughts even as their gazes remained locked. And after several long, searching moments, the parlor door swung open, sending a shaft of golden light across their feet and surrounding them with the laughing voices of his family. Sarah called, "Mama says come in! We're gonna make taffy!" The door slammed, sealing them once again in peaceful darkness. Reluctantly Adam and Samantha stepped apart.

"Come, Samantha," Adam invited, holding out his hand. She placed her palm on his, felt his fingers curl around hers. Together, they went back to join his family.

The wedding day of Frank and Anna dawned bright and clear, one of those crisp windless winter days when the sun bounces off the snow, sending millions of shimmering diamonds back into the air. Samantha pulled aside the lace curtains that shrouded the parlor window and looked out at the perfect day. A hint of melancholy tugged at her. She wished... If only this could be her wedding day! Hers and Adam's...

"Samantha! Samantha!" Sarah's voice intruded into her thoughts, and Samantha turned around to catch Sarah as the child threw herself into a boisterous hug. "Samantha, see my pretty wedding dress?" And Sarah spun an impromptu pirouette in the shaft of sunlight that streamed through the bayed windows.

"It's lovely, Sarah," Samantha praised. The confection pink dress with miles of lace trim was an ideal wrapping for Sarah's china doll prettiness.

Sarah would be the flower girl, with Anna's youngest brother, Benji, as ringbearer. Anna's sister Katherine and Josie were serving as attendants to the bride. Daniel and Adam were standing up for Frank. Arn and Becky would be lighting the candles that lined each window sill and the edge of the altar at the front of the church. Anna's brothers Mort and Matthew were singing two songs, and Teddy would be

responsible for carrying all the gifts that arrived to a decorated table. Frank had exclaimed, exasperated, that if there
had been one more brother or sister to find a wedding
assignment for, they would have eloped. Anna had leaned
over and chided gently, "Would you rather have no family at
all?" Both had looked at Samantha, and Frank had ceased his
grumbling.

Daniel, Adam, and Arn had dressed up the buckboard
with huge tissue paper flowers and crepe paper streamers in
pink, yellow, and blue. Even Bet and Tick had paper flowers
on their ears, and they stamped their feet, blowing billows of
steam from their noses as they pranced, as if to say they
understood the importance of the day.

The ride to the church was full of joyous jabber and play-
ful ribbing. Frank sat nervous and twitchy, fiddling constantly with the perfect black bow tie that rested below his
chin. Samantha thought he looked particularly fine in his
wedding suit of black broadcloth and crisp white cambric
shirt. In her mind, she pictured Adam dressed in such finery,
standing at an altar in readiness for her walk down the aisle.
Sadness threatened to grip her. *Now stop it*, she scolded herself. *This is Frank's and Anna's day. Don't start moping!*

Everyone spilled out of the wagon when they reached the
churchyard. Other wagons and buggies were already there,
with people milling around outside, enjoying the sunshine.
Laura herded the younger children inside. Si, Arn, and Frank
unloaded the food and gifts the family had brought along.
Adam helped Grandpa and Grandma Klaassen down from
the high wagon seat and escorted them into the church.
Daniel and Rose each took a small daughter by the hand and
headed inside behind them. Samantha lagged behind, feeling
out of place and sorry for herself.

The service was brief considering the amount of time
spent in preparation for it. Anna's mother cried through

most of the ceremony, dabbing at her eyes with a lace hand-kerchief. Samantha found herself wondering what all the tears were about—was the woman overwhelmed with happiness or simply filled with regret? If it were Samantha's wedding day, would her mother-in-law-to-be shed tears of regret or joy over the choice her son had made?

She looked at Laura who was seated next to Si, her gently-lined face tipped upward and wearing a hint of a smile. Would she be wearing that same expression of contented happiness if it was Adam and Samantha at the altar?

Her eyes moved to Adam, standing so straight and tall, flanked by his brothers. He stood with his hands clasped at his spine, his eyes on the minister as he advised the young couple on the seriousness of their commitment. She felt tears sting her eyes. He was so handsome! *Oh, Adam, can't you see me as I see you?* her thoughts begged.

As if he sensed her yearnings, he turned his face slightly and his eyes sought her out. When he found her, he smiled, his lips tipping up and the corners of his eyes crinkling. He seemed to glow. Her breath caught. She sent him a timorous smile in return, her eyes shining, and then both turned their attentions back to the minister—at least they turned their *faces* back to the minister; their attention was definitely focused within.

Samantha's thoughts were racing, *I saw something in his eyes. Something different, something special. I saw....* She hardly dared to believe it. *I saw love.*

And Adam was thinking, *It will be our turn soon, Samantha. Soon it will be you and me standing here before our family and friends, exchanging vows that will bind us together for the rest of our lives. Believe it, Samantha. It will happen. Soon....*

Reverend Goertzen turned the couple to face the congregation and announced, "I present to you Mr. and Mrs. Frank Klaassen! Frank, you may kiss your bride."

Frank's face flooded with color as he leaned toward Anna and she lifted her face for his kiss. Their lips touched briefly, and as they separated, a whoop resounded, and the aisles were flooded with well-wishers.

Samantha found herself swept along with the throng. Somebody bumped her hard from behind, and she said, "Oh, excuse me!" as she turned to find herself face to face with Adam. He was still smiling that front-of-the-church smile— the smile that lit up his eyes and told of secrets he was waiting to share.

"I'm sorry I ran into you," he said softly, his hand resting lightly on her upper arm. People continued to mill around them, causing them to shift and move with the tide of bodies. But their eyes remained locked, each unable to look away.

"That's okay," she breathed. "You didn't hurt me."

A pause, and then he replied, "Good. That's the last thing I'd want to do." His brows came down momentarily, remembering the evening in Liz's yard when he'd frightened her so, and he asked, "You do know that, Samantha, don't you?"

She nodded slowly, still lost in the depths of his brown eyes. "Yes, Adam, I do know that." Oh, yes, she knew. She knew it better than she'd ever known anything.

He gave her that smile again, the tender, filled-with-promise smile that made her heart lurch and flutter and rise up into her throat. The wedding party was moving toward the double doors, Frank and Anna in the lead. Adam gently turned Samantha to join them.

They cheered when the others cheered, threw wheat kernels when the others tossed handfuls into the air, and even chased the buggy that bore the newlyweds toward their new home until it rounded the corner and headed out of town. But when their steps slowed, and the merrymakers had turned back to the church for the after-wedding celebration, they found themselves alone, side by side in the middle of Main Street.

Adam grinned and couldn't help teasing, "Remember the last time we ran down Main Street together?"

She blushed prettily, but she laughed. "Yes, you tackled me."

"You deserved it," he countered, and she surprised him by agreeing, "I did."

Her eyes sparkled with laughter. His sparkled with something else.

"Samantha," he said, "I'd like to show you something. Would you mind skipping the party at the church, and going for a ride with me instead?"

Her heart pounded hard in her chest. She shook her head, the movement barely discernible. "I'd love to go for a ride with you," she said, her voice low and full of meaning. She leaned toward him unconsciously, lifting her face, her blue eyes speaking volumes that her lips couldn't speak.

But Adam's heart understood the unspoken message that shone from her face. And he responded in kind. He leaned forward as if in slow motion, the wait agonizing for Samantha who held her breath and let her eyes slip shut as his face came nearer, nearer. Their noses bumped lightly, and his was cold. But his lips were warm when they settled gently on hers. Only their lips touched, a brief, fleeting contact that wakened Samantha's senses and sent her heart soaring. Their mouths brushed once, twice, then they pulled back slightly, foreheads pressed together lightly, smiling with closed eyes.

They opened their eyes at the same moment. Brown eyes met blue, and two faces were split with happy smiles. He brought up his gloved hands and closed them on her shoulders. Her hands came up to grasp his forearms, gripping hard through the layers of clothing. They stood thus, sunlight reflecting off the crystal snow and surrounding them with thousands of tiny prisms.

"Let's go," he said, and ushered her to the waiting wagon.

Chapter Twenty-four

They ran laughingly back toward the church, and Adam grabbed Samantha around the waist to boost her into the wagon. He jumped up beside her and placed one quick, impetuous smack on her lips.

"Adam," she protested laughingly, "what if someone sees you?"

He shrugged, grinning boyishly. "Then they'll say, look at that lucky guy, stealing a kiss from the prettiest girl in town."

"Oh, Adam," she blushed, ducking her head.

He laughed aloud as he raised the reins and flicked them downward. "Let's get movin'," he called to the horses, still looking at Samantha. And they were off.

The air was crisp, clear. It stung their lungs as they inhaled, but they hardly seemed aware of it. They were lost in a world of their own, a shining, shimmering, brighter-than-sunshine world of happy abandon. Never had the sky seemed bluer, the clouds fluffier, the birds as full of cheerful chatter as they were on this day. Hoarfrost coated everything from the tiniest tree branches to the barbed wire that ran from fence post to fence post, catching the sun and bouncing it back into millions of tiny rainbows.

Adam couldn't keep the smile from his face. In minutes—mere minutes—his secrets would be revealed. He would be free to make promises that he intended to spend a lifetime keeping. He glanced at Samantha. Her head was tipped up, watching something in the sky, her breath coming out in white puffs that dissipated as the horses moved them briskly down the lane. *My Samantha*, he thought contentedly.

Samantha had spotted a cloud that looked just like a puffy heart. *How appropriate*, she thought, *when my own heart feels so full it could burst wide open!* She turned toward Adam and caught him staring, smiling, admiring. She smiled and admired right back.

She asked, "Where are we going?"

"You'll see," he said secretively.

She pretended to pout. "You won't tell me?"

"Not a chance," he retorted, looking down his nose at her.

She tipped her head and batted her eyelashes. Being coquettish was new to her, but with Adam she felt new and truly beautiful for the first time in her life. "Pleeeease?" She drew out the word, giving him her best pleading look.

But he just laughed and said, "Don't even try it!" He advised, "Just settle back and enjoy the ride. We'll be there soon. Why don't you tell me what you thought of the wedding."

So Samantha and Adam chatted away as the sun shone down and the clouds floated lazily in the clear blue sky and cardinals scolded the squirrels that danced in the treetops. In time, Adam pulled back on the reins and called in a deep

voice, "Whoa now, Bet and Tick." When the horses came obe-
diently to a stop, Adam turned to Samantha and said, "We'll
walk from here." He tied the reins around the brake handle
and leaped off the wagon. He reached up to Samantha, and
she placed her hands on his shoulders as he lifted her down.
Her feet touched the ground, but Adam kept his hands on
her waist, hers remaining lightly on his shoulders.

"Samantha," he said, a hint of a smile lighting his eyes, "I
have a surprise for you."

Samantha tipped her head at an inquisitive angle. What
was he up to? "A surprise?"

"Yes. I wanted to get it ready for you as quickly as I could,
but it took longer than I had expected. So I haven't spent
much time with you since you've been back. I hope you
aren't angry with me."

The last emotion Samantha was experiencing at that
moment was anger. Her heart felt light and fluttery, and her
stomach was doing happy flip-flops of anticipation. "Well,
what is it!" she demanded laughingly.

He smiled a reply, took her by the hand, and led her
through a small windblock of scrub maples. Samantha recognized the area—this was the north wheat field. What on
earth?... They were at Grandpa and Grandma Klaassen's old
dugout! But there was something different about it. There
was a new door made of white oak, and the shutters had been
repaired and painted dark emerald green. And curtains hung
behind—were they? Yes, there were real glass windows! Who
would have put in those glass windows?

Samantha stopped and looked up at Adam, a look of
puzzlement on her face. "Adam...?" she said questioningly.

Adam was fairly twitching with excitement. "Come
inside, Samantha," he coaxed, tugging at her hand gently.

She allowed herself to be pulled along behind him. Her
mind was racing and full of questions, but she was afraid to

voice her thoughts. They stepped through the new door which boasted a bright white enamel door knob instead of the old rawhide string-through-a-hole rigging to open it. When Samantha got a look at the spanking clean, white-washed interior, she gasped.

Her startled gaze swung to Adam, her mouth hanging open. Laughingly he reached out with one finger to close it for her. "I could see your tonsils," he teased in the softest of voices.

Samantha gulped, staring around the room in amazement. The dirt floor had been covered with wide pine planking. The walls had been lined with muslin and stiffened with white wash. A round clawfooted table stood in the middle of the room, flanked by two pressed-back chairs and topped with a red-and-white checked oilcloth. A familiar rocking chair sat invitingly in front of the stone fireplace. Samantha, frowning, crossed to it and stroked it with her fingers. Why, it was Gran's old rocker!

She looked at Adam, her face an open question mark, but he just smiled, hands thrust deep into his pockets.

In the far corner a black nickel wood-burning stove took up residence, and on new shelves mounted on the wall beside it sat a selection of turquoise graniteware pots and pans, plates, bowls and cups. Samantha touched them hesitantly, wonderingly, a lump in her throat. What did this all mean?

A blue calico curtain split the room slightly off-center. Samantha walked over and pulled it aside, peeking behind it. There was a bed with a tall, carved maple headboard and footboard. Shyly, Samantha stepped over to it and pressed both hands down on the beautiful Trip-Around-the-World quilt that covered the straw mattress. With shaking fingers she traced one diagonally-set row of blue squares, her heart thumping wildly in her chest.

Adam appeared at the curtain. "Well, what do you think?" he asked, his arms crossed casually, his dimples showing.

Samantha straightened and turned an amazed circle. "It's just wonderful, Adam. Why, it's like new in here! And Gran's rocking chair—how did it get here? Did you have it sent?"

"Yes, David arranged to have it shipped here. He knew you would want it."

She shook her head, awed. "And all of this—" She gestured to the curtain, the new shelves, the floor. "You did all of this?"

Adam shrugged in feigned nonchalance, a secretive smile still tipping up the corner of his lips. Under his Sunday shirt his heart was beating a rapid rhythm. "Liz helped a bit with the curtains and tablecloth and quilt."

Smiling but obviously still puzzled, she reiterated, "It's wonderful—a snug, perfect little home. But—" She bit her lower lip. *Who was it for? For me? To live here on my own or with David? Or...dare I hope...?*

Adam gestured to the other side of the curtain with his thumb. "There's something for you on the mantel."

Samantha looked at him, her blue eyes full of curiousity, as she passed him to cross back to the fireplace. Resting on the mantel was an enameled box with a beautiful rose on its top. She lifted the lid, and a tinkling melody poured forth. She recognized it immediately—*Lohengrin*—the traditional wedding song. Her breath caught at the implication.

Adam crossed to her slowly, his steps measured and purposeful. He stopped inches in front of her. Taking her by the shoulders, he turned her gently and helped her sit in Gran's familiar rocker. He then bent down on one knee, letting his hands slide down her arms until he reached her hands and linked fingers with her. The tune continued to play as he smiled gently into her searching eyes.

When he spoke, his words lifted at Samantha's heart, sending it beating high in her throat. "Samantha, this little dugout was prepared over fifty years ago by my grandfather as a first home for himself and his new bride. It was simple, but it was built by loving hands and was offered with a loving heart.

"Grandpa told me that he and Grandma were as happy as could be in this little dugout, because it was their *home*. They didn't have much in the way of material possessions. They'd just arrived from Germany, two young people far away from their family and friends. They were scared and probably lonely, but they had each other. They had a common faith, as well as a lot of love. So when Grandpa dug out the side of this hill and made a house around it, he was building on the promise of love and of better things ahead.

"It took a lot of faith in one another to make their new start a bright one, but they did it! And when the dugout was complete, he painted a plaque for Grandma which they hung beside the door." Adam released one of her hands to reach beneath his jacket and pull out a small, flat package wrapped in tissue. He placed it in Samantha's lap.

She stared at the package nestled in the folds of her dress, afraid to touch it, afraid to speak. She dared not break the spell his words were spinning.

"Samantha," he continued, and her gaze rose to lock back on his, "I've dreamed of the day when I would embark on the same journey my grandparents made—a journey of living and loving and becoming one with a special woman."

Samantha was finding it hard to breathe. Adam's eyes were so filled with tenderness it literally took her breath away. Her own eyes were wide with awe that this man was speaking such words to her—Samantha O'Brien, a nobody. She felt at once undeserving and full of longing to hear him continue his soliloquy.

"I am ready for that journey, Samantha," Adam said, his brown eyes shining. "I've met that special woman, and I know that God will bless the union." He took in a deep, shuddering breath before continuing. "Samantha, you would do me great honor if you would agree to begin a new life with me, here, in this little dugout that I've made ready for you much the same way Grandpa made it ready for Grandma all those years ago."

He paused, tears springing into the corners of his eyes, emphasizing the flecks of green that rested in the velvet brown of his irises. He squeezed her hands. "Samantha, I love you. I am asking you to marry me."

She inhaled sharply, taking in a great, choking breath of joyous disbelief. He'd said it! He'd said he loved her! *He loved her!* "Oh, Adam," she said breathily, her voice shaky. Too overcome for words, she could only duck her head, and the room began swimming through a sudden spurt of happy tears.

He dipped his head to peek at her impishly. "'*Oh, Adam…*'?" he repeated. "Does that mean yes or no?"

Samantha lifted her head, and tears overflowed to stream down her flushed cheeks. "Yes, Adam—oh, yes!" And she threw herself into his embrace. "I love you so much, Adam! I can't believe it—your wife. Your *wife*! Oh, I'm so happy I can't bear it!"

Her chest ached with the effort of containing so much joy. Adam rocked her back and forth in his arms, his face buried in the mass of russet curls he loved. Finally he put her gently away from him and suggested, "Why don't you open your present."

Still kneeling on the floor beside Adam, Samantha picked up the little wrapped package. Her fingers were shaking as she pulled the string that held the paper closed, and she giggled self-consciously. She was giddy with excitement! She pulled back the paper wrapping, revealing a nine-inch square of cedar. It had been sanded smooth and was decorated with a painting of a small yellow frame house at the top, a crude red heart at the bottom, and a verse printed between the two.

She frowned, unable to read it. She handed it to Adam. "What does it say?" she asked.

He cleared his throat, then spoke the words written on the plaque. They sounded melodious when uttered in his even, baritone voice:

"'*Ein Haus wird gebout von Holz und stein;*
Aber ein Heim bout mon von Liebe alein.'"

"It's German, isn't it?" she asked, and Adam nodded. "What does it mean?"

Without looking at the plaque, Adam recited, "'Houses are built of wood and stone; Homes are built of love alone.'"

She echoed the last two words, her voice as soft as a feather floating downward: "Love alone...."

Samantha retrieved the plaque and ran a finger across the painted words, leaving it to rest on the last two words. Her gaze came up to meet Adam's again. "Our home was built with love, and it will always be filled with love, Adam. I promise you that."

From a woman who knew the pain of broken promises, a promise would not be made lightly. It would not be taken lightly, either. Adam's heart swelled. "I make that same promise to you, my Samantha. Forever, and ever."

Tenderly, Adam wiped Samantha's tears from her eyes with his thumbs, leaving his hands cupping the sides of her face. His fingers were buried in her hair. "Miss Samantha O'Brien, you have made me the happiest man in the world today. I feel so blessed to have you in my life."

Samantha brought her hands up to curve around the backs of his. "No, Adam, I am the one who is blessed. You will never know what it means to me to be loved by someone like you."

Adam opened his mouth to speak, but she shook her head to silence him. "No, let me finish," she demanded gently. "I need to tell you this. When I came to Mountain Lake, I was frightened and filled with angry bitterness. I didn't—couldn't!—trust anyone. I didn't know how. Where I come from, if you trusted you got hurt. So I had closed myself off. But a person all shut away inside herself is a lonely person. I was so very lonely, Adam.

"I didn't realize it then, but I was seeking something. They say you can't miss what you don't know, but I think that's wrong. I didn't know what it meant to belong, to be loved, to be accepted.... And I did miss it.

"You asked me one time what I was running away from, and I told you I wasn't running away. You didn't believe me, but it was true. I wasn't so much running *from* something as I was trying to run *to* something—only I didn't know what. I've been looking for that illusive something since I was six years old and they covered my Gran with dirt."

She smiled tremulously through her tears, and her hands tightened on his, bringing them down from her face and clasping them together between her own, almost beneath her chin. "My searching neared its end the day you came dashing down the street after me—when instead of treating me with anger, you reached out to me with kindness. Me, some dirty little thief from the wrong side of the city."

Her eyes were bright with glistening tears and Adam fought to swallow a growing lump in his throat as she continued. "I never could have imagined being loved by someone like you—someone good and kind and virtuous. I never could have imagined deserving the love of someone like you. But because of you, I don't see myself in the same old way anymore. I'm not that same frightened, lonely, seeking person anymore.

"Adam," she said in an emotion-filled voice, her hands squeezing his tightly, "you have given me everything my heart ever longed for. You introduced me, through example and word, to a Savior Who will be ever with me. You found my brother and brought him back to me. You gave me love, and self-respect, and helped me open up to trusting again. You gave my seeking heart a place to call home. I know that I've never done anything to deserve you, but I know that you are mine anyway, and because of the things you've taught me, I can accept you as my own without feelings of guilt or unworthiness. You've even given me *me*. I am so thankful for you. I love you, Adam!"

She kissed the tips of his fingers, clasped between hers, then raised her face to him. Their kiss was salty and wet with tears, but only happy tears. They came together again in a tender embrace, hugging and rocking one another contentedly.

Suddenly a huff of laughter was released near Samantha's ear. Samantha pulled back, startled. Adam threw back his head and laughed again, uproariously, uninhibited.

"What's so funny?" Samantha asked, sniffling a bit as she pressed the palms of her hands against his jacket front.

Adam's eyes crinkled merrily as he replied, "You!"

Her eyebrows rose up and she placed a hand on her chest. "Me!?" she exclaimed, wondering if she should be offended by this unexpected turn of emotions.

"Yes, you, Miss Samantha O'Brien," Adam replied, his voice still holding a hint of suppressed laughter. "When you came to town, you were trying to pass yourself off as Sam Klaassen."

She still looked puzzled, and he leaned down to kiss the end of her nose. Keeping his face close to hers, he finished with a humorous smirk, "Well, now I intend to make an honest woman out of you!"

She burst into happy laughter as well and snuggled herself securely against Adam's chest. When his arms closed around her, Samantha felt as if her seeking heart had truly come home.

THE END

A Note from the Author

Dear Reader,

A Seeking Heart is a story close to my own heart as it is loosely based on my own family history. My grandparents, Henry and Elizabeth Klaassen Voth, raised their family, including my mother, in the small, German-Mennonite community of Mountain Lake, Minnesota. My mother's stories of her childhood on the farm were the inspiration for the Mountain Lake Series.

While I've taken my mother's stories and turned them into a fictional account, there are parts of *A Seeking Heart* that are very factual. The truth that Samantha learned as a result of the Klaassen family's tender care is a truth that is still very applicable today. God does indeed love each of us regardless of our past or present unhappy circumstances. It is His desire to have each of us become a part of His family. As Adam explained to Samantha in the shed behind the railroad station, all one must do to become a part of His family is simply accept the gift of salvation offered through the sacrifice of God's Son, Jesus Christ, and the whole world changes.

If you've never made the decision to accept Jesus Christ as your personal Lord and Savior, it is my fervent desire that you take the steps necessary to join the family of God as a joint heir with Jesus. It truly is as simple as believing and asking. May God bless you richly as you journey with Him.

In His love,
Kim Vogel Sawyer

A Seeking Heart
Order Form

Postal orders: Kim Sawyer
602 Molly Mall
Hutchinson, KS 67502

E-mail orders: dksawyer@ourtownusa.net

Please send *A Seeking Heart* **to:**

Name: _____

Address: _____

City: _____ State: _____

Zip: _____

Telephone: (_____) _____

Book Price: $10.99

Shipping: $3.00 for the first book and $1.00 for each additional book to
cover shipping and handling within US, Canada, and Mexico.
International orders add $6.00 for the first book and $2.00 for
each additional book.

Or order from:
ACW Press
5501 N. 7th. Ave. #502
Phoenix, AZ 85013

(800) 931-BOOK

or contact your local bookstore